FUJINO
OMORI

ILLUSTRATION BY
SUZUHITO
YASUDA

VOLUME 2

FUJINO OMORI
ILLUSTRATION BY SUZUHITO YASUDA

NEW YORK

IS IT WRONG TO TRY TO PICK UP GIRLS
IN A DUNGEON?, Volume 2
FUJINO OMORI

Translation by Andrew Gaippe

This book is a work of fiction. Names, characters,
places, and incidents are the product of the author's
imagination or are used fictitiously. Any resemblance
to actual events, locales, or persons, living or dead, is
coincidental.

DUNGEON NI DEAI WO MOTOMERU
NO WA MACHIGATTEIRUDAROUKA vol. 1
Copyright © 2013 Fujino Omori
Illustrations copyright © 2013 Suzuhito Yasuda
All rights reserved.
Original Japanese edition published in 2013
by SB Creative Corp.
This English edition is published by arrangement
with SB Creative Corp., Tokyo, in care of
Tuttle-Mori Agency, Inc., Tokyo.

English translation © 2015 by Hachette Book
Group, Inc.

Yen On
Hachette Book Group
1290 Avenue of the Americas
New York, NY 10104
www.hachettebookgroup.com
www.yenpress.com

Yen On is an imprint of Hachette Book Group, Inc.
The Yen On name and logo are trademarks of
Hachette Book Group, Inc.

The publisher is not responsible for websites (or their
content) that are not owned by the publisher.

First Yen On edition: April 2015

ISBN: 978-0-316-34014-4

10 9 8 7 6 5 4 3 2

RRD-C

Printed in the United States of America

VOLUME 2

FUJINO OMORI
ILLUSTRATION BY SUZUHITO YASUDA

Prologue **WEAKLING'S GRIN**

Supporter: a noncombatant, dungeon-prowling party member.

Their main role is to collect magic stones and dropped items after battle and bring them safely to the surface.

They shoulder the load behind the action so that party members fighting monsters on the front lines aren't weighed down more than necessary.

In short, supporters are just porters. They carry the loot.

"What the hell are ya doing?! Move yer ass!"

Business as usual today. More verbal abuse.

A male adventurer angrily yelled at a supporter just a few steps behind him, who was almost hidden under the shadow of a massive, bulging backpack.

They were in a labyrinth where the only thing that wasn't a problem was finding sufficient lighting.

The man's voice was full of unhidden contempt as he railed on his supporter. "At least carry my stuff properly, ya good-for-nothin'—!"

This was nothing new, just more of the same porter abuse this particular supporter had heard quite enough of.

But arrogant words could sometimes lead to violence. Adventurers are above supporters and feel nothing for those they outrank.

Adventurers don't even give them a second glance.

In fact, supporters who fall behind are mocked and become the butt of jokes told later on.

Adventurers' cruelty to anyone weaker than themselves knows no bounds.

They can take money, dignity, hope—everything.

This particular supporter had heard these words somewhere:

First, an adventurer could not reach their full potential without a good supporter.

Second, it was the efforts of supporters that allowed adventurers to prowl the dungeon.

Third, supporters had a hidden strength within.

They were very pretty words, and very easy to accept. They stood to reason. They felt true.

Supporters filled the important role of lightening the strain on adventurers. No one could refute this fact.

"Like hell I'm gonna pay a lazy-ass weakling who holds me back!"

But just how many adventurers were there who could even begin to comprehend these facts?

Where were the admirable adventurers who appreciated how much supporters did for them?

Did an adventurer who didn't look down with contempt on a supporter who is lagging behind even exist?

"Listen up! Ya better do your job if we get surrounded, clear?! Useless friggin' supporter!"

Supporters made excellent decoys when being chased by monsters.

The supporter looked up at the honorable adventurer who so honestly made his expectations known, and lightly smiled.

Yes, yes.

They weren't that hard to understand, really.

All adventurers were the same.

Chapter 1

DATE, THEN SUPPORTER

Crunch, crunch comes the sound of something chewing the earth.

Light spills down from the ceiling, lighting up the pale green walls in every direction around me. I'm standing in a square space within the dungeon simply called a "room."

I've got the Divine Knife from Hestia aimed at the ground chewer, the blade coming out the bottom of my hand.

The thing has four legs, two thin arms, and two big eyes. Its body looks like a giant red ant.

What makes it different from a normal ant is that it's as tall as I am when it hoists its upper body up, pivoting around its hunched-over midsection.

A killer ant.

It's a monster that first shows up on lower level seven. I've heard that it's called a "newbie killer," just like the Wall Shadow on the sixth level.

It got that nickname due to its thick skin and strength that puts lower-level monsters like goblins to shame. The killer ant's skin is so tough that it might as well be armor. Halfhearted attacks bounce right off the living shell, and piercing that outer layer is no easy task.

There are four sharp claws at the ends of its arms. Warped and curved, the deadly weapons dangling in front of its body give me the creeps.

Those claws carve people up before they can break through the ant's defenses. That's the usual pattern.

Adventurers who are used to the monsters down to the fifth level don't expect these ants to be all that smart, and tend to become said ant's afternoon snack.

"Gegii!"

Click, click, click. The killer ant snaps its mandibles together, chewing the air.

One more thing—this monster can summon other buddies. It doesn't call out to them but releases some kind of pheromone that humans can't smell to gather its friends. I hear it happens when they're in a pinch.

It's a handy combination of toughness and teamwork. But for an adventurer, it's a recipe for disaster.

Anyway, I have to take it out fast. A quick strike to a vital spot is my best bet.

The ant and I stare each other down, both of us taking a few steps forward.

"—Yah!"

I make the first move. Absorbing the first blow and counterattacking really isn't my thing.

It charges right at me, its right arm raised high. I meet it head-on, jumping in close to its body.

I catch a flash of a white arc out of the corner of my left eye—*slash*!

I'm just a blink faster. The monster's claws, along with a good part of its arm, go flying.

"Giii!!!!"

The monster's right side, its arm—and weapons—are gone. Its shrieks of pain fill my ears as I brace the Divine Knife for impact.

The recommended method for killing a killer ant is to aim for the space between the solid shells at the joints, to hit the soft flesh beneath. It might be hard for a newbie adventurer to pull off, but at least that's the theory.

However, I've decided to ignore that.

No arm—and no weapon—means its defenses are weak on the right side. I jam the jet-black blade between its head and thorax.

"—"

I can feel the thick skin around its neck tear as my blade passes through.

The feeling doesn't last long. The blade glides through the monster's flesh without much resistance. All that's left is to finish it off with a flick of the wrist.

Shing! The blade hits a good note as it slides out from under the ant's neck, sending its head flying to the ground.

A purple liquid dribbles out of the open wound, an insectoid expression of surprise at this turn of events still on the monster's head as it crashes to the dungeon floor.

The headless body stands there for a moment, not realizing something is missing. A few breaths later, it notices and falls like a bag of rocks.

"...Yep, that was good!"

I flick the purple goo off the Divine Knife before taking a closer look at it.

It fits perfectly in the palm of my hand. It's almost like we grew up together, or it grew into my hand.

Its potency, too, leaves nothing to be desired. The blade cut through that killer ant's armor like a hot knife through butter.

Amazing! This is the strength of a Hephaistos-made weapon!

A gift from my goddess!

"—♪"

With the look of a kid who just got a new toy, I set to work on the slain monster to get the magic stone within its chest.

In reality, I'm not all that different from a child. I feel like I did on my birthday when Gramps gave me *Dungeon Oratoria*, a picture book filled with images of famous heroes. It was so special to me, I was afraid to open it at first for fear that it would get dirty.

Of course this present would be wasted if I didn't use it, but the feeling is the same.

Thank you, Goddess...

I smile as her face floats into my mind. She's been so busy lately; I'll have to find time to thank her properly.

I will get strong. Strong enough to be worthy of this weapon— strong enough to make my goddess proud.

Returning the blade to the sheath tucked into my lower back, I set off to find my next target on the seventh level.

"*What* floor?!"

"Agh!" Bell let out a scream. The cause of his pathetic squeal was a frowning Eina Tulle fuming with anger and glaring right at him.

Bell had made a triumphant return to the Guild after prowling the seventh floor with the assistance of Hestia's Knife. He'd gotten the money from all of his magic stones and drop items at the Exchange and went to give his adviser an update with a big smile on his face. But the second he said, "Seventh level," his good mood came to an abrupt end.

"What is with you?! Does nothing I say stay inside that thick skull of yours?! Going from the fifth to the seventh?! Are you *insane*?!"

"S-s-s-s-ssorry!"

Wham! Eina slammed both of her hands down onto the table. Her emerald eyes burned, her head leaning to the side. Bell was little more than a frog being stared down by a python.

Eina was angry because Bell was showing no concern for his safety and lightheartedly entering deeper floors. He was adventuring, and it was that with which she took exception.

"Tell me, just who was it that was nearly killed by a Minotaur only one week ago?"

"Uh, m-me?"

"Then just why are you doing this?! Do you not understand how dangerous it is, after all you've been through?!"

"I-I'm sorry…!" Bell said, his eyes filling with tears. This was by far the angriest he had ever seen her. Eina was going all out. Her desire to keep Bell alive was turning her into an ogre.

A newbie adventurer with not even a month of experience going deeper than the fifth was the same as suicide.

The dungeon layout became more complicated after the fifth level, not to mention there were more powerful monsters. Bell went down to the seventh level—if the killer ant had called its friends, he wouldn't have made it out alive. Killer ants were not a pack of Kobolds; they would tear a solo adventurer limb from limb.

"You don't seem to understand the word 'dangerous.' Not even close. I'm going to fix that, right here and now!"

Bell let out another pitiful cry, as he had become all too familiar with Eina's Spartan-like style of "guidance" in the past few weeks.

Bell had seen everything she taught him in the field, but being able to say "I understand, leave it to me" to his adviser was entirely another matter. Bell rushed to explain.

"Please, wait! I, um, grew quite a lot since then, Ms. Eina!"

"'Quite a lot' is quite a claim from someone who's only just gotten to grade *H*!"

"N-no, it's true! Several of my basic abilities are already at *E*!"

"...*E*?"

Eina froze on the spot, her eyes open wide.

She didn't understand what he said at first, but when her mind sorted it out, she raised her eyebrows in disbelief.

"Do you think you can fool me, making that kind of claim?"

"It's true, all of it! Maybe I'm in some kind of growth spurt, but I'm getting stronger very fast!"

"...Really?"

Eina cast her bewildered gaze at Bell as he nodded with all his might.

She hadn't been his adviser long, but she was able to tell when the boy in front of her was lying.

And according to her intuition, Bell was telling the truth.

"...Really, *E*?"

"Y-yes."

Eina put up her hands, palms forward, as if to say "wait a minute."

The remaining grades were S, A, B, C, D, then E. She counted them out on her fingers, nodding to herself, saying, "Hmmmm." One more time—S, A, B, C, D, E...six again. Same as before.

Eina was now officially confused. She didn't completely doubt Bell, but that rate of growth sounded like it came out of a horror story.

Eina had guessed grade *H* because that was the highest ability level for adventurers with Bell's amount of experience. *H* was the highest believable amount of growth over that span of time, and that was only for the really gifted individuals.

G was already ridiculous, and anything above *F*...That was just too fast, no matter how she thought about it.

If Bell had been a warrior before he'd become an adventurer, with combat training of some kind, then she might have been able to accept it, maybe. But he was a farmer. Still, he didn't look like he was lying at all…

"Hm-hm-hmmm…" Eina said as she stroked her chin with her pointer finger, not able to figure out which was true.

Bell sat there silently, watching her as if she could explode at any moment.

"Hey…Bell."

"Y-yes, ma'am?"

"Would you mind showing me the 'status' on your back?"

"…Huh?!"

A high-pitched gasp escaped Bell's throat as he looked at Eina's serious face.

"It's not that I don't believe what you're saying, it's just…"

She looked away, shaking her hands back and forth, trying to make sure Bell didn't get the wrong idea.

She felt that the most reasonable explanation was that Bell's goddess, Hestia, had made a mistake when transcribing Bell's status.

Or perhaps there was a misunderstanding somewhere.

The idea that Bell had improved to grade *E* stats was just that inconceivable for her.

Eina wasn't going to believe a single word out of Bell's mouth until she saw undeniable proof.

"B-but the number one thing that adventurers aren't supposed to reveal is their status…right?"

All the city's adventurers were under the jurisdiction of the Guild and were forbidden from giving out personal information to anyone, including Guild employees. Their levels and *Familias* were reported, but nothing more than that.

There were also adventurers who had special skills and magic. The relationships of the gods and their *Familias* were constantly changing. Today's friend might be tomorrow's foe. Information was tightly protected to cover potential weaknesses.

"I give you my word that I will not tell a soul what I will see. I'll take full responsibility if your status becomes public. If that happens, I swear I will obey you."

"Obey...? Hang on, Ms. Eina, you can read hieroglyphics?"

"Yes, but only a little. I think I can read enough to understand statuses, though."

Eina had attended her fair share of school and had excelled in theological studies. She could certainly read and write simple hieroglyphs.

"If I don't see it with my own two eyes, I will never clear you to go deeper than the fifth level."

"That definitely would cause a lot of problems for me..."

"I promise I won't look at your magic or skill slots, so, please?"

"I don't have any skills or magic anyway, so that wouldn't change a thing...but okay."

Bell gave in to Eina's request as she bowed forward and clapped her hands together.

Eina had done so much to support Bell in the past; he felt that she deserved his complete trust, just like Hestia. Bell had no reason not to take her at her word.

"Well, um...I'll take off my clothes now?"

"If you're embarrassed enough to blush, don't check with me first! You'll make me uncomfortable, too!"

Both of their cheeks flushed red as Bell stood up and faced a far corner of the wide room. A flustered Bell unhooked his armor and quickly pulled off his undershirt.

Rather than immediately focusing on the status engraved on the boy's back, Eina's eyes were drawn to his remarkably chiseled back muscles for a brief moment. Shaking her head a bit, she forced her eyes back to the hieroglyphs.

Her pointed ears turned a light shade of red as her eyes scanned the markings left to right.

Bell Cranell
Level One
Strength: E-403   Defense: H-199   Utility: E-412
Agility: D-521   Magic: I-0

No way...

She couldn't believe her eyes; her jaw dropped slightly in shock.

With the exception of Magic, he was definitely strong enough to keep up with monsters on the seventh level. Eina tended to judge adventurers by their defensive ability, so Bell's low "Defense" grade made her a bit nervous. However, his hit-and-run combat style fit very well with his ability levels, so she came to the conclusion that he dodged most attacks anyway.

The fact that his "Agility" was already at grade *D* made her a little nauseous.

I can't believe it…

Eina lightly coughed in her throat. It was the sound of her concept of "common sense" being broken; a cold chill worked its way up her spine. Working at the Guild and advising many adventurers, Eina knew just how abnormal Bell's growth rate was.

His growth was more than through the roof. It was otherworldly.

—A Skill?

The possibility popped up in the back of her mind.

Maybe he has a Skill that explains the unusual growth, she thought to herself with a twinge. The only way to check…was to go back on her promise.

If it's just a quick look…

Her eyes glanced below Bell's abilities and took in the hieroglyphs. Where Bell's Magic and Skills were listed.

She had already come this far. It was too late to look away now. Wanting to know what was inside a treasure box after peeking through the lid must be a trait of demi-humans.

Her curiosity was piqued; she looked at all his Skill slot.

…Ahh, nope.

She couldn't understand what was written.

The amount of complex characters was too much for her to make heads or tails of it.

It could be that his goddess, the overprotective Hestia, might have put an extra layer of protection over his status so that others couldn't read it even if they had a chance. Eina didn't have a full understanding of hieroglyphs' size and stroke order, and she didn't realize that Hestia's "protection" was actually just her own bad handwriting.

Eina had newfound respect for Hestia and her strategy for keeping Bell's status a secret.

"Um…Ms. Eina? Are you finished yet?"

"A…ah! Yes!"

Eina's ears jumped as Bell's still-embarrassed voice reached them and she noticed the situation. Eina laughed out of her own embarrassment as she looked away from Bell's status and bowed a few times in apology.

*It's true…*she groaned to herself.

There was no way she could withhold permission to enter the seventh level with a status like that. As long as he was careful, he should be able to go there safely, even alone.

—However, she did have one other problem with him going that far down.

"…"

"W-what is it?"

Fully dressed, Bell heard his voice waver as Eina's eyes traveled his body from head to toe. Her gaze was overwhelming.

But it didn't look like she doubted Bell's ability or strength.

She wasn't looking at his body; she was looking at the poor excuse for armor that was covering it.

"Bell."

"Y-yes?"

"Do you have any plans tomorrow?"

"…Huh?"

A day has passed since our conversation.

I'm standing by myself in a half-circle-shaped park built just off of North Main.

Waiting for Eina.

Yep, I'm meeting her here.

Is this…a date?

No, that's not possible, I reassure myself.

Yesterday Eina asked if I had time to go buy some new armor with her. Seemed like she thought my current set wouldn't be enough. Once again, she's going out of her way to help me. She's looking out for me.

So she's not thinking of this as a date. She's just being kind— kindly failing to mind her own business.

…Still, to anyone who didn't know the details, this really would seem like…

All of the conditions are there.

Conditions like "Let's meet at ten in front of the bronze statue in the park!" and "Just the two of us!"

Whoa! Whoa!!!

"Hey! Bell!"

"!"

And now the time has come.

The owner of the pretty voice comes jogging up to me waving her hand, her figure growing in my line of sight.

"Good morning! Aren't you early? Was the idea of buying new armor that exciting?"

"Ah, no, I just…"

—I just think it's strange to be alone with you, Eina. I don't have the guts to say that to her directly, though.

"Well, I was excited, too. I know this is your shopping trip, but I'm eager to get started."

Eina is wearing clothes I've never seen her in before. Usually she's in a perfectly pressed Guild uniform, but today she's in a cute, lacy white blouse and a short skirt. She's got a good sense of fashion. I can't really look at her the same way I usually do.

Maybe it's because I'm used to seeing her in that uniform all the time, but today she seems more grown-up. How do I put it…she's practically glowing.

Yes, she's very cute.

I am totally taken in by the charms of this new Eina.

"Do you think I'm strange for getting excited about buying possibly dangerous equipment?"

"N-no, not at all!" I vigorously shake my head, but Eina just giggles. *Whoa, whoa…*

Eina is probably a contender for the first or second most popular Guild member among all adventurers. I wonder if all half-elves are like her…

"Ahem. Anyway, Bell?"

"W-what is it?"

"What do you think? Seeing me out of uniform? Anything to say?"

She looks up at me with the eyes of a mischievous child.

Whoa, whoa, now…

"You look…well…much younger than usual."

"Hey! I'm still only nineteen, you know!"

"Owowowowowow!!!!!"

Eina whips her thin white arm around my neck, putting me in a headlock.

As I try to escape, my neck slips into her armpit, my cheek rubbing up against a very soft bulge…

"Hey! Say you're sorry!!"

"P-please, forgive meeeeeeeeeeeeeeeeee!" I yell with all my might over the sound of Eina's amused laughter.

"It's been a while since I've been out shopping like this."

"Really? I'm surprised that people can leave someone like you alone…especially guys."

"Hee-hee, you're good, Bell. But it's true. I've been busy at work ever since I started at the Guild."

The sky is a bright, clear blue.

Perfect for a date…is not what I'm trying to say, but the weather is very calming. I follow Ms. Eina southward on North Main, a cooling breeze at my back.

The main streets are always busy at this time of day. It's difficult to get anywhere. Employees of stores both large and small stand outside trying to bring in customers. I could swear the ground shakes when a dwarf yells out his store's special deals.

A few of them call out to Eina (apparently mistaking me for a manservant) but she just waves them off with a friendly grin. One animal-person clerk looks really happy when she flashes him a smile.

"Um, can I ask where we're going today? If we keep going this way, we'll end up at the Dungeon…"

"Would you be angry if I said 'Not knowing is part of the fun'? Okay, I'll tell you."

Orario has eight main streets all extending out from the core. There's one that goes north, one that goes northeast, east, southeast, south, southwest, west, and northwest. If you think about it from a bird's-eye view, there are four thick lines intersecting in the middle of the city.

The Dungeon is right where they all come together.

But on ground level, the main streets all meet at Central Park. It's right in front of us now. In the center of the park is an overwhelmingly large building. It blocks more and more of my view of southern Orario as I wait for Eina's answer.

"Our destination is…the Dungeon."

"Whaaaaaaa?"

"The tower above the Dungeon—Babel, to be more specific."

Babel Tower functions as a lid over the Dungeon itself. It's that big building casting a massive shadow over western Orario right now.

Being a "lid," Babel is used to monitor and control the Dungeon entrance.

Managed by the Guild, it's a building that adventurers see very often.

"Babel…Isn't it just a public facility and a…shower room for adventurers?"

"You really are clueless, aren't you? But you've only been an adventurer for a few weeks, so I guess it can't be helped. Right, then, you're gonna get some useful information today."

I remember all too well her Spartan style of "summarizing" useful information about the Dungeon, and to be honest, that look in her eyes is scaring me.

Praying that it won't get as intense as that time, I brace myself for the incoming lecture.

"Just like you said, there are shower rooms for adventurers as well as public facilities inside the tower under the Guild's control. Did you know there are a cafeteria, hospital, and even an Exchange in Babel?"

"Huh? I thought that the Exchanges at the Guild's main office and branches were the only ones."

"Nope, there is one here, too. But it is a little understaffed, so I hear the lines get a bit ridiculous. Anyway, one more thing. The Guild rents out open space to shops and merchants, and that's where we are going today."

Okay, now I get it. The reason we've come this far is that we're going to visit one of the equipment shops in Babel Tower.

"Babel was built right on top of the Dungeon, so naturally all the shops there cater to adventurers. Many of them are run by mercantile *Familias* that specialize. I imagine you've heard of *Hephaistos Familia*?"

"Y-yes."

My heart jumps. My hand grabs the knife currently tucked into the back of my armor.

"How much do you know about *Hephaistos Familia*, Bell?"

"Well, um, I know that that *Familia* makes very high-quality weapons and equipment that all adventurers want..."

"Yep, that's absolutely right. As it happens, we are going to a shop run by *Hephaistos Familia* today."

"Wh-whaaaat?"

It's the loudest I've yelped all day. Eina looks at me like a kid who just pulled a prank and I was her victim.

I hurry up to her, hoping for some kind of explanation. But she just steps to the side and reveals a wide-open space at the base of Babel Tower behind her.

"We're here..."

Central Park.

It makes a perfect circle with the massive white tower in the center. With trees planted all over the place and fountains built into the ground, it really does feel like a park.

Back on North Main, all sorts of people mingle together as they go about their business. But most people in Central Park are carrying big swords and long spears—they're adventurers. The truly scary thing is that even though there are enough adventurers here to make my eyes spin, Central Park doesn't feel full at all.

"Eina, what is going on? Do I look like an adventurer who could buy anything from *Hephaistos Familia*?!"

"Not knowing is part of the fun! You'll see when we get there."

"I've been sweating bullets since we met up this morning! I can't take much more of this!"

She looks right at my strained face and crying eyes but is utterly unmoved by them. She won't even slow down.

"Here we go! Man up and stop complaining!"

My face turns red and my mind is blank as Eina grabs my hand and pulls me into the tower.

Her thin hands are soft and warm—the complete opposite of mine. Hands get rough when you work in the field every day. My head swims; I can't grab onto any of my thoughts.

As we weave through the crowd, I can't help but feel like all the male adventurers about to go into the Dungeon are looking at me like they want to murder me…

I take a deep breath and look up at the tower to calm down.

"Ms. E-Eina, m-m-my hand…Please let go. I'm begging you…!"

"Since we're about to pay one of the top forging *Familias* a visit, it would be a good idea to know a little about the smiths themselves, right? Bell, do you know about 'Advanced Abilities'?"

I guess she's going to ignore my bumbling request. I'm a man, but I can't even get her to listen. I feel like I'm dying here.

I do my best to shrink behind her, shaking.

"No…I don't."

"A blessed person receives an Advanced Ability by choice when their level goes up. They're usually more specialized than basic abilities."

Eina simplifies it by explaining that an Advanced Ability is like a reward for your level going up…a "rank up" present of sorts.

"The kinds of Advanced Abilities available for someone to choose are predetermined, but one option is called 'Forge.'"

Burst Ability and Forge. I've never heard these words before.

According to Eina, Forge is necessary to become a smith in today's world. Also, apparently more than half of *Hephaistos Familia*'s smiths have it.

To put it another way, more than half of them are level two or above. That's a very strong group.

"Smiths have been around since ancient times, of course. Most of their works are antiques now, but there are some that can still be used. But blessed smiths with the Forge ability can add special properties to the items they create."

"Special properties...?"

"An ability unique to that individual weapon. You know how adventurers can get skills on top of their statuses? Smiths with the Forge ability can give skills to weapons. For example, blessed smiths can make a sword that will never break or will always be sharp. If they were just shaping metal, they couldn't do that, right?"

Very true, I nod in agreement.

"There are also weapons that produce something very similar to magic—like shooting flames when swung, things like that."

"Huh?!"

"I thought this was common knowledge...Anyway, weapons that can produce magic-like effects are referred to as 'magic blades.' Only a few smiths can make them."

I swallow audibly. What this all means is that if I can get my hands on one of these magic swords, I would have the power to take on experienced swordsmen.

"A quick warning—'magic blades' have a limit. Once they have used up all their energy, they break. And they're not as powerful as spell-based magic from a magic user."

Eina adds that they're both disposable and extremely expensive, a smirk on her face.

I guess that means that most adventurers don't use magic swords. I'm sure that it's not due to lack of popularity. But taking a weapon that will break into the Dungeon, where anything can happen, wouldn't make me feel safe. Yeah, I bet that's why most people resist the urge to get one.

Well, that and the price tag.

"Um, Eina. Are there Advanced Abilities other than Forge?" As an adventurer, I have to ask. I'll be going down that path someday. I will rank up!

"Well, many adventurers gain abilities called Heavy Guard or Magic Control. Other than that, there is also an ability called Enigma."

"Enigma...?"

"Yes, now how do I explain this...It allows someone to perform a special trick—a miracle, if you will. A 'Divine Art' might be a good way to put it. Do you know about the Philosopher's Stone, Bell?"

No, of course I don't. I shake my head side to side.

"This happened a long, long time ago, but a member of a *Familia* with the Enigma ability succeeded in making an item called the Philosopher's Stone. The stone grants the user eternal life."

"...I don't know why, but my jaw won't close."

"Hee-hee, I know, right? But there is more to this story...You see, the maker took the Philosopher's Stone to the god of the *Familia*... The god took the stone in his hand and smashed it to pieces on the floor in front of him...the source of eternal life."

"............"

"According to the story, the god looked at the maker's shell of a face after that and laughed so hard he pulled a muscle in his stomach."

This is the cruelest myth I have ever heard.

When I say myth, I'm talking about a story about the gods that has a completely appalling ending.

I'm so lucky to have met Hestia first...

"The Philosopher's Stone was created by accident, and all attempts to recreate it failed. No one after the maker mastered the Enigma skill, so his Philosopher's Stone became a legendary item."

"Mastered...? So these abilities need experience to grow, like a status?"

"Not quite. The abilities do have an S to I grade, but raising the level doesn't require experience like a status. It takes much more to raise the grade, and is very difficult. It's nothing like raising a basic Ability."

That sounds really hard…but I don't actually say what I'm thinking.

I'm still a ways away from experiencing this myself, but I can imagine.

We arrive at the front gate of Babel Tower during our conversation. "Gate" might not be the best word because the ground floor of the tower has many arches all the way around the circumference, to allow any number of adventurers to enter from any direction at any time. Passing through the nearest arch, a pale blue and white lobby opens up in front of us.

The entrance to the Dungeon is right below our feet.

"From here…?"

"We go up. The shops in Babel start at the fourth floor."

The first floor of the tower is, as I said, a massive lobby. The community center is on the second. We climb up to the third, Eina pulling me by my hand to the middle of another lobby. I catch a glimpse of the Exchange out of the corner of my eye. But I can't see any stairs.

There are several wide, circular pedestals on the floor of the lobby. Eina leads me up onto one of them. A clear tube of something clear rises up around us. I swear it looks like glass…

Eina reaches for some kind of control panel. The instant she touches it, the pedestal leaves the floor and begins floating in midair.

It goes up and up…no, it's growing upward!

"?!"

"A-ha-ha, I was the same way the first time."

It seems the pedestal and the glass are parts of a floor-transport device…Most likely this is another magic-stone device.

That means that there must be a large number of magic stones beneath the pedestal, and their energy is being converted into lift. Eina takes a look at my surprised face and explains that the magic stones needed to be changed out after a certain amount of time. This thing doesn't just work forever, it turns out.

In no time at all we reach the fourth floor of Babel.

"The shop I have in mind is a few more floors up, but as long as we're here, let's take a look around. You want to see the top-of-the-line equipment too, right, Bell?"

The entire floor is filled with weapon and armor shops. I'll admit I get excited looking at all the sharp, shiny things. I nod to Eina as we step off the pedestal.

There is only one sign on the whole floor:῾Ηφαιστος. Don't tell me...all the shops here are part of *Hephaistos Familia*...?"

"I see you noticed the logo. Actually, all the shops from the fourth floor up to the eighth floor are owned by *Hephaistos Familia*."

...The entire floor...Just how powerful is *Hephaistos Familia*?!

By the way, they also have a shop close to my home with the goddess on Northwest Main.

The short sword in the window...is worth 8 million vals. That's enough to buy several houses.

Stepping up to the display window of the closest shop, a crimson sword enshrined there catches my eye. I go up to take a look at the price...

...Thirty million vals?!

All the blood leaves my face. I lift my hand to my forehead, trying to steady myself. I can tell that next to me, Eina is giggling to herself.

I have a Hephaistos-made knife on me right now; it was a gift from my goddess. She told me it was the only one in the world...How much did it cost?!

"Welcome to our store! Can I help you find anything today?"

The store clerk must have seen me staring and drooling at the sight of the crimson sword. She comes up to greet us in a bright, cheerful voice.

The girl is short, but she looks extremely professional, with a very well-rehearsed smile glued onto her glowing face. Twin black ponytails bouncing around her head make her look very cute indeed.

She wears a deep red apron-style uniform, which is being pushed up by breasts much too big for her body type, jiggling with her every movement...

"...Um...Goddess? What are you doing?"

"......"

Her smile instantly freezes.

So this is why. I *thought* she'd been more tired than usual recently. She's been working here…!

"Why are you here?! You don't need two part-time jobs! Didn't I just say that we can start saving money because I'm going deeper into the dungeon?!"

"Listen closely, Bell. You are going to forget that you saw me here and quietly leave right now…! It's too soon for you to be here!"

"It's too soon for you, too! Aren't you getting thirty vals an hour at your other job?!"

"Don't make fun of my career in potato snacks!"

"Forget about that! Come on, let's go home. You're a goddess! You can't be seen like this, it's embarrassing! Are you trying to become a laughingstock?"

"Let go of me, Bell! Let go now!! Even gods have to throw away their pride when times get tough!"

"And when are times ever tough for gods?! Just please, listen to what I'm saying!"

I grab her right arm with both of my hands, turn, and try my best to pull her out of there.

Why in the world is my goddess being so stubborn…?!

I can feel Eina's wide-eyed gaze on my back, but now is no time to worry about that.

"Hey! New girl! Stop playing around! Back to work!!"

"Yes, sir!"

"Huh?"

Boing! The goddess twists out of my grip and bounds away.

I watch her twin ponytails dance behind her for a moment before she disappears into the back of the shop.

"Goddess…"

"W-well, just as interesting a goddess as ever, I see?" Eina doesn't know how to respond to my pitiful voice, and she forces a smile.

I feel a bit dejected, but I then remember I'm not alone today. I force myself to look up.

…I'll forget this trouble with my goddess, for now.

© Suzuhito
Yasuda

"Sorry you had to see that…"

"It's all right. Shall we go upstairs?"

I nod lightly a few times as the still-awkwardly-smiling Eina leads me back to the pedestal.

We board the "elevator" (as the magical lift turns out to be called) and arrive on an upper floor soon after.

"This is us."

"We're here…"

Eina pushes open the glass to reveal another level inundated with shops just like the fourth floor.

Swords, spears, axes, war hammers, blades, bows and arrows, shields, armor, and many other pieces of equipment are on display at all the shops on this wide floor. The only difference is that there are more customers—more adventurers—here.

That thought makes me flinch for a moment.

"You're thinking that you don't have a place shopping at *Hephaistos Familia*'s shops, aren't you, Bell?"

I'm not in the best mood, and I shoot her a look saying *it's a little late for that now*. But then I nod and agree with her.

Eina looks down on me like queen over a servant, grinning.

"Actually, that's not completely true. But, seeing is believing! Follow me."

Eina guides me into the nearest shop—a spear shop by the looks of it.

Leading me to the very back wall of the shop, she stops in front of a spear rack. All of the combat-ready spears stand on end, blades facing the ceiling.

Just as I start thinking *Here we go again*, my eyes catch the price tag: 12,000 vals.

"H-huh…?"

I might be able to afford this…

"Hee-hee, surprised, aren't you?"

"W-well, yes, but why?"

This price is unbelievable. Shocking, even. Eina sounded like she was awfully pleased when she asked if I was surprised, too.

I'm still staring at the spears, though.

"What sets *Hephaistos Familia* apart from other smiths is that they have even their most inexperienced members make items and sell them in their shops."

"Is that…okay? I mean, compared to the masters…"

"Of course, those weapons are not sold next to ones made by master smiths. But the new smiths get valuable business experience and they can sell their work directly to adventurers. It's a real plus for the younger smiths to get feedback—both the good and the really harsh. It all helps motivate them to make better and better weapons."

I'm a bit surprised, but then again it makes perfect sense. Rather than being restricted to experimenting or practicing, getting comments and criticism from people in the real world would be a lot more motivating.

"It's good for the stores, too. They can sell these weapons to very low-level adventurers and get more customers."

So they can bring in newbies along with the all-stars. Once the newbies get stronger, they can afford better weapons from the same shop. Eina says it's like a pyramid.

The shops draw in as many of the new adventurers as they can to build as many relationships as possible. When the adventurers level up, they become regulars of that shop and buy high-level weapons.

That's what's special about Orario. The large population of adventurers brings out all kinds of benefits and possibilities.

"The most important thing here is that new adventurers and new smiths form bonds early in their careers. Doesn't matter if it's weak or strong."

What do you mean by that? I ask with my eyes.

"New smiths are discovered by new adventurers through the items the smith makes. If an adventurer remembers the smith's name, they might have a client. Very talented—but unpolished—smiths can be hidden in the rough of the business, just waiting for an adventurer with an eye for quality to find them. They might not become close friends, but adventurers who have used their items in combat, felt their armor on their skin, will give the most valuable feedback."

…Makes sense when she puts it like that.

At the very least, I feel that way about my dagger and light-armor provisions from the Guild.

"Smiths can bring out special properties in the items they make if they are forging them for someone in particular, especially if there is a strong bond between the smith and the adventurer…Or at least they claim."

Eina lightly sticks out her tongue. I freeze in place.

Never in my wildest dreams would I ever have imagined Eina doing something so…childish.

"Kind of got sidetracked a little bit there, but what I'm saying is that there are items made by *Hephaistos Familia* that are in your price range. How much do you have on you right now, Bell?"

"Um, should be right about ten thousand vals."

"I wonder if we'll be able to find you a full set of new armor. Like I said before, there are diamonds in the rough made by raw ore smiths. We just need to dig them up! Let's go!!"

Eina seems more excited than I am. It's all I can do to force a smile now that I've come to my senses a bit.

She leads me to a shop that has a sign outside equipped with armor and a shield. Eina suggests, with a peppy smile on her face, that we split up to cover more ground. So I set foot inside without her.

The view from my first step inside the establishment is that it's like nothing I've ever seen before.

Just look at these! Were they really all made by lower-level smiths? Everything looks amazing!

Looking into the forest of armor is the highlight of the day so far.

Pure white mannequin chests wear many different shapes and kinds of armor. It doesn't matter that the head and arms are missing, the chest looks very dignified. A few full-bodied mannequins are equipped with the works. I can clearly see myself wearing those armored plates in battle.

Shield and battle helmets on shelves line the walls. Some look impenetrable, some are simply gorgeous—there's something for everyone.

Male and female customers fill the shop, all looking for a piece of armor that suits them. It looks like you can try on the armor, too.

I think…I'm starting to get a little excited…! What do I do now? …Huh?

As I take in the sights and sounds, my eyes are drawn to a spot at the back of the shop.

It's the most ordinary-looking corner of the store. There's a box filled with equipment pieces just sitting there.

Are they…armor pieces?

The rest of the store's stock is equipped on the mannequins, so are these junk boxes? They're just lying here like a pile of trash. Wait, there is another box next to it, and a few more after that. I guess these must be the items that the *Familia* deemed not worth putting on display.

I'm sure they wouldn't sell them if they were faulty, but maybe there are some imperfections or something like that.

"Ah, yep, they're for sale…"

There is a price tag on the bottom of each box: 5,700 vals, 6,800 vals, 3,900 vals…All the prices are written in red ink by different people, but all of them are quite cheap.

The full set of armor that I saw toward the front of the store is 15,000 vals, and my current light armor from the Guild is 5,000… Yep, I've probably got the right idea. These are in my price range.

Then again, Eina would say that this is something that's going to save my life, so I shouldn't be stingy.

"…?"

I suddenly stop in front of a box in the middle of the row.

This armor—its spirit is calling to me from within the line of boxes.

Silver. Rather than having a reddish tint or darker black hues, this one shines like pure white metal.

No flashy colors or fancy decorations, it looks like it just finished cooling from the forge. It's tugging at my heartstrings.

I bend down to get a closer look; it's light armor.

There are knee guards and a small breastplate designed to fit snugly against the chest. Under those pieces I find wrist and elbow guards, along with a plate that covers the lower back. It's built to protect the bare minimum of the body to allow for maximum mobility. Kind of a patchwork armor.

Lifting up the breastplate, I discover it's very light—much lighter than my provision armor from the Guild. Just hitting it a few times doesn't tell me much, but I think it's sturdier than my Guild armor, too. At least it feels like it.

It's just my size…This is almost scary.

I think I'm in love.

It might be because this is the first one I've picked up.

But suddenly all I can see is myself wearing this armor.

I hold the breastplate up to the light for a closer look. Flipping it around, there it is: the maker's signature is on the inside. "Welf Krozzo."

Looks like this wasn't worthy of the ""Ηφαιστος" name.

Welf Krozzo…

I'll remember that.

My brain snatches the name from the armor like a hawk snatches a fish out of water. It's a smith's name I'll be looking for from here on out.

Eina told me about the bond between adventurers and smiths. So this is what it feels like.

I'm already set on this light armor. I want to buy it, right now.

Let's just look and see how much it is…Gasp! 9,900 vals!

That's almost all of my money…

"Hey-y, Bell! I found something really good! A protector and leather armor! They're a little expensive, but it would be a good idea to get at least one of…Oh? Did you find something?"

Eina has returned. She bends down over me, an unimpressed look on her face.

Maybe she doesn't like it because it's being sold in a box, as though that's somehow proof of its poor quality.

"…Are you getting that?"

"Yes. I'm buying this."

"Haaa…You really have a thing for light armor, don't you? Just when I found some good things for you, too…"

"I'm sorry."

Eina sees my shoulders shrink, as I didn't have anything else I could say. She forces a smile and waves it off. "Don't worry about it. You are the one who's going to wear it. I do want you to think about your safety a bit more…but if you've decided to buy this, that's good enough for me."

"…Thank you."

I stand back up again and pick up the box.

After making my way to the counter and paying for it, I only have 100 vals left…

Today has gotten very expensive.

"Huh…?"

Eina's gone. I turn around with my new armor in a box strapped to my back, looking for her.

Just when I start to wonder where she could've gone, I find her. She'd been standing right behind me, a sparkling smile on her face. Maybe she'd just come out of the shop?

"Bell, here."

"…What?"

She leisurely hands me a long, narrow vambrace.

It fits just over the wrist and extends up the arm to the elbow. I can tell from the outer shell it's designed to be used like a shield. The armor is the same color as Eina's eyes, emerald green.

"I-is this…?"

"It's a present from me, so please use it, okay?"

"Whaa? N-no, I can't accept this! I'm giving it back!"

"Whaaat? Are you saying you can't accept a girl's present?"

"N-no, it's not that…I just feel so pathetic!" With sweat pouring down my face, I just blurt out how I really feel. No matter how much older she is than me, getting a present from a girl like this…It feels like I've done something wrong.

Eina flashes a big smile as my shoulders start melting again.

"I want you to have it. Not for me, for you."

"Wha…?"

"The truth is, adventurers never really know when they'll die.

Even ones who are really strong just disappear as if by the whim of a god. I've known many who didn't come back."

"……"

"…I'd like you not to be one of them, Bell. O-ho, I guess this present is for me, after all."

Eina laughs a bit to herself but never takes her eyes off me.

Those tranquil eyes.

"Is that bad?" she asks.

I look at the floor.

My reddening face is hidden by my hair.

I don't have what it takes to refuse her gift after that.

"…And Bell, you said that you loved me."

My face is beet-red now. My neck jerks my head up and I meet her eyes with my own.

Looks like she's blushing quite a bit, too.

"That was, well…I was just so happy that you were encouraging me…!"

"I was happy too, that you said you loved me. I realize you didn't mean it 'that' way."

Both of us are blushing up a storm.

"It's not just because of that, but I want to give you strength. You've been working so hard, and I want to help you. Will you accept it, please?"

Sniff. My nose is starting to run.

I wipe it with my sleeve, nodding.

"Thank you…very much……"

"You're welcome."

I can feel gentle warmth flowing from the emerald protector on my arm.

"It's gotten pretty late…"

The sky is turning red. Late evening has arrived.

I walked Eina back to her dwelling after we finished shopping, and am now close to my own.

I jog down West Main and find my usual side street that leads to the old church.

To think I would get that nervous being around Eina...This isn't good.

I can just see Aiz Wallenstein looking at me with disappointment and yelling all kinds of things at me. This is all in my head, of course.

I don't want to think that I could be interested in someone else... Just a little while ago, I was thinking how great it would be to have a harem. Ha-ha-ha, I laugh out loud a bit and try my best to run away from that fact.

The person for me is Miss Wallenstein; the only person for me is Miss Wallenstein...

"...Footsteps?"

I stop jogging.

Thump, thump, thump. The sound of someone running comes from the other end of the side street. No...two someones, one big, one small. I can tell by the echoes of their shoes.

"Where...?"

I've just come off West Main. Looking back the way I came, I can still see people moving on the crowded street. The footsteps are getting louder, and they're coming this way.

They're still a little ways from me, but I don't like the idea of an incident happening so close to my home.

Being as careful as possible, I timidly look around the corner of my usual route.

"Ow!"

"Huh?!"

A shadow passing in front of my face suddenly crashes to the ground. It must have tripped over my foot as the shadow tried to turn the corner.

Trying to keep my own scream down, I turn around for a closer look.

...A prum?

The person is a bit shorter than the goddess, with limbs so thin that they might break if I touch them. Seeing how small every part of the body is, the name of a certain race of demi-human came to mind.

They are known for loving good food, dancing, and being merry.

"Excuse me, are you okay?"

"Eh...h."

The stuttering prum pulls her body off the pavement.

She's a girl. Her messy, chestnut-colored hair is long enough to hide her neck.

She looks like a child. That would explain her small size. Her oversized spherical eyes make quite an impression on me.

"Found ya, ya piece-of-shit prum!"

I'm just about to extend my hand to help the girl up when a human appears at the other end of the street. His rage-filled voice is making the girl shake with fear. Poor girl.

The man's eyes shine with anger, and he looks to be an adventurer, too.

He seems to be—perhaps twenty years old? He has a relatively large sword strapped to his back and looks much more experienced than me.

"Yer not getting away...!"

The man is like a demon breathing hellfire as he looks down on his prey.

He's not even looking at me directly, and I still lean back a bit out of fright. This guy is scary...

—What was he going to do to this prum girl?

My body moves on its own after that thought runs through my head. I step into his path, hiding the girl behind me.

"...What the?! Kid, yer in the way! Beat it!"

The man had been so focused on the girl that he just now realized I was here.

My cheeks twitch. I've stared down hundreds of monsters, but I'm not used to this feeling.

Facing down the man's powerful aura, I square my stance and lock my legs in place.

"Umm...What are you going to do with this girl?"

"Shut it, brat! If ya don't scram right now, I'll carve ya up along with the piece of shit behind ya!"

—Nope, can't move.

My eyes moisten up a bit, but I've made up my mind.

I don't know the details, but this man is about to do something very cruel to the girl behind me.

I pull my backpack off my shoulders and lightly toss it to the side of the nearest building. Of course the man is surprised, but I can see a look of shock on the girl's face just behind me, too.

The glazed look in the man's eyes vanishes as a new wave of red rage overtakes him.

"Kid…! Do ya *want* to die?!"

"W-wait…just a minute. If you can just calm down…!"

"Shaddup!! The hell is wrong with ya?! Is short stack there yer friend or something?!"

"N-never seen her before in my life."

"Then why the hell are ya protecting that piece of shit?!"

"…B-because she's a girl."

"The hell are ya saying…!"

Really, what *am* I saying…? But I don't think I have a choice. That really is the reason. That's what real men do, right? It's normal to help a girl in trouble. Do I need any more reason than that?!

"Fine…I'll slit yer throat first, kid…!"

The man reaches behind his back and draws his sword.

I can feel his intent to kill all over my body. I pull out the Divine Knife in response.

Ahh…I hear something gulp air behind me. Stealing a quick glance, I see the girl has her eyes fixed on me.

No, not me…the Divine Knife?

The man is taken aback at first, but soon assumes a ready stance and glares at me with pure hatred.

—This is bad.

This is my first time facing off against another human…My legs won't stop shaking. Can I…fight this fight?

I'm already nervous, but his killing energy is starting to make me panic. Sweat pours down my face. I swallow spit in my mouth over and over again. A ferocious smile grows on the man's lips as he sees my pitiful excuse for courage in the face of danger. He probably realizes that his opponent isn't ready for this.

He takes a few steps forward. I would like nothing more than to take a few steps back, but I force the urge down with pure willpower.

I can't see this ending well for me. But I can't back down.

It takes all of my power just to raise my eyes to meet his.

The next heartbeat, the man jumps straight for me.

"Stop right there."

The man never brings down his blade.

A forceful voice fills the area.

The man and I both look toward the source of the voice. An elvish girl holding a large paper bag stands just a few feet away.

Like Eina, her eyes and nose are high on her face. The main difference between her and the half-elf is that this girl's ears come to a full point.

Sky-blue, almond-shaped eyes bore straight through the male adventurer.

Wait, isn't she…Lyu? One of the waitresses who works at The Benevolent Mistress?

"Where do these rats keep coming from…?! What's yer deal?!"

"The one you intend to kill…He is destined to become the companion of a person irreplaceable to me. I will not allow you to injure him."

What did she just say…?

"What the hell is wrong with people today?! Ya really wanna die so bad?!"

"Silence!"

—The air itself seems to freeze.

The man who was yelling at the top of his lungs swallows his words. Lyu stands before us, her eyes sharp slits on her face. The sheer pressure of her presence is intense. A look of panic works its way onto the man's face.

I don't have any room to criticize him; I'm shaking in my boots, too.

"…—…?!"

"I don't want to cross blades with you. I have a bad habit of going too far." Lyu sounds detached, almost bored. She is bathed in red light from the setting sun shining in behind her from West Main.

I'll bet—yes, that's the truth.

It has to be true; I can tell how strong she is just by her posture.

The adventurer starts to flap his lips, like he's trying to deliver on his last warning. I hear a sharp *shing*, and suddenly there's a stiletto in Lyu's free hand.

C-couldn't see it at all…

"D-DAMN IT!"

The man turns slightly blue in the face before making a hasty retreat.

"……"

"Are you all right?"

The girl in front of me managed to fend off an adventurer without having to even throw a punch…I'm more than a little scared of her now.

I wipe off the sweat that built up under my chin.

Whether I'm sweating this much from staring down the man or from Lyu's display of power, I'm not sure.

Is Lyu, maybe, an adventurer herself…?

"Th-thank you very much. I was in a bit of a pinch there…"

"No, I'm sorry for getting in your way. I'm sure you could have dealt with this situation on your own just fine."

"I'm not so sure about that…"

I'd been petrified. I couldn't see myself getting out of that alive.

I scratch my chin and avoid looking at her. "Um, Lyu, why are you here?"

"I was shopping for supplies to prepare for this evening. Unlike in the afternoon, adventurers visit our establishment in the evening. So if we are not fully stocked, many problems tend to occur. I happened to see you in the middle of my errand, and you know the rest."

That makes sense. The Benevolent Mistress is a popular bar, so they would run out of ingredients and wine rather quickly.

Then again, "I know the rest"...We don't know each other very well. Maybe Lyu has a strong sense of justice?

"What about you? Why are you here?"

"Well, you see, this girl here...Huh?"

I spin around, looking for the prum girl, but she's gone. She's vanished into thin air.

"Was someone there?"

"Y-yeah. At least, I thought so..."

She must have gotten scared and run away.

It can't be helped; even I was scared out of my wits.

But that does seem kind of strange...

"If you will excuse me, I will take my leave now."

"All right," I say. "And really, thank you so much."

We exchange a quick bow and go our separate ways.

"Alrighty..."

Bell, fully equipped in the new armor he bought the previous day, took a look at himself in the mirror.

It went very well with his black inner clothing and pants. The new armor was so light that he could barely feel it. He would be able to move freely in combat.

His new emerald-green protector lightly sparkled on his left arm.

Bell ran his fingers down the outer edge of the gift from Eina with a smile on his face.

"Goddess, I'm heading out!"

"Gotcha...Have a good day..."

He grimaced a little at the sight of his exhausted goddess, sinking ever lower into the middle of the bed. Bell reached for the door. He had already given up on getting an explanation as to why the goddess was working at *Hephaistos Familia*.

Bell took one last look into the mirror. Now that he no longer had to wear Guild provision equipment, he looked more like a full-fledged adventurer. Bell smiled at his reflection and gave a nod of approval.

He left the hidden room under the only church, dagger and Divine Knife tucked into the armor behind his lower back.

Nice weather today...

The sky that opened up before him was blue and clear.

A smile perked up his lips as he gazed at the sky. He felt like something good was going to happen today.

He followed the side roads to West Main, and then down to Central Park.

Bell joined the waves of adventurers gathering at Babel Tower.

*Seize the day...*Bell mouthed to himself, a certain blond-haired, golden-eyed girl on his mind.

"Mister, mister. Mister with the white hair."

Bell stopped in his tracks, trying to figure out if the voice was addressing him.

"Huh?"

He turned in the direction the voice came from, but all he could see were other adventurers coming and going, all of them avoiding making eye contact. None of them could have been the owner of the voice.

"Mister, down...down here."

The voice of a little girl tickled his ear. Dropping his chin, he saw she was there.

The girl stood about 100 celch tall, dressed in a plain cream-colored robe. A hood covered most of her face with a little bit of chestnut-colored hair sticking out. A backpack at least twice, no, three times her size, big enough to surprise Bell, was strapped to her tiny shoulders.

Bell's eyes went wide as he felt a strong sense of déjà vu. Memories of the event on the side street the day before came flooding back into his mind.

"A-aren't you...?"

"Pleased to meetcha, mister! If you don't mind me asking, are you looking for a supporter?"

Interrupting Bell's words, the girl pointed an almost infant-sized finger toward the boy's back.

She was pointing to his backpack.

Anyone could guess that an adventurer walking alone and equipped with a backpack was going solo—perhaps thinking *If only I had a supporter...*

So the girl had come to confirm and asked him directly.

"W...what...?"

"Are you confused? This is a pretty simple situation, you know. A poor supporter has come to you, an adventurer, to sell her services in the Dungeon."

Opposite Bell's wide-eyed, confused look, the girl squinted her eyes and smiled from ear to ear.

"No, I mean, but...aren't you...from yesterday...?"

"......? Mister, have you met Lilly before? Lilly doesn't remember."

Many adventurers gave them annoyed looks as they passed by, wondering what these two were doing in the middle of the road.

"Are you sure?"

"So, mister, do you want a supporter?"

"Well...if I could find one...Yeah, I'd like one."

"Really? Then please take Lilly with you, mister!"

The girl looked so happy and innocent, her round eyes shining through her bangs from under her hood. Those big eyes found their way to the knife tucked nicely into Bell's waist.

"I suppose that'd be okay..."

"Ah! Names? Sorry, Lilly didn't introduce herself."

The girl took a few steps back and cheerfully smiled at Bell.

"Lilly's name is Lilliluka Erde. What's your name, mister?"

The eyes looking up at Bell twinkled suspiciously under her hood.

Chapter 2

THE SUPPORTER'S SITUATION

"So, you aren't a free supporter...?"

"Nope, Lilly's in a *Familia*."

We're on the second floor of Babel Tower, in the cafeteria. It's mid-morning; most adventurers are prowling the Dungeon. The cafeteria is mostly empty. The small girl and I sit facing each other across a table in the middle of the wide-open lunchroom. I have a few questions I want to ask this Lilliluka Erde.

"What's the name of your *Familia*?"

"It's *Soma Familia*, mister. Lilly thinks her *Familia* is pretty well known."

It seems like this girl who's approached me about going into the Dungeon together had been released from a contract with members of a different party. She has spent every day since then making trips between the Guild and Babel, trying to find someone to hire her to make money. She's in dire straits. Today, she happened to see me.

She saw someone without a party or a supporter, a solo adventurer.

She jumped at the opportunity without a second of hesitation.

Sure, I said I'd like a supporter, but to have someone just show up right when I wanted one...I'm not that naïve.

I take another look at her. Her body is very thin, and the slender lips that I can see beneath her hood always have the same happy smile plastered on them. While I can't see her eyes, she's got a cute little nose in the middle of her small face. She seems like an adorable kid.

I don't want to doubt what this innocent-looking girl is saying, but I don't think it's right to just agree to something straightaway without asking a few questions first. It's just common sense.

Something just doesn't feel right, so I keep asking the girl more questions.

"But, why me? I'm not in your *Familia*. It's not good for two members of different *Familias* to have a connection like this. Why don't you join adventurers in your own group?"

"Eh-heh, Lilly is so tiny, and not strong at all. 'Lilly is slow and will hold us back,' all the honorable members of Lilly's *Familia* always say. Lilly is treated like a burden. Even if Lilly asked them, they won't say yes."

She's being left out? Now I want to help her.

"Lilly's so useless in a fight it's embarrassing. The air at home is so bad; Lilly has been going from cheap hotel to cheap hotel every night to sleep."

Wait…She can't sleep at home? Not even relax…? What's with that?!

Her words shock me to the core. I can't believe anyone would treat a member of their own *Familia* like that.

For me, a *Familia* is a family.

Sure, there are only two members of *Hestia Familia*, but there is a strong bond. Not just a friendly connection but a real, warm family tie between us. Even if another person were to join our *Familia*, I don't think that would ever change.

A *Familia* is there to help you through thick and thin, that's how it should be.

But this girl's family is…shutting her out?

I feel a little dizzy. I know I shouldn't just take her at her word, but my whole world just turned upside down. I'm shaken.

"Lilly doesn't have enough money to stay at the same hotel tonight. So please, please, please, mister! Take Lilly with you into the Dungeon today!"

"Well…um…"

"Ah! If you're worried about the *Familia* thing, there shouldn't be a problem. Lilly's god, God Soma, doesn't talk to any other gods or goddesses, ever. So, unless your god already has something against God Soma, I don't think any fighting will break out between our *Familias*."

She must have misunderstood why I was mumbling. Lilliluka didn't let any silence into the conversation and added that piece of information.

…I do have a few thoughts on this, but for now, let's change the topic.

Now's as good a time as any to put some of my misgivings about her to rest.

"I understand your situation, Lilliluka…but can I check one thing?"

"Sure, what is it?"

"We seriously haven't met before?"

Is she really not the prum girl I met in the side street yesterday?

That's what has been bugging me. I don't know the face of the prum girl or her voice, but physically Lilliluka looks almost exactly like her. It happened yesterday; my memory isn't that bad.

"Today was the first time Lilly met you…Are you confusing Lilly for someone else?"

"…If it's okay, could you take off your hood?"

If I could see under that long hood, then I could make up my mind. I feel like they could be the same person because I have only seen half of Lilliluka's face.

Lilliluka looks at me for a moment after my request. Looking all around the room very quickly, I hear a soft "Okay…" come from beneath her hood. Her tiny hands reach up and pull it back.

"…Huh?"

"T-this enough?"

On the top of her head, cutely fluttering from side to side, are two animal ears.

My jaw drops. If this is true…

"…So, you're animal people?"

"Y-yes. Lilly is a Chienthrope—a dog person."

A few second pass until…*pop*. I stand up and lean over the table.

Lilliluka fidgets in her chair; maybe she can feel my gaze. A tail is swishing back and forth under her robe. I can see the chestnut fur on it poke out from under the hem.

She's no prum…But a little animal girl?

…*No way.*

My mind is still in shock, but my hands move on their own. They reach up and grab hold of both of the girl's animal ears, barely noticing how her small shoulders cringe.

"Hnnn…"

The ears between my fingers are soft and warm. They're tender.

I rub my fingers up and down the ears, Lilliluka getting redder and redder.

…They're real.

The soft fur, the muscles beneath the skin, the pink and moist inner ear—everything is real. There is no mistake.

It's not her…

I have no doubt. They may look similar, but they're not even the same race. There's nothing left to ask.

I let go of all of the trivial questions and just go with it.

"Ummm…mister…?"

"—?! S-sorry!!"

A little voice makes me realize what I was doing, and I let go and fly back to my chair like a frog jumping away from a fire.

She holds the ears I'd been fondling tightly against her head, looking up at me with a little bit of anger before an evil smile spreads across her lips.

"To think a man would play with Lilly's precious things like that… Lilly's going to make you take responsibility for this."

…I can't make a sound.

Blinking a few times, I feel like my face is on fire. My voice suddenly comes back, and I apologize over and over again on the spot.

"…If you don't mind me asking, why do you hide your race like that…?"

"Lilly's fur is dirty and matted—don't want people to see it…"

I ask her after finishing my series of apologies, whereupon Lilliluka pulls her hood back up, hiding her face in shame.

Personally, I think her fur looks very nice and kind of cute…But then again, I'm a guy, and there's no way I can wrap my head around what girls think about their own hair or fur.

It would be one thing if she were a prum, who are widely known to be the smallest race—but Lilliluka is still the smallest animal child I've ever seen. She can't be more than ten years old.

"So what will you do, mister? Will you hire Lilly?"

"...All right, I'll bring you along. For right now, just for today, I'll hire you as my supporter."

"Thank you, thank you, thank you!!"

After what I did to her ears, how can I refuse? If I left right now, I'd be the scum who did that to a little girl, then ran off.

...And on top of that, if I'm being honest, I want a supporter more than anything right now. I want to get as strong as I can, and I can't do that unless I can focus completely on combat. Lilliluka's proposition is a godsend.

"Well, um, isn't there an advance payment or something I have to give you before we go?"

"Sometimes that's true, yes. But today is a trial, so we can just divvy up the money after we get back from the Dungeon. If you'd give Lilly thirty percent, Lilly will jump with joy!"

"That's all? Fine with me. I'd just like to be more professional..."

From there we put our heads together to work out the details for a while, the same carefree smile plastered on Lilliluka's face.

Each section of the Dungeon was its own world, with unique layouts and characteristics.

The walls on levels one through four were a pale blue, and monsters that appeared there were usually just goblins and kobolds. There weren't many types of them, either.

The monsters closer to the fourth level were a little stronger and smarter than those higher up, but it could still be said that this area was the easiest for newbie adventurers to conquer. If they went in alone and avoided being surrounded—or better yet, formed a party—then there was very little risk in prowling these floors.

Everything changed on the fifth level.

The walls turned a slimy green and the layout got more complicated, but that wasn't all. More unpleasant monsters, like the seventh level's killer ant, appeared in larger numbers.

Plus, the birthing interval of monsters was much shorter on the seventh than the fourth. The moment an adventurer ventured into a dead end, they could be swarmed from all sides by monsters pouring out of the dungeon walls.

Many adventurers who grew overconfident on the upper levels met their doom here. Even if they didn't let their guard down, newbies got their first glimpse of the true threats inside the dungeon on lower levels five to seven. It was their first major obstacle to overcome.

They couldn't just go lower when they got bored on the upper levels. Adventurers needed to build a strong foundation before going deeper. Not just a strong "status," they needed experience, good equipment, fast reflexes, and general adventurer knowledge— among other things—to survive.

Newbie adventurers needed to spend time learning and growing on the upper floors first.

This was even truer for solo adventurers.

However.

"Hya!!"

"Gyshaaaa!!!"

In Bell's case, things were a little different.

His growth speed broke all the rules to such a point that he couldn't be compared to other newbie adventurers.

A killer ant's thin abdomen was caught by a long sweep of Bell's knife and split in two.

Prowling the seventh level, Bell charged into an incessantly advancing horde of monsters alone on a floor where a party was all but necessary.

"Jigigigigigigi!!"

"Not today!"

"Byugii!!"

Bell nimbly dodged a purple moth that came from above, the Hestia Knife connecting with its wing as the boy spun backward.

The now one-winged giant moth lost its balance and was slain as Bell plunged his dagger straight into its body.

"You two, stay put!!"

Bell kicked off the ground in the direction of two killer ants.

The monstrous ants flared open their mouth pincers to intimidate him, but Bell only sped up his assault.

He charged forward as if to take on both of the killer ants at once, but lunged for the one on the right at the last second.

The ants were a moment too late to react.

"—Giya?!"

Bell's leading blade plunged into the ant's upper body like a skewer.

Its hard outer shell crumbled under the power of the Hestia Knife; the flesh beneath was torn to shreds in an instant. The creature didn't even have time to writhe in pain or let out a dying shriek. The lights in its eyes cut out, and the killer ant fell silent.

Bell immediately turned to face the other ant—but his knife wouldn't budge.

"Huh?!"

The knife was jammed in a piece of the dead creature's thick shell-like skin. Bell couldn't move.

At the same time, enraged by the death of its brother, the remaining killer ant turned to face the boy and brought down its sharp claws on a collision course with Bell's face.

Bell jerked his left arm up to protect himself in the nick of time.

"Giii!!!"

"A...AAHHHHHH!!"

Shing! The killer ant's knifelike claws slid harmlessly off Bell's emerald-green protector.

A trail of sparks popped up in the claw's wake. Even with the creature's strength, it couldn't make a dent in this piece of armor.

Bell launched a counterattack.

Ignoring the jolts of pain in his left arm, he tossed the blade lightly into the air and let go of the Hestia Knife at the same time. His now free right hand caught the dagger in midair.

Slash.

The dagger's edge found a weak spot between the well-armored abdomen and thorax of the killer ant. Purple liquid spilled out from the wound.

Even though Bell's dagger was one of the weakest weapons available to adventurers, it was strong enough to inflict a mortal wound on a killer ant.

"—Gii!"

"Next!"

Bell delivered the final blow to the dying monster before yanking the Hestia Knife from its previously slain comrade. He then charged forward into another incoming group of monsters without stopping to catch his breath.

"Mr. Bell is so strong!!!"

While Bell tore into his next group of foes, Lilly was busy gathering all of the slain bodies into one spot.

She was very efficient. Even with a big smile on her face, she was very aware of her surroundings as she dragged the bodies into a line but never let them touch. Wearing specially made brown supporter's gloves, she grabbed onto the arms and legs of the lifeless beasts and hauled them across the dungeon floor with no problem.

"Sha!!!"

"Kyuu?!"

Thanks to Lilly's work, Bell didn't have to worry about footing and slew a needle rabbit with his dagger.

Bell was a humble person. Even though he possessed the strength to slay a monster in the same class as a killer ant, he wasn't letting it go to his head. He was following his adviser Eina's instructions to the letter: Slay the killer ants quickly so that they can't call for reinforcements. Do whatever it takes to avoid taking on a group by yourself.

Bell had the entire battle within this wide room firmly within his grasp.

"—Gushyuuu…!! ShyaaaaaAAAAA!!!!"

"Yikes!! Mr. Bell! One's about to be born!"

One of the dungeon walls had split open; a killer ant's ominous cries were coming from within.

Bell responded swiftly to a situation he had encountered countless times before.

He delivered a finishing blow to the remaining monsters before rushing up to the giant ant attempting to emerge from the crack in the wall.

© Suzuhito
Yasuda

After sprinting ten meters across the room, Bell leaped skyward and drove his left boot into the beast.

"One, two...!!!"

"Guweiii?!"

Echoes exploded on the kick's impact.

Crack! The ant's neck shattered. Its lifeless body hung from the side of the wall.

"Ohh, Mr. Bell, what should we do? That killer ant is stuck up there?"

"Hmm, what can we do?"

A bead of sweat ran down Bell's face as he tried to figure out how to get the ant's body, which looked like it was too big for a small hole, out of the wall. It was well out of Lilly's reach, but when she looked up and saw the confused look in Bell's eyes, she couldn't help but giggle.

"Mr. Bell's very strong, but weird. Ha-ha-ha-ha-ha-ha!"

"...Don't laugh!"

Realizing how dismal he looked, Bell cracked a small smile, too.

With the floor almost conquered and the room fully cleared, the two of them set to work on retrieving magic stones.

But now it was Lilly's time to shine. All Bell could really do was keep an eye out for any monsters that might try to sneak up on them.

"Whoa...You're really good at this..."

"It's because this is all Lilly can do to help. Mr. Bell, you slew all of these monsters, so you are the one who is really good."

Her experienced hands used a knife to cleanly and efficiently remove only the magic stone from the monster in front of her.

Her tiny hands moved with speed and precision, opening a small hole in the monster's chest before its body turned to ash.

Bell watched her work while thinking about his own woeful way of doing the same task, but decided to comment on something else.

"...Can I ask you a favor? Could you stop calling me 'Mr. Bell'?"

"Sorry, but that won't do. It goes against the contract, and it shows who is higher ranking in this party. Supporters cannot be condescending to adventurers."

"But, Lilliluka..."

"Mr. Bell, please call Lilly Lilly. Other names are okay too, but not by full name."

"Why are you so concerned about names?"

The third killer ant turned to ash as Lilly looked up at Bell. Her eyes hidden completely by her hood, Lilly forced a smile and said, "Are you listening, Mr. Bell?" before continuing.

"The word 'Supporter' sounds pretty, but underneath it all, Lilly and other supporters just carry the bags. Compared to the brave adventurers fighting monsters on the front lines, we're just cowards who watch from a safe distance and reap the rewards of battles that we didn't fight in. We're no better than parasites."

Given that just by going into the Dungeon, supporters were exposed to the same level of danger as adventurers, Lilly's speech wasn't necessarily true. Still, she continued without any hesitation.

"It is arrogant for Lilly and other supporters to think that they are equal to adventurers. The brave adventurers won't allow it. If Lilly tries, then the honorable adventurers get angry and won't give Lilly her share."

"Th-that's horrible…!"

"Lilly knew Mr. Bell was a good person as soon as we met. But there has to be a line. If word got out that Lilly wasn't treating Mr. Bell as a superior, Lilly won't get any contracts to go into the Dungeon with adventurers other than Mr. Bell from now on. Lilly would have to work for free."

"……"

Bell had his own morals, and they weren't about to change. However, he couldn't speak for other adventurers.

Something that seemed wrong to him might very well be common sense to someone else.

"It might be hard for Mr. Bell, but can you accept Lilly's request? Think of it as helping Lilly."

"…Sure thing, Lilly."

"Thank you very much!"

Bell gave in. If it meant helping Lilly, he had no choice but to ignore his own trivial opinions.

He decided that he would talk to her like a friend around his age rather than a business partner.

"On an unrelated note…Is Mr. Bell really a newbie adventurer? Lilly can't believe Mr. Bell slew all of those monsters alone…"

Lilly stopped working on the monster in front of her and counted the dead bodies with her tiny fingers.

If she counted the monsters already turned to ash, Bell slew four killer ants, three purple moths, and five needle rabbits, for a total of twelve monsters.

Leaving out the human-sized killer ants, the remaining monsters were all classified as "small," so it wasn't that difficult for adventurers to take on all of them.

But the icing on the cake was that Bell slew them all alone. Lilly couldn't look at him the same way after seeing what he could do.

"Yes, I won. But they almost had me more than a few times…"

"Mr. Bell is fighting by himself, so of course that's going to happen. Most distinguished adventurers like you come into the Dungeon in a party of three or more, you know? They don't want to fight solo down here."

"That's because they don't want to, right? Doesn't mean they couldn't do it. There are tons of Level One adventurers who are stronger than me, too."

"That…may be true."

"You've accompanied many parties into the Dungeon, right Lilly? So you've seen adventurers who are much stronger than me."

"…Yes. Lilly has seen adventurers stronger than Mr. Bell…"

"So, I've still got a long way to go."

Lilly looked up at a grimacing Bell with frustrated confusion. He had completely missed her point.

There were, in fact, solo adventurers who prowled the Dungeon on their own. However, Lilly wanted to know if Bell had really only started the job less than a month ago.

Common knowledge said that Level One adventurers could conquer lower levels one to twelve.

To put it in terms of which levels were appropriate for which statuses, adventurers with a status of *I* or *H* could work in levels one through four, *G* and *F* in five through seven, *E* through *C* in eight to ten, and *B* through *S* in levels eleven and twelve.

However, this was merely the received wisdom. Level Two category monsters would appear beginning with level thirteen and below, so it was generally accepted that Level One adventurers had no hope of clearing any of those floors.

If one were asked to state the average level of an adventurer in Orario, the answer would have to be "One." More than half of all adventurers worked on the top twelve floors.

Half of the remaining adventurers were at level two, with the remainder a mix of those who had become even more powerful.

The line between Level One and Level Two separated the lower-class adventurers from the upper class, and there was a significant difference. This was because they entered the "Third Tier" class of adventurers from Level Two. Since Level One was average, going beyond that point required a good amount of talent and skill.

Since adventurers' statuses were considered personal information, they were well protected. Figuring out an average status was very difficult. However, most adventurers who hadn't yet leveled up to Two spent the bulk of their time on levels seven to ten of the Dungeon.

To put it another way, the average adventurer's status grades were somewhere between *G* and *C*. That was the line that beginners had to cross to become experts.

Bell was already standing shoulder to shoulder with these "advanced beginners" after only a few weeks of working as an adventurer. It was understandable that Lilly would have some trouble believing what she had witnessed that day.

"Also, Mr. Bell has a good weapon to go along with his strong status."

The tone of Lilly's voice made a sudden but subtle change.

Bell didn't notice, and shyly laughed at her words.

"Yeah, you've got that right. I've been relying on this knife a bit too much. At this rate, I won't get much stronger, will I?"

"No, no, it's a weapon's dream to be wielded by a worthy master. The point is, Mr. Bell's strength is wielding that weapon without wasting movement. Today is proof of your strength."

"Do…do you really think so?"

Bell had his back to Lilly, keeping a sharp lookout for monsters. His hand reached around and stroked the knife.

Black from end to end, it was a very rare knife indeed.

Bell's fingers ran along the Ἥφαιστος insignia on the sheath of the weapon.

Lilly's eyes went wide and flashed a fiery blaze.

"Lilly doesn't know much about weapons, but Lilly knows that knife is special. How in the world did you get it? Lilly doesn't mean to be rude, but Mr. Bell is still a newbie, and newbies don't have much money…"

"The goddess…the goddess of my *Familia* gave it to me. Apparently she went through a lot asking one of her goddess friends for it. I think she tried a bit too hard."

"What a…nice goddess you have."

"Yes. She's very important to me."

Bell didn't notice the hidden twinge of jealousy or the shaking in Lilly's voice.

Lilly finished off the last needle rabbit a bit more roughly than necessary before standing up and sneaking up behind Bell's back.

"Mr. Bell?"

"Oh, you finished?"

Lilly flashed another big grin as Bell turned to face her.

"Since we're here, we might as well get the magic stone from the killer ant in the wall."

"I agree. But how?"

"If Mr. Bell cuts open the thin part of its chest, that will be enough. The magic stone is in there, anyway. Lilly will take it from there."

"I gotcha. So…"

"Here, Mr. Bell."

"Eh…Ah, okay."

Bell took the knife that Lilly handed to him. He was about to draw the Hestia Knife, but Lilly's knife would work. Bell walked over to the killer ant, the lower half of its body still inside the wall. Grabbing the thick skin on the monster's upper body, he lined up Lilly's knife with the thin area between the killer ant's upper and lower body.

Hmm...This knife is really hard to use...

Bell stood on his tiptoes as he fought with the shell-like skin, struggling to cut it open.

He was completely focused on cutting the ant open, never once looking behind him.

With his arms up and in front of him, his sides and back were completely open and defenseless.

"Huh?"

Something didn't feel right. A shock ran through his brain.

His head flipped around.

"Have you finished?"

Lilly was standing right beside him, looking up at the ant's body with big eyes and standing as tall as she could.

Bell blinked his wide eyes a few times and chuckled to himself. He held out his hand, gesturing. "Just a moment."

Bell finally guided the small blade to the top of the killer ant's chest. Lilly quickly moved in to claim the stone.

"Well then, shall we call it a day, Mr. Bell?"

"Eh? Already? I can keep going, no problem."

"No no, you're being overconfident. Today, Mr. Bell has slain many purple moths, a monster that spreads poisonous wing-scales during battle. The effects are not immediate, but if you breathe in too much, your body will be poisoned."

"N-no way!"

"It's true. Lilly was careless and forgot to buy more antidotes... Lilly suggests going back to Babel Tower for treatment."

As soon as Lilly finished speaking, Bell remembered Eina saying that he should be aware of where he was while battling moth-type monsters. Bell put his hand to his head with a small gasp and agreed with Lilly's proposal.

"What is being poisoned like...? Wait, when do the symptoms show up? I'll need all of my strength to slay monsters, otherwise..."

"There is no problem, Mr. Bell. Lilly knows a fast way to get back to Babel without having to fight any monsters."

"Y-you do?"

Lilly nodded her head in a resounding "yes" and pointed toward the exit of the room. A group of adventurers stood just outside the archway. They turned and left upon seeing that Bell and Lilly had already slain all of the monsters within.

"If we trace the path of other strong adventurers, there won't be any monsters. They prowl the Dungeon for monsters...I mean, dropped items and magic stones, right?"

"Oh, I see."

"Even if monsters come out, we can just hide in the shadow of another party and they will take care of them for us. The idea is to choose a path with people, and we can avoid all battles."

Usually, Bell would avoid adventurers from other *Familias* to prevent any difficult situations from happening. But in times like this, it might be the best option.

This was a good way to get out of a bad situation, if they could pull it off.

"Many honorable adventurers are in the Dungeon at this time of day. If Mr. Bell sticks close to Lilly, he won't have to use his weapon even once."

Lilly looked up at Bell with one of her big smiles, and he was struck by just how reliable the girl was.

"Lilly, you really are amazing. You are a 'supporter' for a reason: I can count on you."

"Mr. Bell will learn many things too with experience. Now, let's get moving!"

Lilly snatched Bell's hand and half pulled him out of the room. Following the footprints on the dungeon floor, they ran past a few groups of adventurers on their way to the top. Whenever a monster showed up, they were always close to the battle party. Lilly's instincts were spot-on.

She was so efficient, it was almost as if she had done this hundreds of times.

"Mr. Bell, Mr. Bell. About today's payment..."

"Well, you have helped me out a lot. So I think we should split it fifty-fifty..."

"All magic stones and dropped items collected today are yours, Mr. Bell. May your wallet be warm tonight."

"What?! But that leaves you nothing! Didn't you say you wanted at least thirty percent?!"

"Your trust is worth much more to Lilly. Today was a day for Mr. Bell to learn about Lilly, and think of this as a thank-you gift."

"To...learn about you?"

"Everyone gets this trial day, not just you, Mr. Bell."

So today was just a test for Lilly. Bell didn't feel right about it at all. Bell blushed as he looked at the girl, wanting to apologize.

"...Besides, everything else is a parting gift."

A strong breeze blew through the lobby and carried her words with it.

"...? Did you say something, Lilly?"

"No, nothing at all, Mr. Bell. If it's okay with you, please hire Lilly in the future!"

"Sure, I'll think about it and come back with a good answer."

Lilly turned and ran, but looked back over her shoulder and waved at Bell.

"Please do! Lilly is always in Babel, so you can always find me! Lilly's not going anywhere, so take your time!"

The girl was grinning from ear to ear.

"Aah, another *Familia*'s supporter..."

"So, this wasn't a good idea after all?"

I'm in the very familiar counseling room at the Guild main office, talking with Eina about Lilly. After visiting the medical facilities (they cost money, by the way) and the Exchange, I'd hurried straight here.

It sounds sad, but I don't think I can make a good decision about something like this on my own.

The best way to solve this is to get another's opinion, and who better to ask than Eina?

"I know you are concerned about a problem between *Familias*, but there have been plenty of cases of both sides benefiting from a healthy and respectable contract...Bell, what do you think of this girl, Lilliluka?"

"Well, she's a good girl...and her skills as a supporter are very high."

I think back to what I saw her do in the Dungeon. She'd made a good impression on me.

On top of that was her situation...I felt so sorry for her I couldn't just ignore her.

I know it's not good to do something just out of pity, but still...

I'm pretty sure that she wasn't lying when she told me about how her *Familia* has been treating her, ignoring her. My gut feeling is she was telling the truth.

"Do you know what *Familia* she belongs to?"

"She said she's a member of *Soma Familia*."

"*Soma Familia*, huh...I can't strongly support or oppose that one."

"Um...Ms. Eina? What kind of *Familia* are they?"

She says, "Wait a moment," as she pulls out a large file from the desk that was already prepared and opens it in front of her. Eina pulls a pair of glasses out of her pocket and with a quick flick of the wrist and a light *click*, she slides them over her eyes in one fluid motion.

It seems like she isn't just going to give me her opinion, but some accurate public information as well.

"Looks like *Soma Familia* is your model dungeon-prowling *Familia*. They are a little different from other *Familias* in that they also dabble in the retail industry."

"Retail? What are they selling?"

"They sell wine."

"Wine...?"

"Yes. They don't supply very much product to stores and market-places, but I hear the taste is extraordinary. Apparently there is a very high demand in Orario."

She keeps on talking, adding that with a product like that, they shouldn't even need to go into the Dungeon.

Since danger always follows adventurers, the best thing for gods to do when they make a *Familia* is to go into a safe industry. Sure, it's a gamble to go into retail, but relying on adventurers for money is like walking on a suspension bridge that can be cut at any moment. Adventurers brush shoulders with death every day.

On the other hand, adventurers change everything. If the god is not afraid of the high-risk, high-return atmosphere of the Labyrinth City Orario, then adventurers are the best way to strike it rich in a hurry.

"That *Familia* is in the middle of the pack in terms of strength. No one stands out above the rest, but everyone has above average power. Whoa…They have quite a few members, too. I had no idea."

"So if they have a lot of members, then that means…"

"Their god, Soma, has a good following. I haven't heard anything good or bad about that god at all, though…"

"Um…the girl, Lilly, said this to me, but is it true that the god Soma doesn't interact with any other gods or goddesses?"

"I would actually say he is rather famous for that. It feels strange to say that a god stays apart from this world, but that really is him. He's never attended one of the other gods' Celebrations, nor has he responded to social calls. It's a challenge finding someone who has even seen him."

Well, that's…an extreme case.

Didn't Lilly say that Soma never talks to other gods and goddesses?

And then Eina said that she couldn't strongly support or oppose my involvement based on this *Familia*. Must be because they're safe—too safe, even. They aren't on "friendly" terms with any other *Familiar*, but they're not on "bad" terms with anyone else, either…

"There doesn't seem to be anything wrong with the *Familia* itself…just."

"Just?"

Eina furrows her brow like she's deep in thought, but makes up her mind and starts talking.

"This is just my opinion, but the members of *Soma Familia* seem different from members of other *Familias*. Fighting among one another, almost like they're frantic…"

"……"

"They don't seem like 'live fast, die young' types, but…I don't know how to describe them. At any rate, every single member of that *Familia* seems desperate, somehow."

Eina's face looked troubled as she spoke. I could only listen and wonder.

But as I hear all of this, I kind of feel like I can see how Lilly's circumstances turned out that way…

"For now, I will give my support in hiring that girl as a supporter."

"Eh? Is it all right?"

"Yes. Surely there are a few questionable things about *Soma Familia*, but I think the problems between *Familia* members that you've been worried about won't happen. I'm basing that on Soma himself."

Lilly said the same thing.

"As long as you are careful around other members, you should be fine. And personally, I'd prefer that you form a party with a supporter rather than going solo, so I'd encourage you to hire her."

"Ms. Eina…"

"After that, it's up to you. You'll have to take responsibility for whatever you decide."

…Isn't that obvious?

Waiting for someone else's permission to interact with Lilly would be rather rude to her. I have to make a decision myself now. I need to relax, get my thoughts together, and make a final call.

"One more thing. I looked around to see if I could find a free supporter for you, but I couldn't find anyone. I knew of a few, but all of them entered a *Familia* very recently."

Eina forces a smile and says, "I'm sorry about that." We've talked about me hiring a supporter before; she must have been thinking about that since then.

"Must be that Free people don't usually want to set foot in the Dungeon. Their income depends entirely on who they make their contract with, and it's very dangerous. There have to be safer, higher paying jobs all over the place."

A "Free" person is someone who doesn't belong to a *Familia*. This goes without saying, but they don't have Falna—the mark of a god's blessing—or a Status. They're no stronger than townsfolk.

There are some races like the naturally powerful dwarves or the magically adept elves that can fight monsters on their own, though, so I don't want to say all Free people are powerless.

As all my thoughts come together, something Lilly said pops back into my mind.

"Ms. Eina. Do adventurers look down on supporters?"

"...In a way, yes. Full-time supporters are not very highly respected. I'm sure you can figure out the reason why..."

We just carry the bags. Lilly's voice runs through my head.

Is that really true? I've always admired adventurers, but now I feel kind of disappointed in them.

"Normally, adventurers who aren't powerful become supporters. Most *Familias* delegate their weaker members to the role of supporter, even if they level up."

But in that case, it's a way for weaker adventurers to go deeper into the Dungeon and learn. By carrying the bags and accompanying their stronger peers, they can see both high-level monsters and advanced combat techniques up close and personal.

"It's not like everyone who receives Falna will keep getting stronger without a limit. It depends on what that person is made of, if they can stand in front of a monster and not crumble under the pressure. In fact, it's quite common that an adventurer who can slay weaker monsters all day can't lay a finger on anything after that."

"……"

"The fact is that these weaker adventurers become support specialists...So, yes, they're an easy target for discrimination."

The mood in here is getting heavy. Eina's face tells me everything I need to know about her thoughts on the matter; she doesn't like it at all. I don't think she likes talking about it, either.

But it's all coming together now. This explains why Lilly was so humble—she was labeled a "weak supporter" by those around her. So she stays away from her *Familia*. Everyone.

......I hate this.

Just what the hell is this feeling? It's not even my problem, but I can't sit still or calm down.

Resisting the urge to yank out my hair, I do my best to pull myself together and stand up from the chair.

I would have been lost in thought for hours if I sat still.

"Thank you, Ms. Eina. I will think about what you said and make a decision."

"It's no problem. You can see me anytime, so when you have something like this on your mind, come and talk with me. Okay?"

She gives me a nice smile. I bow one more time in thanks.

Standing back up, I lightly turn to face the door.

"Um...Bell?"

"Yes, what is it?"

"What happened to your knife?"

"Eh?" I'm still lost in thought, so my reply sounds kind of stupid.

Eina is now halfway out of her chair, her face filled with worry and her eyes on my lower back.

"Knife...?"

I reach around my back.

My dagger, there.

Pouch for magic stones, there.

Divine Knife, there.

...But only the sheath.

".........."

There is only dry air where the handle should be.

Sssss...Blood drains from my face at an alarming speed.

Eina watches as I frantically pat down my body, mouthing the words "It can't be..."

The Divine Knife is...gone.

My face turns blue.

"...I *dropped* it?!"

The thief continued on through the backstreets.

The overall atmosphere back here was completely different from the big shops and bright colors of Main Street.

Looking up, the thief saw only a long strip of the sky was visible between long brick houses. The bottoms of the clouds were dyed orange by the evening sun's weak light. The day was ending. A group of cats gathered around a shabby garbage dump, their golden eyes all pointing this way. Nyaaaa-nnn. They all scattered at the thief's approach.

Thump, thump, thump. The echoes of small feet bounced down the alleyway.

The thief ran through streets even more complex than the Dungeon itself, entirely certain of the destination. After turning many corners, the thief found the looked-for building.

An ancient dwelling stood in the middle of a small clearing. The thief didn't know whether it actually was ancient or not, but it certainly had that feel.

A dusty, hard-to-read sign could be seen above the one-story wooden house.

The thief opened the door and entered, causing a sad little bell to ring.

"Ooh, it's you, my friend."

"I have some business."

A completely bald gnome with a white beard looked up from a newspaper. He was wearing a red hat, but the thief knew he had no hair. Without a word, the thief set a knife on the counter.

"You've brought me somethin' strange again today, I see..."

Adjusting his glasses and thoroughly inspecting the blade, the master of the shop said, "Back in a jiffy," and left the counter. His round head disappeared into the back of the shop—a space filled with hundreds of antiques. Looking around, the thief saw there were many breathtaking jewels lined up in a glass case.

The gnome was very quick to return.

His face seemed surprisingly sour.

"Just what is this? Did you pick it up at the garbage pile on your way here?"

"Huh—?"

"The blade won't cut, stab, or slice. And it has no special attributes to it at all. And…I don't know how to put it, but…this blade feels… dead."

Placing the weapon back on the counter, the old gnome scratched his white beard for a moment before saying, "This is trash, nothing more. This is unusual for you, my friend. Bringin' somethin' like this to me."

"W-wait a minute! That can't be right…!"

"Even so, I can't show this to my regulars…If you still want to sell it, it'd make a fine decoration. How's thirty vals sound?"

"I…I'll be back!"

"O-ho! I'm lookin' forward to it…But these markin's look like earthworm trails, this geezer thinks he's seen them somewhere before…"

With shaking shoulders, the thief took the blade downstairs. The door slammed closed in the thief's wake.

Thump, thump, th-thump. The thief's footsteps reentered the back alleyway, a bit more roughly than when they had come in.

Thirty vals? The same price as a potato snack from that street stand? That idiot! This is a weapon that easily sliced through the carapace of monsters like it was tissue paper! It should be worth enough to build three palaces and still have change left over!

Had the old gnome gone mad? Then again, just yesterday he gave a very satisfying appraisal. Did his head go bad overnight?

His appraising eyes never failed. The fools at the Guild didn't even come close.

There was no one better than him in this city.

So why…?

The thief looked down at the knife.

Not a single glint of light came from the weapon. The blade had a series of complicated characters carved into it. Pitch black from tip to tip; it was hard to tell how long the blade was in the dark alley. It was the same color as shade.

For this blade to be such a rotten shade of black—something didn't feel right.

Earlier it had carved arcs in the air and glowed a darkly purple glow...

If only it had the "Ἥφαιστος" signature...The sheath, I need the sheath...

If there was undeniable proof of its value, then even if it were trash, the blade could be sold at a very high price.

The sheath. This blade was worthless without it. All these thoughts came together in the thief's mind while looking at the black piece of junk.

The only option now was to change the plan: take a major risk and make contact once more...

"I apologize, Syr. I never meant for you to carry the groceries."

"I really don't mind, but...Lyu, do you always come through here?"

"Indeed. I have found that I can reduce time in transit by learning the layout of these backstreets. They are not as inconvenient as you are thinking, Syr."

"That's not exactly what I was worried about..."

The two of them were coming from the front, an elf and a human. Both of them were holding large paper bags. The bags were so full that apples and a variety of other fruits and vegetables were in danger of falling out.

The thief looked away and hid the knife in a sleeve.

Can't believe anyone would cut through an alley this deep. Just act natural and walk past them...

"—Stop right there, prum!"

A voice with overwhelming presence lashed out from behind.

The thief came to a sudden stop. Cold sweat ran all the way down the thief's back.

Why did she call out? Something unbelievable occurred to the thief.

"That knife hidden in your sleeve—I would like to take a closer look at it."

Inwardly, the thief made a great tongue-cluck of irritation.

"Lyu...? Um, Lyu?"

"...Why do you ask?"

"Because it bears a strong resemblance to a possession of someone I know. I would like to confirm that it is a different weapon."

Just how damn good is your eyesight, anyway? The thief wanted to curse at the elf.

The elf could see a pitch-black blade in this darkness? Even prums with their tremendous eyesight would have difficulty doing that.

"I'm sorry to inform you that this is mine. You are mistaken."

Flight without leaving any time to react—yes, that was the key.

Completely ignoring the elf's request, the thief made a break for it.

"Draw."

The air in the alley cracked.

"......?!"

"I only know of one person who wields a weapon engraved with hieroglyphs."

It was as if a blade of ice were pressed against the thief's neck. The thief's ankles felt frozen.

Even the human girl drew back in shock. The elf was just that intimidating.

Can't turn to face her. Don't want to turn and face her.

"Be still."

The thief's jaw was locked in place, breath ragged and shaking, heart beating fast enough to break ribs.

The elf's footsteps drew near. There was no longer much distance between them now.

It's do or die. No time for a plan, just get away.

The thief's knees bent, ready for action. Suddenly, the elf's foot slammed down onto the road just ahead, cutting off the escape route.

"I warned you."

The thief ran to the nearest corner and was just about to turn when a strike of terrible force hit the thief's hand dead-on.

"Gwahhhhh!"

An apple?

It *exploded.*

The red fruit hit the thief's left hand, which was carrying the knife. The shock sent pieces of the apple soaring in all directions, so fierce was the impact.

"You may wish to brace your stomach."

"—"

The knife fell from the thief's hand. The thief looked back.

Calm, sky-blue eyes looked down from above, her leg bent far behind her body.

So that's how it is. I'm the ball. You've gotta be kidding me.

Her leg swung forward and hit, just as she warned, right into the small of the thief's back.

"Hnggaaah?!"

"Wh-what was that?"

He heard it when he was running like a maniac down West Main in front of Guild headquarters.

A piercing scream, echoing from the backstreets.

Bell was retracing his steps to see if the Hestia Knife had fallen on the street somewhere, but he knew in an instant that what he heard was not a normal scream, and he stopped on the spot.

The demi-humans in the area all followed suit. The next moment, a large number of cats came pouring out of one backstreet entrance, running as if their lives were at stake. Bell looked down that alleyway as far as his ruby-colored eyes would allow.

"Meow! Meow!" the wave of cats cried as they ran away from whatever was inside. The panicking felines weaved in and out of the legs of people on the busy street, turning the whole area into chaos. Bell carefully worked his way through the throng of people toward the backstreet, sweat rolling down his cheek.

Bracing himself to face whatever was coming this way, Bell inched into the alley. All of a sudden, a small shadow collapsed with a loud *thud* at his feet.

"L-Lilly?"

"Haa-aah?"

Jumping back for a moment after finding one of the most unlikely of people, Bell kneeled next to the girl.

"Hey, what happened?! What's wrong?!"

"Th-that voice...Mr. Bell?"

Her small body shook as she tried to get up, like a newborn fawn trying to stand for the first time. Her face looked frightened at first, but she soon showed him her usual smile.

"Actually, I was attacked by a violent lady...Er, I mean, a stray dog..."

"A-are you okay?!"

"Somehow..."

Her cream robe wasn't all that dirty, but it was obvious to Bell that Lilly had taken some serious damage. For now, he wrapped his arm around her shoulder and helped her out of the middle of the street and off to the side.

Just when Bell was reaching for his leg holder to see if he had a spare potion...

"I cannot believe he managed to escape..."

Crick, crick. The sharp sounds of shoes on stone accompanied the elf, Lyu, as she turned the corner.

"You too, Lyu?! What the hell's going on back there?"

"Ah, great timing. I just happened to have found your..."

Lyu had said that much before her eyes found a hunched-over Lilly sitting on the ground.

Lilly was shaking like a scared child, rubbing her hands over the hood covering her face.

"Mr. Cranell, please step aside."

"Eh? What? Hey?!"

"Eiiikkkk!"

Lyu pushed Bell to the side and grabbed ahold of Lilly, pulling her hood back with no hesitation.

Big, round eyes and disheveled chestnut fur emerged, followed by two doglike ears. Lyu stared down the traumatized girl with unwavering eyes before saying, "My apologies," and pulled the hood back to its original position.

"What the hell do you think you're doing?! Lilly! Are you okay?!"

"Y-yes…"

"I mistook you for someone else. I seem to have lost my temper in the moment."

Bell was utterly confused by the course of events. He did his best to support a wobbly Lilly as his eyes flicked back and forth between Lyu and deeper into the back alley.

In no time at all, more light echoes came from within. Syr emerged from the backstreet, carrying large paper bags in both hands.

"Lyu! Lyu—!! You can't use food like that! Mama'll get mad at you, you know!"

"That would be…a problem."

"Umm, can someone give me an explanation already…?"

"Oh, Bell."

Syr smiled and did a small curtsy. Bell responded with a simple "Hi…"

Lyu waited for their greetings to finish before giving Bell a straight answer.

"Mr. Cranell, is that black knife currently in your possession?"

"Oh! That's right!! Have either of you seen a knife that's completely black from top to bottom?!"

Suddenly coming out of his confusion, Bell frantically looked both girls in the eyes.

Lyu withdrew a dull, lackluster black knife from the fold of her robe and held it up for Bell to see.

"Is this the weapon?"

"—WAAAAAAAAAAAAAAAAAAAAAAHHHHHHHHH HHH!!"

Bell's scream of jubilation pierced the evening sky.

The shoulders of three different races of girls simultaneously flinched in surprise at the sheer volume of his voice.

Even the ever-calm and aloof Lyu's sky-blue eyes opened wide.

"THANK YOU! Thank you so much!"

"...Mr. Cranell. You are putting me in an awkward situation. I should not be receiving this praise, but Syr..."

"I'm saying it to you, Lyu!"

Bell looked like he was about to cry. He had both his hands clasped around Lyu's smooth, white free hand. An uncharacteristic look of panic grew on the elf's face as Bell came closer to her, crying like a child.

Hearing Syr's screams, Bell took the knife and wiped his face on his sleeve, sniffling.

"I'm so relieved...Goddess, I'm sorry. I swear I'll never drop you again...!"

"Drop...?"

Bell brought the knife up to his cheek as he swore to it. The piece of trash suddenly came alive again and began to emit a purple glow.

Like the spirit of a dog finding its long-lost master, the Hestia Knife had come home.

Lilly's big eyes grew even wider.

"Thank you for going out of your way, really. Where did you find it?"

"I did not find it, *per se*. It was being carried by a prum."

"Prum?"

Bell gave Lyu an inquisitive look after hearing her answer.

Tension grew beneath the hood of the girl behind him.

"Was it, maybe, the one from before...?"

"Yes, I was in pursuit, but I lost the prum...and mistook the girl here for that person. I was too quick to judge. You have my apologies."

"Quick to judge? So that means...?"

"Yes, this girl is obviously a Chienthrope. The one I was chasing was a male prum."

A lightbulb came on in Bell's eyes as he finally understood what had happened. A look of relief swept over Lilly's face under the cover of her hood as she let her body relax.

"Did you happen to see a male prum come through here? Is he close by?"

"Sorry, I haven't seen anything…"

"Well then, it would seem that said prum found the knife that you dropped. He seems to have had the good fortune to notice your knife before today. It is a strange weapon, so he must have remembered it after seeing it but once."

"Ah, that makes sense."

Lilly seemed very uncomfortable during Bell and Lyu's conversation.

Syr quietly watched the girl from between the two paper bags in her arms.

With the situation resolved, Lyu and Syr needed to finish their shopping. Bell said another thank-you to the both of them. Lyu did a slight head bow in response; Syr chuckled softly and said she hadn't done anything to be thanked for.

Bell stepped out of their way as Lyu and Syr started back into the alleyway.

It was as they were leaving that Syr bent down and whispered into Lilly's ear.

"—No more mischief from you, all right?"

"!!"

A cold chill shot through Lilly's skin.

Her tiny body shook pitifully.

Syr stood up as if nothing had happened and joined the stern-faced Lyu as they went into the backstreet again.

"Lilly, what did Syr say just now?"

"N-nothing…Um, Mr. Bell?"

"Yes?"

"Who are those two?"

"They're waitresses at a bar. It's called The Benevolent Mistress. It's pretty popular—have you heard of it?"

"…Mr. Bell."

"Yeah?"

"Never, ever take Lilly there, okay?"

"Uh, er, okay…" was all Bell could say to the half-laughing, half-crying Lilly. He could tell that something was still wrong with her, and quietly broke a sweat.

With the sun setting in the west, Main Street had finally calmed down and returned to normal. Bell and Lilly stood there for a moment, a strange air between them.

The next day.

Lilly and I make our way to the Dungeon early in the morning. We walk side by side down the first floor of the Dungeon, the light spots in the ceiling shining down on us like the magic-stone lamps around the city above.

In the end I decided to hire Lilly as my supporter.

I've had to consider all sorts of things, but after collecting my thoughts this is what I honestly want to do. The goddess even granted her permission. Once I got that far, there wasn't any point in saying no.

Lilly and I signed a party-member contract with each other that didn't have a specified time limit. Today is day one.

"…Mr. Bell?"

"Hm?"

"That knife—where did you put it?"

"Ah. The knife and its sheath are in my breastplate. There's a slot under the outer layer and they fit nicely. That way, I won't accidentally drop it again."

"I…see."

I tilt my neck out of confusion as her head droops down.

She hasn't had any energy at all today. She's smiling like usual, but it feels empty. I wonder if something happened.

"Mr. Bell. Let me thank you again for hiring Lilly as your supporter. Lilly will work very hard so that Mr. Bell doesn't abandon her in the Dungeon."

"Abandon?! I wouldn't do that to anyone. Besides, you're the only supporter I have, Lilly."

"Lilly's glad to hear that...But Lilly already knows Mr. Bell wouldn't do such a thing because Mr. Bell is surprisingly gracious."

I don't think I'll ever get used to this hierarchy thing.

Lilly is also starting to close the gap, but "gracious"? Being called something so polite makes my skin crawl.

"Mr. Bell, may I ask about today's plan?"

"Well, I was thinking that we'd go to the seventh level again today and work until evening. Is that okay with you, Lilly?"

"If that is what Mr. Bell has decided, then Lilly shall obey. However, are you sure? As you know, Lilly is only a supporter and isn't any use in battle. You'll be fighting off wave after wave of monsters alone, Mr. Bell."

"That's okay with me. I'm used to fighting alone, and last night my goddess updated my status with yesterday's experience."

I didn't spend the last few weeks as a solo adventurer just for show.

Fighting alone for long periods of time is just another trip into the Dungeon for me. Thanks to Eina's rather severe teaching methods, I've gotten very good at managing time as well. I feel like I can brag about that a little.

But above all, the goddess updated my status with her own hands last night, so there's no way I'll be outmatched by any monsters on that level. To be honest, I'm itching to test my new power.

My status grew just as much as before. It's almost scary how fast my abilities are growing. It's the best feeling in the world.

...But for some reason, when the goddess sees how much I've grown, she gets upset and her mood turns sour...I really have no idea what's up with that.

"I'm more worried about you, Lilly. Drop items will pile up pretty quickly, and your backpack will get very heavy..."

I glance at the girl at my side. Her tiny body only comes up to my stomach. It can't be easy for someone that small to carry all that loot up and down the Dungeon floors.

"You don't have to worry, Mr. Bell. Because Lilly has a Falna, too. No matter how much is in the backpack, Lilly won't get tired."

I'm sure she's telling the truth...but still.

Lilly's backpack is well beyond the standard size, so even now with nothing inside, it still makes quite an impression.

"On top of that, Lilly has a Skill. So Mr. Bell won't be held back at any time during transport to the surface even if the unthinkable happens."

"Huh?! You have a skill, Lilly?"

Amazing! I'm jealous! I can't hide it in my voice.

Lilly laughs a little at me before shaking her head.

"It's better than nothing, but a pitiful skill. It's not the wonderful 'blessing' you are thinking of, Mr. Bell."

"Even still! I don't even have one skill…"

"Skills" are different from "Magic" in that, as long as you have the excelia—experience—you can learn many of them. I've heard that there are adventurers with five (!!) skills. So even if it's a skill like Lilly's that doesn't have much impact, as long as it doesn't have a negative side effect then you are stronger than you were without it.

"I'm so jealous right now…Skills and Magic are really hard to learn, right? I don't have Magic, either…Ah, speaking of which, do you have any magic, Lilly?"

"…Unfortunately, Lilly doesn't have magic, either. There are many people who never see their own magic; Lilly is probably one of them."

That's right. Tens of thousands of people may gain the possibility of learning magic with their Falna, but it's only a possibility. Many people, it seems, weren't lucky enough to have that possibility become reality.

As someone who pictured himself using all kinds of magic while reading about heroes of adventure over and over again since childhood, it's a truth I don't want to face…Lilly looks up at me, my shaking shoulders sunk on my body as my mind filled with the thought of never having magic.

Telling the details of your status to someone outside of your *Familia* is a violation of manners and also prohibited—even if said someone is under contract with you.

It's kind of obvious if you think about it. An adventurer's status is both private information and their lifeline.

I feel like a jerk for bringing this up, and I regret it.

"One other thing: Are you sure you don't want a signing fee or an advance payment?"

Keeping an eye on the road ahead, I ask Lilly about the details of our contract.

Lilly said it during our sorry excuse for a signing ceremony in Babel Tower. That she only wanted a share of the income after taking our loot from the Dungeon to the Exchange.

I'm the one hiring her. There should be more to this...

"Yes, that's fine. Mr. Bell isn't working with any other party members, so there won't be any problems figuring out who gets what at the end of the day...and then."

"And then?" I repeat back to her like a parrot.

Lilly's cheerful mood changes all of a sudden...I feel like I see a little hesitation in the eyes hidden behind her bangs.

"...Also, this is the best arrangement for Mr. Bell, yes?"

"Eh?"

There's a strange mix of sneering and self-mockery in her words.

I'm a little flustered, hearing Lilly talk to me like that for some reason. I don't have a clue why.

Less than a second later, Lilly smiles her usual smile, like nothing had been said and her usual cheerful personality floods back in.

"Alrighty, let's go! There will be no problems as long as Mr. Bell's hard work helps Lilly eat something good tonight!"

"S-sure..."

The best for me...?

So that means, basically, I don't have to pay her?

Or maybe something else entirely?

I don't know what she's trying to say.

I'm not her, so I have no idea what she's thinking or what she might be hiding.

It's just—

—You're no different from the other adventurers.

I get the feeling that that's what her eyes were saying to me.

"Eina. Hey, Eina."

"Hm?"

Eina was hard at work at the reception desk of Guild headquarters when one of her coworkers working at the same desk got her attention.

She lifted an eyebrow to say, "What is it?" Her coworker mouthed, "Look at that!" while pointing across the room.

Eina's eyes followed the direction her coworker indicated to see a Guild employee having a heated argument with an adventurer in front of the Exchange.

"See, it's them again. That guy's in *Soma Familia*."

"……"

Eina frowned at the situation unfolding across the way.

Their angry words reached her ears as Eina tilted her head forward to listen in.

"A measly twelve thousand vals?! Come on! Are you blind?!"

"You fool! How long do you think I've been doing this job, huh? My eyes are just fine!"

They were arguing about the terms of an exchange, that much was certain.

This kind of thing wasn't all that uncommon. Adventurers bet their very lives every day prowling the Dungeon. After working all day, they came to the Exchange with hopes great or small, but many tended to get upset and raise their voices if the amount offered for their Dungeon loot wasn't as high as they were expecting, complaining that it wasn't commensurate with the effort.

The Guild was used to this kind of thing, and all of the appraisers lined up close to that counter had a lot of guts. This particular appraiser was yelling just as loudly as the adventurer.

This kind of argument was just another day at work.

However, whenever *Soma Familia*'s adventurers made a scene, a normal argument tended to become anything but normal.

There was no point in adding up all the times members of *Soma Familia* had criticized an appraiser's offer. It was a daily occurrence. The Guild employees were long since fed up with this daily farce.

All of *Soma Familia*'s members had the same issue with the Exchange's terms: "Give us more money!"

They had an obsession with money that went beyond rationality.

Their demands for large sums of money were fierce enough to make all the bystanders' blood run cold.

"Ugh—just watching this makes me want to tear my eyes out! It's sickening! Sooo glad I'm not in charge of *Soma Familia*!"

"……"

Eina scowled at her human coworker's choice of words.

Eina was not herself an adviser of any *Soma Familia* members, but due to some recent events, she couldn't just write them off as someone else's problem.

"Damn it! This is all…This is all I get…?!"

Eina massaged her temple, feeling a headache coming on as she watched the adventurer clasp both hands around his head from a distance.

He might have been a little hasty…

The supporter Lilly's presence had a dramatic impact.

First of all, since she carried the backpack, I didn't have to take loot back to the surface to exchange it for money when my own pack got too heavy. So I stayed in the Dungeon much longer than usual.

Every floor I passed through on my way to a deeper Dungeon level meant that the distance to the Exchange was longer (and my time in the Dungeon was shorter). So even though I was going deeper than before, I wasn't getting more money for my efforts. There was too much lost time in transit.

Today, all of those problems were cleanly solved.

Thanks to Lilly, I didn't have to equip a backpack. I felt so light and free as I slew monster after monster on the seventh level that I can't even remember how many I took down.

Whenever a monster appeared, I swung my knife and Lilly quickly extracted the magic stone and collected drop items.

The result:

The money we received from the Guild's Exchange—

" "……" "

Lilly and I each grab the lip of the pale yellow bag, opening it together and peering inside.

Our eyes are greeted by…moneymoneymoneymoneymoney.

More coins of various sizes are crammed into that bag than I can count!

So shiny!

"Twenty-six thousand vals…"

Our eyes meet just inches apart as we look up from the bag at the same moment.

We take a deep breath and……

"YYYYAAAAAAAHHHHHHHAAAAAAA!!!!!!!!!!!!!"

We jump with glee!

"Amazing! Absolutely amazing! Lilly could count all the drop items on her fingers, but Mr. Bell passed twenty-five thousand vals all by himself!"

"Wow, wow, WOW! This is really happening, right? I'm not dreaming?! All of this money in one day…This is all thanks to you, Lilly!"

Hurray for supporters!

"You shouldn't say stupid things, Mr. Bell. It depends on the monsters, of course, but a party of five Level One adventurers usually makes twenty-five thousand vals in a day. That means that Mr. Bell did more work than all of them put together!"

"Hey, now. Even rabbits can climb trees if they're flattered enough. Same thing!"

"Lilly has no idea what Mr. Bell is saying, but for now, Lilly agrees! Mr. Bell is amazing! Let's do even better!"

"Lilly, that's too much flattery…!"

I'm way too excited about this, but I just can't calm down.

We're not in a bar, but we're making noise and really whooping it up.

It's late enough to be completely dark outside, so Lilly and I are about the only adventurers in Babel's cafeteria. Everyone else has probably made their way to a bar by now.

Our good mood rising even higher, Lilly stands up in her chair, yelling "Yayyy!" and we high-five over and over.

"Well then, Mr. Bell, can Lilly get her share now?"

"Yes, of course!"

I take 13,000 vals out of the bag, set them on the table with a *thunk*, and slide them over to her.

"………Huh?"

"Ahhh, with this kind of money I can finally feed the goddess some delicious food…!"

I can just see the look on her face when I give her food we've never been able to afford.

I can actually do something to thank her!

Lilly's staring at me with eyes about the size of marbles, but I don't care. I'm too wrapped up in my own fantasy.

"M-Mr. Bell. What is this…?"

"Your share! It's what we agreed on! Ah, that's right! We should celebrate! Lilly, let's go to a bar! I know a great place!"

Lilly's eyes glaze over as my jubilant invitation reaches her ears.

Oh yeah, didn't she say she didn't want to go to The Benevolent Mistress?

Oh well, no matter! It's just for today!

"Come on, let's go!"

"M-Mr. Bell!"

Lilly raises her voice as I start to quickly pack up our belongings.

Huh? I look at the girl in confusion. Her small lips quiver as she struggles to get words out.

"…D-doesn't Mr. Bell…want all of the money…? …Take it all for himself?

"Eh? Why would I?"

I don't understand at all. That seems really strange.

Having her question answered with a question, Lilly looks lost for words.

"I couldn't have made this much money all by myself. We did this together, right, Lilly?"

I flash a big smile before saying, "Thank you so much!"

Even the words "I'll be counting on you!" come out of my mouth.

I'm so glad I met Lilly that I can't stop smiling at her.

"......"

"So, Lilly, shall we go?"

Swish. I stick out my hand in front of Lilly.

She stares at my hand for a moment before carefully extending her own and taking it.

"...Mr. Bell's weird."

I do a fantastic job of pretending I don't hear her last murmured words.

[Bell Cranell]

Familia: *Hestia Familia*

Race: Human

Job: Adventurer

Dungeon Range: Level Seven

Weapons: Divine Knife

Dagger

Income: 18,900 vals

[Status]

Level One

Strength: D-591   Defense: G-233   Utility: C-607

Agility: B-702   Magic: I-0

Magic:

[ ]

Skill:

Realis Phrase

- Rapid Growth
- Continued Desire Results in Continued Growth
- Stronger Desire Results in Stronger Growth
- Equipment:

"Pyonkina" Rabbit Armor MK-II

- The first in an armor series by Welf Krozzo, a smith working for *Hephaistos Familia*.
- Due in part to its name, the armor was put in a box on a shelf to be sold. Bell felt sorry for the way the armor was treated.
- It was forged from the drop item "Metal Rabbit Hair." According to Bell, it's "extremely light."
- In fact, its defensive capabilities were highly rated by *Hephaistos Familia*.

"Green Vambrace"

- Value of 7,700 vals
- A gift from Eina. Has the emerald-green color of her eyes.
- Serves the same purpose as a shield. While not as strong as a pure shield, it's much lighter.
- It has a long, thin compartment that can fit small weapons including knives, daggers, and short swords.

Interlude CRY OUT, GODDESS

The sky's hue shifted from deep red to blue-black as night fell.

Western Orario. West Main was alive with groups of townspeople and adventurers back from the Dungeon, all letting off steam after yet another day.

"I...I made it again..."

Hestia stumbled along on tired feet among the crowd walking down Main Street. Babel Tower loomed behind her as she made her escape and trudged toward home on wobbly legs.

She had completed her shift at *Hephaistos Familia*'s Babel Tower Branch Store and was headed for her room.

"That Hephaistos...Can't she cut me a little slack...?!"

While it might have been nothing more than the repayment of a loan, this had still been the most stressful time in Hestia's life. She was used to an almost lazy lifestyle up until now, and her current situation bordered on torture.

Whether it was her goddess "friend" Hephaistos's lectures or the children who worked alongside her showing no respect, she couldn't catch a break. In fact, they seemed to go out of their way to give her extra work. It was to the point that she wanted to scream on a daily basis.

She was getting a glimpse at just how serious Hephaistos was about fixing Hestia's habit of relying on others.

"Ahhhh, I wanna see Bell...!"

Worn out from consecutive days of hard labor, thoughts of her own "child" popped into the exhausted Hestia's mind.

Until just a few days ago, she couldn't wait to warmly welcome Bell back from the Dungeon every day, often leaving her part-time job early to do just that. Now their roles were reversed.

She wanted nothing more than to jump into his arms as he walked through the front door. Knowing that wasn't going to happen, she dragged her tired limbs toward home.

"—Eh?"

Hestia was brought out of her own thoughts when a flash of white hair like a rabbit caught her eye.

She noticed a very familiar shape in the middle of all sorts of races of people crammed into the street in front of her.

—It was Bell!

Her round eyes lit up the second she realized it was him.

Bell had to be on his way home from the Dungeon. He was still wearing his new armor. Since his back was to her, he must have been on his way back to the room.

Hestia got her energy back like a fish returned to water, and was about to run to his side—and then...

"?!"

Thanks to the crowds, she hadn't seen the person walking right next to him, but now whoever it was came into view.

The person was shorter than Hestia and wore a robe that was too big with a backpack. It was impossible to tell the person's gender or any other detail from the back, but it was a girl. Hestia *knew*.

The mystery girl probably had an aura that made all men want to protect her. What's more, she had a firm grip on a hand being held out to her.

Hestia could see the side of Bell's face as he looked down at the girl and she looked up at him. He was smiling happily.

Boom! It was like a ton of bricks fell on Hestia's head.

She was already at her physical and mental limits, so this was the final blow. Bell, her last oasis, was holding hands and laughing with some girl who wasn't her. The heavens had come crashing down to earth, leaving Hestia with a wound too deep to measure.

Missing out on a chance to observe Bell with the supporter he had talked to her about, Hestia turned her back to them and took off running. This misunderstanding weighed heavily on her heart.

"—Listen to this, Miach! Bell, he—he cheated on me!!"

Slam! Another empty glass hit the table as Hestia wailed tearfully.

They were in a bar that stood a little ways off Main Street. The cramped, old wooden building was filled with mostly shabbily clad adventurers who were conversing in loud voices that weren't very polite.

She was drinking cheap alcohol alongside them, sitting at a table across from another god and reciting all the events that just transpired.

"Cheating is very serious. I cannot imagine a situation where Bell would do such a thing."

The handsome man who spoke in a polite, calm voice was Miach. He had been listening to Hestia's story very carefully, and interjected his opinion into the conversation. His worn-out, ash-colored robe fit in very well with the décor of the bar.

Hestia and Miach were the lowest of the low—the poorest of all the gods living in Orario. This gave them a very strong bond. *Hestia Familia* was on such good terms with the potion-making *Miach Familia* that each of the gods knew about the other's "children" in great detail.

Hestia happened to run into Miach on the street and practically forced him to join her in drowning her sorrows in alcohol. Through all of this, Miach never once made an angry face as he lent the goddess his ears.

"I saw them with my own eyes! They were holding hands, smiling, laughing! That's proof; he's guilty, guilty, guilty!!"

"We don't know Bell's situation, so it could be something harmless. I think it's too early to declare him 'guilty'…And you're not husband and wife or lovers to begin with, so going on and on about 'cheating' seems strange to me."

Hestia was too busy downing her next glass of alcohol to hear the second half of Miach's words.

*She's at it again today…*thought Miach with a sigh, his sea-blue hair shaking with his head.

"Damn it! Just who is that girl anyway! Bell belongs to me; he's mine! MINE!"

"Now, now. You may be his goddess, but those words are tyrannical. Bell is no one's possession."

"You think I don't know that? Well, I do! I just wanted to say that; I've always wanted to say that!"

"Are you already drunk?"

"Yeeeep!"

Hestia drank like she couldn't stand being sober—as if she were showering in the stuff. In no time at all the table was covered in empty glasses and the reek of alcohol lingered in the air.

The effects of the liquor hit the red-faced Hestia like a steel wall. Her eyes watered up again as she took in a massive breath.

"WAAAAAAAAHHHHHHHH! Bell Bell BellBell BE—L—L! Don't leave me alone—!"

"H-hey! Quiet down, Hestia!"

Even the composed Miach had to try to calm down the goddess; her cries were loud enough to interrupt every other conversation in the bar. All the eyes of other patrons were locked firmly on the two of them.

"I'd live in a sewer if it would make you happy, you know! I love you that much! I want to share the same bed with you and rub my face all over your chest! I'd live on three pieces of bread a day if it made you smile—!"

Miach shifted backward in his chair.

"I love you, BELL!...Hee-hee-hee...Just once, I wanted to let the world know how I feel. Much better!"

"I'm glad he wasn't here for it...Barkeep, check please."

Miach looked at the check and smiled in relief; they hadn't been scammed out of money. Hestia's head was on the table, her face hanging loosely as she laughed happily to herself.

Miach muttered "Good grief..." under his breath as he looked down at the plastered goddess. He diligently supported her limp body and guided her out of the bar.

"Miach, what about the cheeeeck?"

"No need. I covered it all."

"We're buddies, right? That means...we split the...check!"

"Again, no. You only have twenty vals with you."

Miach responded quickly to Hestia's slurred words. He lifted Hestia into a four-wheeled cart he had been using to carry items when they met earlier. It looked more like a baby stroller with Hestia curled up inside.

The two gods made their way down the street, accompanied by the sound of wooden wheels on stone and illuminated by magic-stone lamps under the evening sky.

"Mia...ha. Make me a love potionnnn. I'll brainwash Bell!"

"No. I'm going to pretend I didn't hear that."

"Aaa-oooouuuuuch...!!"

A throbbing headache greeted her the moment she opened her eyes.

Letting out a moan of agony, she stared up at the ceiling from the bed. She recognized it as her own and knew she was at home. The clock on the wall said it was already morning.

It was the morning after her night drinking with Miach, and she had one heck of a hangover.

"A-are you okay, Goddess?"

Bell was right next to the bed.

A glass of water in his hand, he looked at the goddess with worry in his eyes.

"I...I'm sorry, Bell. I'm sorry you have to see me like this..."

"It's okay, I don't mind...Um, yesterday, Miach came here and talked with me. So it's true, then?"

"...Yeah, looks like I drank too much."

Bell held out the glass of water for her. Hestia drank it still lying on the bed, a grimace on her face.

The night before, Miach had arrived at the old church and told him, "She's very...tired. Let her lay down, even if for just a little while." He left after leaving behind these meaningful words.

I can't remember a thing...

All of her memories of the previous night were gone. She had no idea what she had done or what she had said to Miach. After hearing what Miach had told Bell, she couldn't help but feel a little anxious.

Memories of Miach's silent but sad smile made her feel like she had caused quite a few problems yesterday.

"…Bell, are you sure it's okay for you to be here, not the Dungeon?"

"I couldn't leave you like this, so I took today off."

Bell softened his eyebrows and smiled as he explained he'd already come back from informing his supporter.

While Hestia was a little embarrassed by everything Bell was doing for her, inside she was overjoyed. She could spend an entire day alone with him. In that instant, she decided to take the day off as well.

The consequences, aka the wrath of the goddess of the forge, she'd worry about later.

"Goddess, can you try to eat this?"

"…Might be too hard. Bell, could you help?"

"Um, sure. I'll do my best."

Bell put a chunk of apple onto a spoon and raised it to her lips. Hestia propped her body up on her elbows and watched him with glee. She clamped her mouth down around the spoon, a look of pure delight on her face.

Normally, doing this kind of thing would be very awkward because it was just one step below nursing. However, Bell did it with a smile. It made Hestia happier and happier to see Bell hide his embarrassment and show this level of devotion to her.

"Ou…ohhh…My head…"

"G-Goddess?"

After what was one of the worst bits of acting in history, Hestia grabbed her head and "fell" onto Bell's chest. Bell was now holding her in his arms.

She could feel the unease in Bell's eyes, but that just made her want to bury her face even deeper into his torso. He smelled like a gentle forest. She pressed her luck even further by embracing him and giving a tight squeeze.

And so began a short, awkward tug-of-war between the elated goddess and the ever-squirming Bell.

"Hmm…So then, last night you went out to eat with that supporter?"

"Yes. Something very good happened yesterday…"

It was already the middle of the afternoon. Still lying in bed, Hestia was deep in conversation with Bell. Her hangover was almost gone.

While she was relieved to hear this, just thinking about how they were holding hands like that gave her some doubts…But most of all, her heart was uneasy when she updated his status. His growth was just as fast as ever. That meant his thoughts were still focused on Aiz Wallenstein, that blond-haired, golden-eyed girl. He was deeply mistaken about the reciprocity of his feelings.

But for now, she put aside all of her feeling about the kenki—the sword princess—and focused on getting to the bottom of this supporter situation. She wanted to know everything about what Bell thought of her.

Even though she had yet to meet this supporter girl, Hestia was starting to get seriously jealous.

"It's so great, isn't it? It must have been really fun to eat delicious food, just you and your supporter. I wish I could have been there…"

Sprinkling her words with irony, Hestia turned away from Bell, shuddering her shoulders and clearing her throat. But that performance didn't match Bell's reaction.

He sat there for a moment, body shivering slightly. He finally made up his mind and opened his mouth to speak.

"Well then, um, shall we go? The two of us, and, you know, eat at a high-class restaurant…"

"…Eh?"

"How about an…extravagant dinner?"

Hestia was in a pinch, watching Bell doing his best not to blush next to her.

She couldn't believe her ears.

"T-the truth is…I got a lot of money from the Dungeon yesterday…! And I, um, wanted to say thank you, so I…!"

Hestia didn't hear another word.

She was too busy replaying Bell's invitation over and over in her head.

Is this possibly...a d-d-d-d-date???

And from Bell directly? Dinner?! Hestia's thoughts were going a mile a minute.

She was ecstatic.

"Once you're feeling better, Goddess, let's go sometime soon."

"Let's go today!"

"Uh?"

"Today!"

Hestia threw off her bedclothes and sprang to her feet.

Bell sat there in shock.

"G-Goddess...your body needs to rest..."

"I'm better!"

She wasn't lying. The excitement and nervousness that come with a date, with Bell no less, had filled her body with energy. Bell sat, stunned, in his chair next to the bed as Hestia flew around the room getting ready for the evening.

—Wait a second.

Hestia stopped in her tracks and lifted her collar from her chest up to her nose, drawing in a big whiff.

It smelled horrible, like alcohol. It wasn't the way any self-respecting goddess wanted to smell, and she was covered in it.

Her eyes shot open.

"Bell, six o'clock!"

"Y-yes?"

"Southwest Main at six! I'll meet you at Amour Square!"

Bell broke out in a cold sweat as he watched Hestia go out the door, carrying only a small bag with her.

In a word, this was paradise.

"Wonder if mine'll get any bigger?"

"Well, it's not like us gods and goddesses are growing up any more— Hey, no groping!"

If any of the children of the mortal world had set foot in this spot, they would have fainted from blood loss owing to the nosebleeds it would inspire.

Here goddesses, under the cover of cloudy steam, revealed every inch of their beautiful bodies without a second thought, naked as the day they were born. Light glistened off their clear skin; toned arms and legs shined through the mist.

This place was the very definition of heaven that all men dream about at least once.

"Haah…This feels amazing!"

A relaxed smile grew on Hestia's face as she sank shoulder deep into the hot water, causing small waves to caress her body.

The Divine Bathhouse. It was a pure bathing facility where only gods might enter—just as the name would suggest.

There was one main, wide "pool" surrounded by smaller tubs of many sizes. Large trees and natural rocks were interspersed around and among the tubs, making the whole place feel like an isolated oasis. Constructed completely out of stone, intricate designs carved into the walls and pillars made the bathhouse even more majestic.

The Divine Bathhouse was built and maintained for the gods and goddesses living in Orario by the Guild. Money was collected from each of the *Familias*, a tribute to the gods, to make this place a reality.

Of course the male and female gods had their own baths, but due to the lack of male gods using the facility, the "Divine Bathhouse" usually referred to the goddesses' side. Ever since one perverted old god had gained entrance to the goddesses' bath at some point (he had since become legendary), the Guild upped security to the point that a single mouse couldn't find a way in.

Hestia had joined the other goddesses, completely vulnerable without a thread of coverage, in the hot water. Her glistening skin turning pink from the heat, she let out a deep, relaxed breath as the water flowed over her.

"Can it be? Hestia? This is quite a surprise, seeing you here."

"Ahh…Oh, Demeter, it's been a long time!"

Hestia greeted the goddess she knew with the first thing that came to mind, her face as slack as it could be.

The goddess named Demeter hid her lusciously curvy body with one thin towel as she took a seat next to Hestia.

"Ooo-h? Your bosom is as big as ever, I see."

"Look who's talking!"

Hestia slapped the wrist of the hand reaching toward her chest.

The shock from the hit shook Demeter's impressive breasts, sending large ripples out through the surface of the water.

"So what's the occasion? Today is your first time here, I presume?"

"Umm…"

Hestia pulled her face together as she turned toward the other goddess, who happened to be adjusting her fluffy, honey-colored hair.

It costs money to enter the Divine Bathhouse, so Hestia had avoided coming here at all. However, now that she had plans for a romantic night with Bell, she decided to use what little savings she had to bathe here.

It was that important to her not only to get rid of the smell of alcohol, but to refresh her body and mind as well.

Everything had to be perfect tonight.

"I have plans to meet someone for dinner after this. Thought I'd go all out."

"…Could you possibly mean with a gentleman?"

"What would you say if it was?"

Hestia shot an irritated glance at the look of shock on her friend's face.

As a small waterfall on the other side of the pool made a merry little sound, Demeter's eyes lit up like a child's.

"Well, I'll be! Who would have guessed, Hestia with a gentleman! Goodness! Hey, everyone—!"

"Wh-what are you doing?"

Hestia lost her calm at seeing Demeter get a little too excited.

The goddess's voice echoed around the chamber, and other bathers started to gather to find out what was going on. After Demeter told them the news, they too joined her in hysterical frenzy.

"Hestia and a man?!"

"What's happened?!"

"Hestia, the girl who had no interest in men whatsoever back in the heavens, she's—!"

"The Hestia who spent all year cooped up in her room, *that* Hestia?"

"Baby-face Loli-girl Hestia!"

"What is going on?!"

"Spill everything, now!"

In a blink of an eye, all the bathing goddesses swarmed around Hestia.

Completely ignoring the rules and manners of the Divine Bathhouse, some of the goddesses jumped into the pool, others pushed and shoved their way past the others' peach-colored skin to get a closer look at the girl.

"What's the big deal? Is it that strange that I have a date?"

"It's not that, Hestia, my dear. You've rejected all invitations from men up until now, yes?"

"You're one of the top three virgin goddesses, alongside Athena and Artemis!"

"To be frank, we want to know what kind of man brought down your impenetrable fortress."

Hestia shrank away from Demeter and all the other goddesses piling on questions with a cynical look in her eyes.

She tried to tell them that there were no worthwhile gods trying to woo her, but she soon realized that none of the goddesses would settle for a run-of-the-mill answer.

In situations like this, the entertainment-seeking nature of deities completely took over.

"...He's a member of my *Familia*, a human."

A chorus of "Ooohh!" and "Whaaa?" rose from the ring of deities. Even before the echoes of their voices died out, the goddesses started giving opinions like "I knew it!" and asking questions like "Is he taking advantage of your urge to protect him?"

"Are you sure he's not playing you? It would be horrible if you fell for a bad man..."

"What do you take me for? I'm a goddess! I know how to read people."

"The children can hide nothing from us goddesses; we see everything."

"Okay, so what made you fall for that child?"

"His personality, I guess."

Now that she thought about it, there was no one thing that drew her to him. She answered the question quietly to herself under her breath, that if there *was* one thing, it was his pure honesty.

The goddesses kept up their relentless chatter after that, and Hestia was getting tired of it. So she decided it was time to get out. Besides, it was good timing for her to finish getting ready.

Escaping from the ring of goddesses, she stood up. Water droplets remained on her slender limbs and body, reflecting light that shone down from a skylight over the bath. Her normally tied jet-black hair hung wet and loose behind her, shining gorgeously in the light.

Hestia closed her eyes and stood there for a moment.

It was a scene an artist would have painted: a glistening young goddess standing in a pool, bathed in sunlight and surrounded by others looking on in delight.

"Hey, Hestia. What's your favorite part about him?"

One of the goddesses raised her hand to get in one last question.

Hestia looked back over her shoulder and gently smiled.

"His...everything."

Amour Square was located one block from Southwest Main. It was a straight shot down a side street.

The area itself was paved with stones of many colors and was surrounded by a green border of various plants and flowers. All this came together to produce a gorgeous atmosphere. As the sun sank in the west, magic-stone lamps came to life around the square, illuminating it under the darkening sky.

It was just before six o'clock. Surrounded by couples walking hand in hand, Bell tried to make himself as small as possible as he waited in front of a statue of a goddess in the middle of Amour Square.

"Bell!"

"Ah...!"

Hestia spotted Bell and walked up to him.

At first, Bell was relieved to hear a familiar voice. But when he looked up at the owner of the voice, he did a double take.

Hestia had changed her hairstyle. Her usual twin ponytails were let down, and her glossy black hair flowed freely down her back. The young fairy had grown up, and she took Bell's breath away.

The ribbons with bells that she normally used to tie her hair up were wrapped around her wrists like bracelets. She wore the best clothing she owned. Hestia had pulled out all the stops.

Hestia held her breath for a moment, standing in front of Bell. Her cheeks turning a bright shade of pink, she worked up the courage to ask him a question.

"W-well, what do you think? I'm trying out a new look, so..."

"...Ah, yes, you look great! Very, very great! How should I put this? You look much more refined than usual, Goddess! You're... um...p-pretty!"

Bell's face turned red as he stumbled over his words, trying to praise the goddess.

He was doing his best to show respect to the head of his *Familia*, but there was a great deal of shyness in his voice. At this moment, Bell was captivated by Hestia.

Hestia may have looked calm on the outside, but inside she was pumping her fist with a big "Yessss!"

"I meant to get here earlier—sorry, Bell. Did you wait?"

"N-no, I just got here a moment ago."

They looked away from each other, fiddling with their own clothes.

This was beginning to feel so much like a real date that Hestia's cheeks were starting to go numb.

No matter what happened from this point on, nothing could bring down Hestia's high spirits.

"Well then, Bell, you'd better be a good escort for me tonight!"

"I-I will!"

Then he smiled and extended his hand. Hestia was about to take it—then it happened.

They rounded the corner of the square like a pack of wolves.

"There they are!"

"Hestia's here!"

"So then…that guy next to her is…!"

It was the goddesses from the bath. All of the insanely beautiful girls' and women's eyes sparkled with the same fervor as they charged en masse.

Bell froze at the onslaught of deities. Hestia stood next to him, her eyes as wide as they would go.

"Awww! He's so cute!"

"So he's Hestia's type!"

"M-mmpph!"

The swarm pushed Hestia out of the way and swallowed Bell in one swift motion.

Arms from all directions pulled Bell into their owners' breasts, each goddess embracing him one by one.

Oxygen was hard to come by, trapped in the heavenly cage from hell. Bell's face was burning red in a matter of seconds as he struggled to come up for air.

"Nah…Hnnnnn…Hahhhh?!"

"Sorry, Hestia! We wanted to know who it was so badly we couldn't help it. So we followed you…My, my, my! He really does look like a rabbit!"

"Nnn—hnnnn—!"

"B-BEEELLLL—!"

Echoes of Hestia's scream bounced around the square.

Bell's life was hanging by a thread. He had fallen into the valley that was Demeter's massive cleavage. None of the other goddesses even came close to her overwhelming chest canyon. Every time Demeter stroked Bell's white hair, pressure built up within Hestia. Veins in her head were bulging to the point that blood should have been shooting out her eyes.

The spearhead of the goddesses' desire for entertainment had struck her personal life, and it was mercilessly trampling everything in its path.

Just when Hestia was about to hit her breaking point—

Clothing disheveled, face beet red and hair going in all directions, Bell popped out of the group through a small opening.

"God...dess..."

"B-Bell! Are you all right?!"

"...I can die happy...!"

Whack! Hestia buried the tip of her shoe in Bell's shin.

"Sorry...!"

"Accepted. Now, time to get out of here!"

Pulling a one-legged Bell out of the swarm by force, Hestia started their escape.

It took a moment for the goddesses to realize their prize was gone; their moment of surprise was the opening that Bell and Hestia needed to get out of Amour Square.

The two of them took off at full speed through the city, keeping an eye out for the pursuit of the relentless deities.

"Ahhh! Why are they always like this?! Goddesses have no self-control, really!"

"Ha-haaaa..."

Bell grimaced next to a frustrated and yelling Hestia.

The two of them had finally shaken their pursuers in an old bell tower just off West Main. Made of brick, the now silent tower stood by itself with the original—but broken—bell still hanging overhead.

They hid themselves inside the tower until the goddesses passed by, allowing Bell and Hestia to finally relax for a moment.

"It's already the middle of the night…Aww, and tonight was supposed to be our date, too."

"D-date?"

There wasn't much time left before midnight. Hestia let out a long sigh as she fumbled with her hair, which had gotten tangled from running around so much.

The day had come to a lamentable end, and she stewed in it for a moment.

"Oh…! Goddess, take a look at that!"

"……?"

Bell enthusiastically pointed outside to get Hestia's attention.

What unfolded before her as she turned around was the city itself, lit up by magic-stone lamps like stars in the night sky.

More lamps than she could count shone with dazzling colors on every building of Orario.

In the center of it all, a massive white tower pierced the darkness to reach well into the black sky.

Hestia lost herself for a moment in the beautiful view from the top of the old bell tower. She didn't say a word as she looked over at Bell sitting beside her. She could see the entire city's reflection in his shimmering eyes.

Bell felt Hestia's eyes and turned to meet them. Seeing this amazing view side by side with Hestia made him feel warm inside. Harnessing its power, he opened his mouth to speak.

"Um, Goddess…Let's go again sometime. For sure."

"Bell…"

"Until then, I'll work as hard as I can to save money. We can eat delicious food, have delicious drinks, and then let's come here."

"……"

"We found this amazing view today…so let's come here again, together."

He continued, telling her that the day had not been wasted.

And that he was glad to share this moment with her.

Bell was trying to keep Hestia's spirits up. It wasn't just for show, either; he really felt that way.

A carefree smile lit up Bell's face and struck a chord with Hestia. She slowly closed her eyes, butterflies dancing in her stomach.

That innocent, stupidly honest smile made her even more attracted to the boy, right then and there.

She felt love in the memories she'd made that day, and in Bell's promise of tomorrow.

"I'm looking forward to it, Bell."

"Yes."

She smiled back at him with a grin wide enough to split her face in half.

The two of them looked back outside at the beautiful city and enjoyed what was left of their time alone.

Hestia had succeeded in getting closer to him. The feeling made her blush and let her mind be at ease.

I was going to ask him about that supporter tonight, but...I just don't feel like it anymore.

Now wasn't the time for anything so uncouth, she thought to herself, and took in the view once again.

Feeling the warmth of the boy next to her, she closed her eyes and smiled.

The bells on the hair ribbons she'd tied around her wrists rung faintly, shaking in the cool breeze that flowed through the tower, caressing them both under the old bell.

Chapter **3** MAGIC, MAGIC THAT **SUMMONS A LAP**

There was a flash of silver light.

"Grrooaaaaahhhhhhhh!!!!"

The light carved a line from the head of the skeleton monster—the spartoi—straight through its body. The monster let out one last dying cry.

Spartois looked like human skeletons, with the exception of pieces of armor attached to different places all over their bodies. They were truly fearsome beasts. With sharp angles at every corner of their frame and wielding white bones as weapons, they were every inch the cursed, skeletal warriors they appeared to be.

This beast was categorized at level four, and it guarded its territory in the deep levels of the Dungeon very well. This time, however, it was slain in the blink of an eye.

"……"

The warrior whipped her sword to the ground, the overwhelming power of her attack causing everyone around her to break out in a cold sweat.

Bones, bones, bones, bones.

Bones littered the ground as far as the eye could see. These white fragments of their former forms were all that remained of a group of at least ten spartois that met their demise at this spot.

Blond hair, golden eyes.

A girl with beauty to rival the gods stood in the middle of this gruesome graveyard.

"…And she did it all herself."

"She'd be a lot cuter if she pretended to be in trouble every now and then…"

In the time it took for her allies to speak those words, the blond girl—Aiz Wallenstein—silently sheathed her narrow sword and turned to join them.

"Nice, nice! Good work, Aiz! Need a potion? Or an elixir? How about one of your favorite sweet-bean-flavored potato puffs?"

"I'm fine, Tiona, thanks…But I want the last one."

"Why would she need a potion anyway? There isn't a scratch on her."

"In any case, the monsters have been taken care of…What should we do now, Fynn?"

"Hmm, should we head home? We came here for fun, so it would be a real buzzkill if we ran out of food and had to go back hungry. What're your thoughts, Reveria?"

They were standing in the thirty-seventh level of the Dungeon. Members of *Loki Familia* had journeyed down to the level known as the "Lower Fortress." The party was very small, only seven members including their supporters. Aiz Wallenstein led the group of only five top-class adventurers.

This time was indeed just for fun. Unlike their earlier expedition, a few *Loki Familia* members with some free time on their hands had gathered together to do a little dungeon prowling.

Why were they here? They were bored.

Countless adventurers make it this deep into the Dungeon only to lose lives. The fact that any of them could say this was "for fun" spoke volumes about their true power.

"I'll go with the leader's decision…Hey, you two, we're packing up!"

The normally aloof elf, Reveria, raised her voice.

Tiona and Tione, two Amazonian sisters with skin the color of wheat, nodded in acknowledgment. Aiz, holding a potato puff in both hands, slumped her shoulders in disappointment.

Food provisions were a common problem whenever a party of adventurers journeyed this deep into the Dungeon.

"But ya know, if Bete were here he'd be putting up quite a fuss right about now. He always tries to act like a big shot in front of Aiz. It pisses me off, seriously."

"After that night at the bar, when we told him after he sobered up that Aiz flat-out rejected him, he almost cried! So depressed!"

"Ohhh?! I really wanted to see that! Why didn't you tell me, Tione?!"

There wasn't much for them to do in terms of getting ready to leave. This was because collecting magic stones was the supporters' job, and Aiz had already annihilated all the monsters in the area. The sisters created a very relaxed atmosphere as the two supporters, who just ranked up to Level Three, went to work on the remains of the spartois.

Aiz looked up from her potato puff to voice her own opinion.

"Fynn, Reveria. I would like to stay behind, alone."

The two people she named had very different reactions to her request. Fynn's eyes opened a little wider; Reveria's expression remained unchanged, save for her closing one eye.

Ignoring the stunned Tiona and Tione, Aiz expanded on her request.

"You don't have to leave any food for me. I don't want to cause any problems for anyone. Please."

"W-wait—! You're causing us problems just by saying that! If we left you behind, we'd be too worried to think straight!"

"I agree with Tiona. No matter how low the monsters' levels are, I can't abandon an ally this deep in the Dungeon. It's much too dangerous."

Aiz looked sad, facing Tiona, who stood with her hands on her hips and leaned in to within inches of Aiz's nose. She couldn't refute Tione's opinion, either.

She knew what the girls were saying was unquestionably right.

"Why do you want to fight that much? It's such a waste, Aiz! You're so lovely! You should act more like a lady! How can you be losing to me, an Amazon, in fashion sense?"

"I...don't care about that..."

"Why not? Don't you want a good strong male...or some fellow you favor, at least? Is that pretty face just a decoration?"

"Stop telling others to do things you wouldn't do yourself."

Reveria took in a deep breath, standing one step away from the silent, slouching Aiz.

Turning to Fynn, the elf opened her mouth to speak.

"I will ask on her behalf as well. Please respect Aiz's wishes."

"Reveria?!"

"Hmm?"

The shortest of the group, a prum, looked up at Reveria as if trying to figure out her intention.

"This one doesn't often make selfish statements. I want you to listen."

"You can't treat her like a parent looking after a child, Reveria. Tiona and Tione are in the right. As long as it's my responsibility that everyone gets back safely, I can't approve of this."

"I'm aware that I'm spoiling her...So."

Reveria let out a second sigh and looked in Aiz's direction.

Looking at the sad eyes of the girl who normally didn't show emotion, the elf laughed a bit inside at herself.

She then locked eyes with Fynn.

"I shall remain as well."

She declared her intention to support Aiz.

Fynn looked back into the elf's eyes, her hand on her chin. She slowly nodded, as if this decision was extremely important.

"Okay, go ahead."

"Huh? Fynn, talk some sense into them!"

"As long as Reveria is with her, I doubt the worst will happen. On the other hand, we might run into trouble on the way back."

"Because I can't attack or heal anyone, right, Captain?"

Things happened quickly after the leader made up his mind.

Fynn's group with the supporters said their good-byes to the two staying behind and left.

Standing in the only entrance to the room, Tiona turned around and gave a big wave to Aiz and Reveria.

"Thanks, Reveria."

"While I would like you to stop, it's too late now. I will say this, though: I better not have to fight."

"...Sorry."

The two girls didn't look at each other, but there was a great deal of trust within their words.

The thirty-seventh level was different from the upper floors in that it was almost completely dark. The ceiling was so high that it couldn't be seen with the naked eye. A black abyss hung over the heads of adventurers who passed through these halls.

Small spots of phosphorescence, flickering at equal intervals like candles along the milky white dungeon walls, were the only visual cues.

The two of them stayed at that spot in silence as a questioning look grew on Reveria's face.

Sensing something, Aiz withdrew her sword.

"It's here."

"What's here?"

Aiz's eyes squinted, ready for battle. She was going to respond to the elf's question, but there was no need—Reveria quickly realized what was happening.

The floor beneath them was starting to crack.

"Can it be…"

Reveria's whisper reached Aiz just as the blond girl's golden eyes fixed on a point in the middle of the massive room.

She blinked and the ground split open.

Dirt and gravel were pushed aside as a giant stuck its head out of the floor.

Crack, crack, crack. The horrible sound of the earth being torn apart echoed through the chamber. Pieces of the floor that were lifted up by the thing's massive frame fell to the dungeon floor like a landslide, a deafening roar growing louder by the second.

A skull, then collarbones, ribs, and a pelvis appeared. A black skeleton was being born from the dungeon floor.

Every movement it made sent a shock wave through the room. The entire thirty-seventh level was shaking.

It was as if the Dungeon were howling in celebration of the birth of its favorite son.

"NGOOOOOOOOOOOOHHHHH!"

The two adventurers stood below as the giant monster let out an awful groan of a birth-cry.

The gargantuan monster howled at the ceiling. It stood more than ten meters tall.

It was black from head to toe—a giant skeleton from hell. Most of its lower body was still within the dungeon floor, and two large projections emerged from the top of its skull. It was like a spartoi had just kept on growing.

Two bloodred sparks flickered to life deep within the skull's eye sockets.

The creature's magic stone hovered weightlessly inside the chest, protected by a cage of bones.

"So then, three months have passed…"

As a general rule, the number and type of monsters on each floor didn't change.

A single type of monster couldn't overrun a floor, and new monsters were born to replace those slain by adventurers. While there was some difference in time required for new monsters to spawn on each floor, it never took more than one day.

In the middle of all that, there was a type of monster that did not revive immediately after being slain. Its interval of rebirth was much longer.

Also, there was only one of this kind of monster on each floor at a time.

Perhaps because they were too strong or too big, the Dungeon only allowed one of them on a floor, and never more than that.

The Guild had known about these special monsters from ancient times, and had a name for them.

"A Monster Rex."

"Reveria, leave it to me."

All varieties of Monster Rex look different but have two things in common: They had a long revival interval and were *extremely* powerful.

It had been said that each one was fully two levels above the rest of the monsters on their floor.

Even the highest-level adventurers respected and feared them, calling them "floor bosses." Usually many adventurers had to work together to bring one of them down.

"Aiz, do you really intend to fight alone?"

A worried Reveria looked at the girl with severe eyes.

Aiz raised her sword and walked calmly toward Udaios, the Monster Rex threateningly roaring in her direction.

"Not a problem."

The gods sung the praises of this, their "boss character, second class." But the girl now faced it down alone.

"I'll be done in a moment."

A week later, rumors of a Level Six kenki would spread throughout Orario.

"......?"

Bell came to a halt.

He turned his neck to look back over his shoulder, down the stairway connecting the lower first and second floors.

"What's the matter, Mr. Bell?"

"...Did the Dungeon just shake?"

Lilly looked up at Bell as he tried his best to look deep into the second level—no, even farther into the Dungeon.

"Shake? Lilly didn't feel a thing."

"...Was it just me?"

Bell's senses were on full alert. Even waiting for a few moments didn't calm him down. Craning his neck and cocking an eyebrow, he decided that it really just was his imagination.

"It was a long day today."

"Yes, it was. But not just a long day, a very long day! It's already twelve o'clock at night."

"Huh? Really?!"

She nodded yes, her golden watch necklace clasped in her hand.

The big and small hands on the clock face were very close to overlapping.

"Whoa, I had no clue..."

"Because the monsters kept coming at the end."

Lilly said that there was no time to look at her watch, her bulging backpack shaking with every word. They had picked up many drop items that day, and there was no room left in her oversized backpack.

Several days had passed since they signed their contract.

With Lilly's help, Bell had had some very productive days in the Dungeon. Perhaps he had adjusted to the life of an adventurer. His daily kill count was increasing by leaps and bounds, far greater than it had been when he worked solo. Now he was going full speed toward his own goal.

Bell was continuously surprised by how much difference the presence of one supporter could make.

Meanwhile, Lilly was confounded by the freakishly high kill count of this supposed newbie adventurer every day.

"So then, fifty-fifty on today's loot?"

"...Mr. Bell, I think you need to learn about the value of money and common sense. It may not be Lilly's place to say, because Lilly is very grateful...but Mr. Bell is too generous."

"But you need money now, right, Lilly?"

"That's true...But it's like Lilly can't stand to see you vulnerable, like Lilly's taking care of someone else's pet rabbit and is worried about every little thing...Lilly feels like she's being poisoned."

She's been giving me a lot of these lectures recently, Bell thought to himself.

Their relationship had been like an ordinary person working with an aristocrat until a short while ago. But the etiquette and protocol for interacting with strangers had been long-since discarded. Bell felt as though the gap between them had been bridged—like he and Lilly were becoming friends.

Bell and Lilly traveled through level one, tossing any goblins that appeared in their path aside like tissue paper, and left the Dungeon. After a quick shower and a trip to Babel's Exchange, the two of them left the front gate.

"Wow, you weren't kidding! It's very late..."

Central Park, the open area around Babel Tower, was covered by a curtain of darkness.

Amid the lights of the magic-stone lamps embedded in the walls of the city, there was a silence that was completely different from the afternoon.

On the other hand, all the bars in the distance looked as lively as ever even at this hour.

"…It really is huge."

Bell's eyes did a circuit around Central Park until his gaze finally landed on the tower itself.

It pierced the evening sky. Babel stood calmly, looking down over them.

Even though it was impossible to see at this time of night, Bell knew that there were meticulous designs carved into the tower from corner to corner.

The outside was almost a work of art; it didn't match the practical facilities on the inside. Bell took a deep breath, staring at the tower that embodied the extravagance and dignity of the gods themselves.

"I wonder, why is Babel Tower so tall? It's great that the Guild rents out spaces to tenants, but hauling things all the way up to the fiftieth floor seems like more trouble than it's worth…"

"Mr. Bell, the Guild's tenants only go to the twentieth floor, you know?"

"Um…is that right?"

Lilly lips twitched ever so slightly at the look of cluelessness in Bell's eyes.

Slightly embarrassed, Bell decided to ask her directly.

"If it's not filled with stores, then what the heck is above the twentieth floor?"

"Gods and goddesses reside on those floors, Mr. Bell."

"…The gods?"

"Yes. Just the heads of the many *Familias* in Orario are allowed to live there, but their rooms go up to the top."

It seemed only natural that gods, who had a taste for the extravagant, would want to live in Babel Tower, the symbol of the Labyrinth City Orario. Each room was equipped with the most advanced and elegant amenities, but the real draw was the view. No other buildings were allowed to climb that high, so the gods could see the entire city from out their window.

Gods paid a very high rent to the Guild in order to live there. However, if they had enough money to ignore that detail, then they could inhabit the highest-class dwelling in all of Orario.

In other words, only the richest, most powerful gods and goddesses could live there.

"Ohh…So there are gods who don't live at home but choose to live apart from their *Familias*."

"Think of it like a private room, Mr. Bell. While there are gods who like to talk and interact with us, there are other gods who like their privacy. That's how their image has been since ancient times."

Bell nodded in understanding.

"Lilly has heard that Babel Tower wasn't always this high. It used to be the lid over the Dungeon, but it wasn't any bigger than the other buildings around it."

"Well, then why is it so big now?"

"When the first gods came down, the tower was destroyed…They came down like shooting stars and hit the tower."

Like they did it on purpose.

Those gods completely *destroyed* the finished tower and laughed at the crying faces of the ancient people of Orario. In his mind, Bell could see the citizens' faces, mouths half open, tears rolling down their cheeks, as well as the cackling gods trying to apologize. He let out a dry chuckle.

"Since then, it's been known as Babel the Falling Tower. That could be another reason why gods live here now."

Lilly continued by saying that the gods apologized by contributing to the rebuilding effort…and by deterring the Dungeon monsters. Their method: Falna.

The people of the time revered the blessings of strength they received from the gods and allowed them to live in Babel as a way of showing their appreciation.

Soon, many gods and goddesses began appearing on Gekai—the lower world, to them—and created the groups known as *Familias* in many places around the world. Their worshipper–worshippee relationship continued as Babel was built higher and higher to represent the gods' influence on Gekai.

Babel Tower grew to its current height as a result, as well as gained the image of a shrine to the power of the gods.

"I think I understand…Whenever I hear stories about the gods, I can't help but wonder just how boring their world is. They'd have to be bored enough to want to leave the heavens and come down here, right?"

"Maybe they hated their jobs enough to run away?"

Bell had been looking at the tower during their conversation, but these words got his attention and he turned to face Lilly.

"Lilly's heard that the gods had many responsibilities in Tenkai— the upper world. Their most important one is taking care of us, their children, when we go to eternal sleep."

"Isn't that…?"

"Yes. They're in charge of guiding people after they die."

Hearing those words, Bell felt his heart speed up a little.

That was not the typical reaction to this topic, but he sensed his destiny in Lilly's voice.

Lilly's point, in short, was that the gods would decide what happened to mortals after death.

To put it another way, they judged everyone's souls.

The treatment of a soul could vary wildly, depending on the god responsible for it. It might be allowed to live on in Tenkai, or it could suffer unimaginable pain, or be forced into endless, meaningless hard labor…If one were to begin listing the possibilities, the list would never end.

The fate of all the souls released from the bonds of Gekai hinged on the caprices of the gods. The concept of being a good or bad person during life didn't enter into it.

The gods either liked you or they didn't. Their mood determined heaven or hell.

A "judgment" free of rules and regulations, instead based on whims and opinions, awaited them.

"Then again, most souls just get reincarnated anyway...Since there is all this work to be done, the gods still up in Tenkai have to pick up the slack left behind by the gods living down here. They're overworked with no time to rest. They'd be angry, wouldn't they? The next ones to come here will have a very intense 'discussion' to determine the order they leave."

*I don't wanna go there...I don't wanna die...*Bell was deep in thought.

If he were to go up there now, they'd put him through to hell. For fun.

As if she could see where Bell thoughts were taking him, Lilly reached up and shook his shoulder.

He snapped out of it and gave her an embarrassed smile.

Something was off.

"...But there was a time when Lilly longed for death."

That was it.

Those words were like a punch in the gut.

"...eh?"

"If Lilly went before the gods...if Lilly could be reborn...the new Lilly would surely be better than the current one..."

Lilly stared at the top of Babel—no, farther out into the heavens as she spoke.

Her hood folded back as she looked up, exposing her chestnut hair and big, round eyes. They were blank.

It seemed like she was looking into the sky, yearning to go home.

"L-Lilly!!"

Bell suddenly yelled.

He felt like if he didn't, Lilly might just disappear.

Lilly slowly closed her eyes, breaking off her staring contest with the stars, and looked up at Bell with her eyes hidden behind her bangs.

"Sorry for saying such an odd thing."

"......"

"That was a long time ago. Please don't take Lilly seriously. Lilly's stronger now. Lilly doesn't have those thoughts anymore."

Bell couldn't say anything.

She had to be telling the truth. Lilly puffed out her chest with a small grunt, and there was no sadness in her body language whatsoever. She must have recovered from something in her past.

That was yet another reason Bell couldn't put his emotions into words or action.

"Well, it's already very late, Mr. Bell. Let's hurry on home. Lilly has to go back to her *Familia* tonight, too."

A bright and cheerful Lilly turned her back to the tower. She moved away from it, taking little steps.

Bell glanced down at her shoulders, shoulders that were much too small to be carrying that much weight.

He watched her carry that backpack, unnaturally large on the girl's tiny frame, with a heavy heart. A moment later, he ran after her.

"So, you've gotten even stronger."

A voice from above whispered.

Below, a white shadow, running after another shadow and getting farther away.

A woman's excited eyes followed this shadow with the utmost intensity.

Clouds in the night sky shifted, flooding the woman's room with moonlight.

The entire outer wall of the room was made of glass. The woman standing next to the glass wall was so clearly illuminated it was as though the moon were casting a spotlight on her.

Her thin yet luscious body was wrapped in a sheer black nightgown.

Her fair, light skin gave off a mysterious air as it was bathed in the lunar glow.

Silver hair reaching almost to her waist sparkled as if made of ice.

"That's wonderful. You must shine even more…"

Clap. The woman—Freya—put her hands together, her outrageously beautiful figure reflecting off the glass.

It was the highest floor of Babel Tower.

Freya resided in the highest, most glamorous room in the whole building. She watched Bell from her window wall.

"More, more, shine even brighter, child. It's your duty, now that you have my attention."

A deep love was in her eyes, along with the absolute authority of rank.

Freya was obsessed with the boy, with Bell.

Obsessed enough to ignore other trifling things and to be caught up in a burning passion of love. The goddess of beauty was entranced by him.

Freya possessed the Eyes of Insight, an ability that allowed her to see the truth inside the souls of the people of the mortal world.

This was a natural gift of hers, not one of the abilities known as Arkanam. The gods had an agreement forbidding the use of these powers on Gekai, but Freya's Eyes of Insight weren't affected. She had once used those eyes to judge souls of dead people that came to her temple in Tenkai, especially the souls of warriors who fell in battle, and to transport them.

Into her collection, that is.

Freya could determine the nature of a soul faster than any other god, and she quickly embraced her favorites.

Souls who received her judgment after death were the lucky ones.

Those who caught her eye as they were dying were extremely fortunate.

This is because they would be loved by the goddess of beauty for all eternity.

Even if they were forever restrained and denied their freedom.

Freya controlled both love and beauty.

For better or worse, she was a wild and cruel goddess.

"Grow stronger, grow more befitting of me…That is your task."

Like many other gods, Freya had left her temple and Tenkai itself to come down to Gekai, but that didn't mean her "hobbies" had changed. She used her eyes to see the true colors of the children and to add the most talented, brightest souls to her own *Familia*.

No one refused her. No one *could* refuse her.

No one had ever been able to resist the magic that was her beauty.

For that reason, members of *Freya Familia* had strength and power completely separate from those around them. Even among the powerful *Familias* of the Labyrinth City, *Freya Familia* stood apart in its might.

The goddess Loki knew perfectly well about Freya's eyes, and called it the "rot in hell, you lousy cheater" power.

"I just happen to like strong men."

She had discovered Bell by coincidence.

It was early one morning. Her silver eyes spotted him walking down West Main.

—I want that.

That emotion went through her at first sight.

It had been a long time since she felt like that. Her whole body lightly shook in anticipation; her stomach jumped; a breath of euphoria escaped her lips. Just as it had always happened with her, she became no better than a child who'd found a new toy in a toy store. A pure but ugly urge to possess him consumed her.

Bell's soul was a color that Freya's eyes had never seen before: clear.

What color would he become? Or would he stay clear? Anything with an element of uncertainty could keep a god interested indefinitely.

That's why she couldn't stop.

So she decided to wait and watch. It would be fun to turn him into her own color, but she felt as though there would be plenty of time to do that later.

"I can't wait. How strong will you get? How bright will you shine? What color will you become?"

There was indeed love in her silver eyes as she watched the boy from her room, but it was a corrupt love.

She placed a finger on her full lips and playfully bit the tip.

For a moment, a provocative scent filled the room.

"What's this…? …Ha-ha-ha, noticed again, did you?"

The boy was already quite small in the distance, but he had come to a complete stop and was looking around.

It was as though he'd lost something and was frantically searching the area to find it. Freya's eyes closed slightly as a large grin enveloped her face.

He'd done the same thing the first time she saw him on West Main. He noticed her gaze when she focused on him with all the excitement built up in her body. His perception was better than she thought.

Almost as if her gaze had been too strong.

He doesn't have the talents of other children before him…Why, then? Could everything be due to his growth? Mmm…very intriguing.

Looking back on that moment, she should have made her move.

She felt like she could have easily controlled him like a puppet as she'd watched him speak with some familiarity to a girl on the street. Even though he had another god's blessing, she had no doubt she could have persuaded him.

She restrained herself because she didn't know which *Familia* he belonged to—which god would move to protect him. She didn't want to quarrel with someone like Loki and her *Familia*. That, and—

After seeing his innocent smile, her urges waned, and she didn't feel like it.

I'll have to remove Hestia from the picture…but that boy is mine.

But for now, changing the plan and watching him from the shadows wasn't such a bad thing. Freya nodded to herself.

One would tire of always having a cat in one's lap. It was good to let it play to its heart's content outside in the garden from time to time.

After all, it was *her* garden.

She could retrieve him at any time.

"I will wait for a while before I make you mine…It's strange, part of me doesn't want you to come. Now might be the time when thoughts of you dance in my mind the most."

Just like everyone before him, once he became hers, she would lose interest over time. He would become a favorite toy on a shelf, one of the dolls sitting in a row. Occasionally she would remember him, take him off the shelf to play, and then put him back.

The hope and excitement of the first moments would always fade away. Emotion deteriorated.

The same was true of love. Once it hits its peak, it was fated to crumble. No one longed for a love that had gone cold.

However, Freya didn't feel that it was pointless.

That was simply the nature of love, and she was the goddess of love.

She felt that having a collection on the shelf that was a little too big was somehow just right.

She hooked a few strands of hair that had fallen to her cheek with her finger, and pulled them back behind her ear.

Her bare shoulders were showered in moonlight.

Looking like a girl falling in love for the first time, she continued watching Bell with loving eyes.

"…However, yes. It might be about time for you to learn magic."

Tap. She hit her finger on her chin as she thought out loud.

After tilting her neck, deep in thought, something came to mind. She took her eyes off the boy far below and walked away from the window.

Freya's Eyes of Insight couldn't decipher statuses given by other gods or goddesses, but she could infer their strengths and abilities by their color and brightness.

She could tell by looking at Bell that he had no magic. Freya felt this was a flaw.

She decided to act, and quickly.

"I wonder if this will do?"

A heavily adorned bookcase stood in the corner of her room. It was very wide and tall, so much so that it would cover her body if it fell over.

Her thin finger reached for the middle shelf and pulled out a thick book by the spine. It fell into her waiting arm with a *thud*.

Thumbing through the pages, Freya made a satisfied nod.

"Ottar."

"Ma'am."

A rigid voice responded to Freya's call.

A person had either been standing inside the room the entire time or was just outside the main door.

Boar-like ears stood out above short, rust-colored hair. This male animal person stood more than two meters tall and had a body as solid as a rock.

He stood like a statue next to Freya, a guard dog waiting for his master's commands.

"I want you to take this book…"

She was about to hold out the book when her words trailed off.

Closing her mouth, she looked down at the book in her arms.

"Does something trouble you?"

"Hee-hee, no, it's nothing. Please forget it."

"Ma'am."

Ottar gave a short nod and took a step back as Freya smiled at the book.

That's right. It wasn't necessary for her treasured servant to deliver the book directly.

Plus, if this behemoth were to show up silently in front of Bell and attempt to give him a book, the boy would be terrified. While entertaining to think about, it wouldn't do.

There was no need to place it in his hands. He merely had to take it.

She knew just where to leave it.

It would be right where she first saw him, on the big street where they'd "met."

There was a certain bar very close.

If the book were there, it would end up in his hands for sure.

In the dark stillness of the room, her servant watched as Freya turned to the window wall, laughing quietly to herself.

"Ah-choo!"

Syr let out a cute little sneeze.

She blushed behind her hands, covering her mouth. All of the staff in the bar around her stopped what they were doing to look her way. Syr's face got even redder, and she looked at the floor.

"Syr, have you caught a cold?"

"N-no. I'm fine. Nothing to worry about."

Syr forced a smile through her rosy cheeks in response to the elf Lyu's question.

Syr's blue-gray hair was tied into its usual style, a bun with a ponytail in the middle. Her ponytail shook as she waved her hands, trying to convince the elf she was okay.

"Maybe someone's talking about you?"

"The answer's obvious! Mya-ha-ha, it's that adventurer boy, meow!"

"You're going to make me angry, Chloe."

Syr hung her shoulders, glaring at the catgirl who wore a very feline grin on her face.

The girl named Chloe did nothing in response, simply staring back with that same smile. Moreover, she was moving one of the bar's tables and playfully whipping her tail back and forth under her skirt.

Syr let out a heavy sigh.

"But that adventurer didn't come in last night!"

"Even though he always returns the empty basket after eating Syr's lovey-dovey lunch, meow!"

"Syr even opened early and looked for him, meow!"

"I didn't go looking for him!"

All of the staff was setting up tables to prepare for the day, but they took turns teasing the human girl from all sides. Syr yelled at them from the middle of the bar, but the girls showed no signs of learning their lesson. They continued circling her like cockroaches, the same grin on their faces.

"Do not worry, Syr. Mr. Cranell is not the type of man who would neglect your feelings for him. I'm positive he was just late coming out of the Dungeon and didn't have time last night."

"If that's supposed to make me feel better, Lyu…No, never mind, I give up."

The elf watched in confusion as Syr got frustrated. "It's just a misunderstanding," said Syr, but the always serious Lyu didn't seem to understand.

Syr had been making lunch for Bell every day since she first gave him her own lunch. She didn't really know why, but everyone around her had come to this conclusion.

Bell usually returned the basket at night after eating the lunch in the Dungeon. However, he hadn't shown up the previous night. And now this morning she was getting teased by her coworkers.

"You don't think he bit the dust, do you, meow?"

"You shouldn't say that, Ahnya. You're being imprudent. That adventurer would never leave Syr behind!"

"I'm tired of this…"

"Syr, hold yourself together. I'm sure Mr. Cranell is fine."

"No, Lyu, that's not what I meant…"

"What Lyu said, meow! That boy's too strong to die! If he did, my heart will be torn apart…"

Suddenly all the girls started talking at once.

"No way…" "Chloe, too…?" and other phrases of disbelief were muttered in every corner of the bar.

A very frustrated and confused Syr turned left and right saying, "Eh? What?"

"He is irreplaceable, meow! You couldn't find another like him anywhere."

"Chloe…? What are you saying?"

The catgirl looked to the sky as she spoke. Now Syr really had no clue.

The catgirl took her eyes off the ceiling and planted them firmly on Syr.

"Syr, I need to make a confession…"

"A-and that is…?"

"I…sure do like his tight li'l bod! His booty turns meow on…!"

"……"

"When I think about the ripe fruit inside his thin pants…mya-ha-ha! Ah, all the dirty things I would do…! I want— Oww! Ouch—!"

"……"

"A...wait— Oww, s-sorry! I give up! Uncle!"

All the other employees stopped what they were doing and rushed to stop Syr.

The Benevolent Mistress had been filled with an unusual amount of noise this morning.

"Oi! You dim-witted lasses! Quit playin'! Back t' workin'!"

The owner Mia's voice boomed from the backroom door as she looked over the girls' lack of progress.

The "dim-witted lasses" jumped in surprise before hurriedly returning to their duties. "Of all the..." the dwarf woman started to say as she shrugged her shoulders.

"......Hmm? Syr, what's that?"

"Huh?"

Syr's human coworker pointed behind her, and she spun around to look.

It was at the counter, right where Syr had prepared a special place for Bell the first time he'd visited The Benevolent Mistress.

On the chair where Bell had sat that night was a book.

"What's this...?"

"Someone dropped it?" "What's that, meow?" "Something wrong, meow?"

Syr picked up the book with both hands, her coworkers peering over her shoulders to get a look for themselves.

"I'm not clever enough to read, meow." "Me too, meow."

"Yes, I know, so shut up."

"Why I oughta—"

"Syr, what is it?"

"There's a book here...It's not one of ours. Maybe a customer left it behind?"

"Ohh...? It wasn't there last night..."

"Right, right! Runoa's mistake, mistake, meow! If it's not a customer's book, what would that mean, meow? Somebody snuck into the bar and left it there, meow? The idea's so full of holes, me feels sick..."

"As always, the idiot with useless knowledge, meow..."

"What?! I'll cut you!"

Ignoring the commotion behind them, Lyu and Syr took a closer look at the book. Completely white and very thick, it smelled like old paper.

It was lined with many undecipherable figures and patterns. There was no title.

"…Wait a moment. This—"

Lyu realized something, but before she could get it into words, Mama Mia's roar of anger filled the room.

"How many times ya gonna make me say somethin'?! Words not good enough for ya?! Time for this dwarfess t' beat some discipline into y'all!"

Everyone froze with fear.

"W-wait, Mama, meow! We found something suspicious, meow!"

"This! This here!"

"Syr, hurry up and show her already!"

"Huh? Somethin' suspicious?"

Ushered on by peer pressure, Syr gave an "Um, okay…" and stepped a few paces forward, the rest of the girls behind her. Syr's blue-gray hair shaking, she showed a very serious-looking Mia the book in her hands.

"Mama Mia, it looks like someone left this book behind by accident. What should we do about it?"

"…Whaaa?"

The entire staff watched with bated breath as Mia thoroughly looked over both Syr and the book with a deep scowl on her face.

…?

Lyu couldn't understand why Mia would have that look on her face. It was because the dwarfess had once been an adventurer herself and could still run with the best of them. But Lyu had never seen Mia wear this expression before.

As the elf tried to make sense of it all, Mia's sharp eyes hadn't left the book. She then gave instructions to Syr in a voice so gruff it was more suitable for a battlefield than a peaceful café.

"…Put it somewhere it can be seen. If the owner's not an idiot, they'll realize it's gone and come lookin' for it."

"Yes, understood."

After Syr lowered her head in a polite bow, the staff scattered.

The fear of this new kind of anger in Mama Mia's eyes drove them to work harder than ever.

Lyu stopped for a moment when she happened to see two of her coworkers having a friendly chat, but sighed and got back to work by herself.

"Mr. Bell! Look out! Your feet!"

"Huh?"

Lilly's scream hits my ears.

We're currently on the seventh level. I was about to dive into a killer ant with the Divine Knife in my hand, so my reply was a little clumsy.

I've slain so many monsters on this level that it's basically become my playground. I was so confident that I didn't realize what was happening.

"—Kiihiii!!!!!"

"?!"

I knew what she was talking about right away.

A needle rabbit.

The rabbitlike monster with tusks growing out of its cheeks crept up to me in my blind spot. The tusks often become very valuable drop items used to make weapons, but if those bloodred protrusions hit me, I'll be lucky to escape with my life.

It's making a beeline for my left leg, its eyes glaring red.

"Keh!"

I just planted that foot so I can't dodge! Being in the middle of an all-out run, my right leg's safe from the monster's attack but swimming uselessly in the air.

I quickly bend my left knee.

The only armor plates on my lower body are protecting my knees. It's a last-ditch effort to block the needle rabbit's attack. Just as I had hoped, the monster's tusk hits the plate and bounces off.

SHING! The sound of bone on metal reverberates in my ears as pain shoots through my body.

The rabbit passes by with a high-pitched metallic clang, but my balance is completely broken.

"Gyaaaaaaaaaa!!!"

Great timing…like it saw that coming.

My original target sees the opening and is charging me along with his friend.

I've slain dozens of these killer ants in the past few days. I took on four of them at once at one point.

When it was just one, I didn't think much of my enemy. Now there are two.

As a result, now there are four sets of merciless claws heading right for my eyes.

"Keehhh!"

Guard! I snap my left arm, equipped with my green vambrace, in front of my face just in time to block the attack.

The protector is very durable, and there's not a scratch on it. But the impact of the blow not only shoots waves of pain through my arm, my whole body shoots off to the side.

I don't spin at all. Landing gracefully on the balls of my feet, I slide straight back, my protector still in front of my face.

It's the other killer ant's turn now, and it's charging!

Oh, shi—

I'll be pinned down!

Once it plows into me at full force, holds my limbs down with four of its legs, and skewers me with its claws, there'll be no hope of escape. The killer ant's body is like armor, and just as heavy.

Eina warned me about this.

With my thin body type, getting pinned is the same as defeat.

—Ah.

This is the second time.

This feeling of an unavoidable death, the same as when I fought the Minotaur.

Body shivering, cowering in fear. Can't breathe. Time standing still.

The killer ant's hideous mouth suddenly opens.

I can see sickening rows of teeth, all dripping with saliva.

My mind goes blank. All that's left is to absorb the incoming blow, and I brace myself for impact.

"NO—!"

The next moment, Lilly's high-pitched yell and a ball of flame fly in from beside me.

"Huh?!"

"Degggyaaaaaa!!!!"

"Mr. Bell!"

Time comes back to me as the fireball hits the killer ant's head, and it lets out a scream of anguish.

The Divine Knife in my right hand flickers to life as if responding to Lilly's call.

"Gyuu?"

"Yeeeaaahhhhhhhhh!"

Slash! The killer ant's flaming head flies off with a very satisfying sound. I roll forward to engage the other one, aiming for a one-hit kill.

My blade pierces its armor, splitting it in two. But I don't have time to watch it pop, because the needle rabbit is coming in from behind. Drawing my second blade, I counter the advance with a strike to its head.

"Gii. Gaah…"

"…Hah-haaaaaa!"

I exhale the breath that's been stuck in my throat, now that all monsters in the room lay slain on the ground.

Breaking out in a cold sweat that's much too late, I hunch over and wipe my face.

I almost bit the dust there.

My heart's beating like mad inside my ribs. I try to smooth out my staggered breathing with the pulse beating in my ears.

"Mr. Bell! Are you hurt?"

"…Lil-ly. Thank you, you saved my life…"

The tension in my body leaves as I see her running up to me. Once she reaches me, I plop my butt down on the floor.

"That was careless! It was a dangerous situation, but Mr. Bell made it worse!"

"Sorry..."

I have no words to defend myself.

I got too comfortable, and it made me overconfident.

I thought I could take out the two of them in one shot, and I underestimated them.

Just like the books—and Eina—said. As long as I took them one at a time, it wouldn't matter if a needle rabbit suddenly jumped in. This wouldn't have happened.

Now I know the real terror of the Dungeon: Nothing is certain.

If I had made one wrong move, or if Lilly hadn't been there, I'd be dead right now.

A shiver rolls down my spine with that thought, making my whole body shake. I'm burning this feeling into my memory. Careless decisions lead to deadly consequences.

I only half hear Lilly's latest lecture and let out a long sigh.

"Are you listening, Mr. Bell?"

"Ahh, yes, sorry... I'm reflecting on my decisions. I'll never do that again..."

"Mr. Bell does look like he regrets his actions. In that case, Lilly will keep her mouth shut. It'll be Mr. Bell's responsibility if he doesn't learn anything from this."

I make one big nod, promising her I'll remember, and stand up.

I'm about to thank her one more time for saving me when I remember something important.

"Lilly, you used magic just now, right?"

"...eh?"

Lilly flinched when I pointed that out.

"Was that by any chance a magic sword? So that's how you saved me...Really, from the bottom of my heart, thank you. I feel so happy right now."

"...! L-Lilly didn't save Mr. Bell because she wanted to! Without Mr. Bell, Lilly wouldn't get any money and she'd have to find a new contract! Don't get the wrong idea!"

"...What are you talking about, Lilly?"

How am I supposed to respond to something like that? Lilly's eyes widen when she sees the look of confusion on my face. "What is Lilly saying...?" she mutters under her breath as she pulls her hood forward, grabbing her head. Yep, she's lost me...

"Umm...You have a magic sword, Lilly?"

"Ha-ha-ha-ha-ha, one thing led to another and it just sort of fell into Lilly's lap, you see..."

"I see. But don't magic swords break if you use them too much?"

"Yes, they do. So Lilly only uses it at times like this. But Lilly will use its full power to save Mr. Bell!"

That's the exact opposite of what she said before, but oh, well. No matter.

With that, we decide to eat lunch, as both of us are hungry.

After Lilly cleans up all the slain monsters, we take up a spot in the middle of the room. When resting inside the Dungeon, we usually find a place out in the open to avoid any surprises being born from the walls.

Plus, this room is so big that even if an enemy walked right through the entrance, we'd see it coming.

Come to think of it, I haven't returned Syr's basket yet...

As I stuff my face with some plain food, thoughts of the lunch Syr gave me yesterday flood my mind.

I was late leaving the Dungeon last night, and I'd overslept this morning, so I haven't had any time to swing by The Benevolent Mistress. I'll feel bad if I don't return the basket today.

Lilly and I start up a conversation.

The Dungeon is quiet; I don't feel the presence of any monsters at all.

Lilly looks like she's in a good mood. She's laughing and everything. I think this might be a good chance to ask her about something that's been on my mind.

"By the way, Lilly, you said you had to go to your *Familia* last night. Did something happen?"

I mean to ask the question as casually as possible, but Lilly's face freezes on the spot.

It only takes a second for her usual smile to return, but it looks clumsy somehow.

Maybe I shouldn't have asked after all...

"Why do you ask, Mr. Bell?"

"I know that your relationship with members of your *Familia* isn't very good, so I was kind of...worried. Sorry."

The impact of when Lilly told me she was living separately from her *Familia* is still fresh in my memory. Enough to make me worried about her well-being when she told me she was going there last night.

I quickly apologize, out of reflex. She relaxes her shoulders and smiles.

"Thank you for your concern, Mr. Bell. But everything is okay; nothing like what you are worried about happened."

"Really?"

"Yes, it's true. Last night was *Soma Familia*'s monthly meeting."

"A meeting...?"

"...The details will get long, but the main thing is to announce how much money to make in the next month. Everyone combined has to make a certain amount and work hard to make the quota."

It must be the *Familia*'s operational expenses.

It seems only natural that members would have to contribute a fraction of their income—it's a lot like the money I pay to support the goddess at home. So there is nothing strange going on at all.

And the reason that Lilly has to sell her services as a supporter is probably to make this quota on her own. She's left out of parties by her own *Familia*, after all.

"But that's gotta be rough, having a personal quota you have to meet every month, especially for those members who can't save up much money."

"Lilly thinks so, too. Especially for supporters, or adventurers without much bite..."

AH! My eyes pop open for a moment.

I wouldn't call it a breakthrough, but I think I've finally figured something out.

Before, when Lilly made a slightly ironic comment about needing money...?

Perhaps the reason that her relationship with her *Familia* is so rocky is because of money.

A twinge of dread fills my mind; I have to ask now. "What happens to the members who don't reach their quota?"

Almost as if she can see right through me, Lilly smiles and answers, "Nothing at all, really."

So there's no penalty...I relax a bit too much, like an idiot. But the fact that a small animal child like Lilly has to work alone to fill her quota makes me think that something is amiss within *Soma Familia*.

I'm thinking so hard about it that my forehead wrinkles up. Lilly looks at me and pulls her hood down with a pitiful look on her face. Why a pitiful look...?

"Um, one other thing I wanted to ask. *Soma Familia* is in the wine business, isn't it?"

I want to clear the air a bit, so I change the subject.

I force my face into a smile. Not a very good one, either.

"Ahh...That's the rejected stuff."

"Re...jected?...Wait, what?"

"That's right. It leaks out of the container while it's being brewed. So it's collected and sold to stores. It would be a waste to throw it away."

Now just hold on a second.

If I remember right, Eina said that their wine was extremely good and was always in high demand...The wine's cult following has been seeking...a reject?

How could something like that be a reject?

Lilly looks at my confused face with a clouded smile.

"It means the wine is so delicious that even the failures are that good."

The word "failure" doesn't apply here, or at least it shouldn't. I sit there in disbelief, rubbing the back of my neck with my hand.

But wait, that would make the "successes"...

"Lilly's god, Soma, completely neglects other gods and isn't interested in anything...except one. And that's making wine."

"......"

"It's not going too far to say that the only reason he made *Soma Familia*, our one and only purpose, is to assist him in his one and only hobby."

So then the reason that he gives members of his *Familia* a quota to fill is to cover the expenses of making large amounts of wine.

I don't think it's that rare for a god or goddess to use their *Familia* to pursue their own interests. It's understandable that gods, who came to this world for entertainment, would need more money than what was required to just live here, like rent and food. It has to take a good deal of curiosity on the god's part to want to dive into an industry.

But...I still can't shake the feeling that something is wrong with *Soma Familia*.

It could just be everything I know about Lilly's situation is making me suspicious, but I can't help but see *Soma Familia* as the bad guy.

—"Fighting amongst one another"—"Live fast, die young"—"Frantic"—

I still remember Eina's face when she spoke those words not too long ago.

"A-ha-ha-ha-ha-ha...If the stuff's that good, maybe I should have a taste...?"

I can feel my face changing to a frown, so I decide to lighten my mood by joking around a bit.

Lilly gazes at me with a blank stare and makes a little laugh that vanishes in a heartbeat.

"Lilly doesn't think that's such a good idea..."

"......"

Our conversation ends with her muttered words.

I'm about to strike up a new one when monsters appear in our room. We don't have much choice but to engage them head-on. Lilly is soon back to her usual self, and I guess I respond to that.

There's still a gap between us.

I don't know if it can ever be filled in.

I get that kind of strong feeling from her.

It feels like any manliness I ever had is gone, and my weak, useless self is exposed once again.

Two days have passed.

It's been a full day since I went into the Dungeon with Lilly.

Yesterday morning, Lilly told me that she had something to take care of and wouldn't be able to go. I don't know if it had something to do with her *Familia*, but I clearly remember the apologetic look on her face.

After seeing that, I just couldn't bring myself to prowl the Dungeon solo.

I keep telling myself a long break is a good idea, since I've been spending so much time in the Dungeon…but what is this feeling?

Whenever I think about Miss Wallenstein, a little voice in my head says, "There's no time to just be sitting around!" Even still, I don't feel like getting up. I'm a balloon without any air.

"…Ahhhh, this isn't good."

I pull my body up from the sofa, roughly fixing my hair.

Forcing out a deep breath, hoping to get this pent-up feeling out of my body at the same time.

I just need to move. What can I do? I'll get rusty if I just lay here.

If I can't clear my head, I can at least change my focus. I need to stop worrying about Lilly for now.

Been a while since I've done any cleaning…

Since the time I spend here has gone down dramatically, I feel like I haven't done any chores recently.

I shouldn't leave it all up to the goddess, seems unfair. I force my legs off the sofa and onto the floor…only to catch a glimpse of Syr's basket, still sitting on the shelf.

"…Oh."

I'm such an idiot.

"I'm so, so sorry!"

"Ah-ha-ha-ha…"

Clap! I bring my hands together and lower my head as far as it will go.

I raced over to The Benevolent Mistress under the daytime sun, and am now apologizing directly to Syr. There's nothing I can do to rationalize forgetting to return the basket for days.

"Please raise your head, Bell. I don't mind."

"Yeah, but…"

"If that's how you feel, be more careful from now on, okay? What's done is done, and nothing can change that. So concentrate on what you can do from now on."

She's absolutely right. I timidly raise my eyes before slowly standing back up.

Syr looks at me kindly, a soft smile on her face.

It's times like this that make me realize she's older than me.

"But, yes. Without any news, I was starting to get worried about you. So worried that I was making mistakes at work."

"I'm really sorry about that…"

"…Do you know how much they teased me?"

She suddenly has a twinge of resentment in her eyes. Huh? My eyes open wide in confusion. She blushes, turning her cheeks a pinkish red before she does one of her very obvious coughs. I hope that means she'll cut me some slack.

Still having no idea what she meant, I return the basket and pick up a menu.

Saying good-bye right after returning the basket after all of this would just be wrong. It wasn't exactly a way of apologizing for forgetting about the basket for so long, but ordering something simple still seems like the right thing to do.

Most of the other patrons at the bar right now are women. Seeing animal-person mothers and their children makes me smile. Their plates are overflowing with fruit—that is, until the kids dig in with fang-filled grins.

"Hey, was that decoration there before?"

I sit at a counter seat in the corner and am looking around the place, when a big white book catches my eye.

It's leaned up against the wall behind me. It doesn't match the interior very well.

"Hee-hee, well, that's…"

I ask Syr about it when she comes to take my order. Her words cut off for a moment, but she continues before I can wonder why.

"I believe it was left behind by one of our customers. We wanted to make sure they could see it when they came back for it, so we put it there."

"Oh," I respond in a weak voice. So there really are people who can forget something like that when at a bar.

Syr comes back with my cake and tea a moment later. She stays at my seat and we have a small conversation. A cat-person waitress comes over by herself and seems to offer Syr a break. I wonder if everything's all right.

The catgirl is grinning, too, for some reason.

"Well then, are you convalescing here for a while?"

"Nothing all that fancy…"

I decide to bring up Lilly, and the fact that I had no motivation to do anything.

It wasn't by accident. I just want someone to listen to my problems, I guess.

Maybe I have some kind of shameless hope that she'll give me a bit of helpful advice.

After lending an ear and staring at me as she listened, Syr smiles.

"Why don't you try some literature?"

"Literature?"

"Yes. You don't read books very often, right, Bell? Why don't you take a chance and read?"

She tells me that books might provide the stimulation I need right now.

Literature…The thought has never crossed my mind. But she has a point. It could be just the medicine I'm looking for.

I need to get back to the feeling I had whenever I read about the heroes in tales of adventure; I never could sit still.

Who knows? Going into a book's world might just get my heart racing and cure my couch potato syndrome.

"Yeah, I think I will. Thanks for the idea, Syr. I'll read a book."

"I'm happy to be of service."

I'm glad I asked her and I'll take her advice.

Seeing that I was open to her advice rather than just thinking things over by myself, Syr followed that up with a question of her own:

"Do you have a book in mind?"

"Not really. My goddess has plenty of books at home. I'll probably borrow one of them…"

Going to the bookstore is also an option. As soon as those words leave my mouth, I hear Syr say, "In that case…" She reaches over and picks up the white book.

"Why don't you try reading this?"

"Huh? But this book, it's someone else's, right? They forgot it here."

"As long as you bring it back, there shouldn't be a problem. Books don't disappear after someone reads them. Plus, I think it belongs to an adventurer, so there might be something useful for you in here."

Many adventurers come to this bar; more than likely the owner of this book is one, too.

Because it's a personal possession of an adventurer, it might stimulate my mind. At least, I think that's what she's saying.

It's a rare book that I've never seen before, that's for sure. This might be my only chance to read something like it.

Then again, I'd be getting my fingerprints all over someone else's book…

"Nothing to worry about. Honestly, Mama Mia doesn't really like having it here, so if you take it, you'd be doing us a favor. And…"

Syr suddenly looks shy.

"…I want to help you any way I can, Bell."

"……"

"But this is all I can do for you, so please, take it. For me."

Didn't she say something a lot like that not too long ago? I grimace when that thought hits me.

Well, if she's going to go that far, I may as well let her spoil me.

It would be rather cruel of me to refuse her goodwill, and her embarrassed face. So I take the book from her.

But when I reach up to take it, my hands accidentally sweep across hers. The feeling of her soft skin makes my heart skip a beat.

"T-thanks. Umm…well then, I'll see you later?"

"Yes, thank you for coming today."

I'm flustered, but I do my best to hide it as I stand up to leave.

After a quick "The cake was delicious," I leave the bar.

It was the same with Eina…I can't help but get nervous when I touch a girl's skin. I blush like there's no tomorrow. Just how innocent am I?!

"*Syr, you gave him that book…?*"

"*Yep, I did.*"

"*For someone as straightforward and honest as you to give out the bar's property like that…Never thought it would happen.*"

"*Don't you two know love is blind, meow? Syr, you should let your hair down more often, meow!*"

Still flustered from the feeling of Syr's warm hands, I hurry home.

I open the book the moment I get home.

Since the goddess isn't home yet, I set the book down on the table with one hand.

Getting a little anxious, I pull out a chair, sit down, and look over the title page without a title.

Mirror, Mirror: The Fairest Witch in the Land Is ME: An Autobiography (With Appendix: Awaken Your Magic!)

Right off the bat, it sounds childish…

Chapter 1: Modern Magic Even Goblins Can Understand!

Teaching magic to goblins. No one should do that…

I want to close the book right now, but I decide to bear with it. I can't let Syr's good intentions go to waste. I force my eyes across the characters on the page with all the endurance I can muster.

The top parts are painful, but the content actually isn't that bad.

Just like the words on the title page said, this book seems to be about magic.

"Ooohhh!" My eyes light up with sudden anticipation and I dive back into the pages.

There are two types of Magic: innate and acquired. As the term "innate" suggests, this type of magic can be used by various races based on genetics. From ancient times, these races have had the potential to become magic users within them and are trained in magic at a young age through rituals. While the types of magic they can use are rather limited, the strength and scale of these spells are often very high.

It's written in Koine, the common language, so even I can understand it, with some effort.

But what are these characters between the lines...?

Not wording...maybe some kind of equation?

Next page.

Acquired magic refers to the possibility of Magic given to those people who receive "Falna," and appears on its own. With almost no restrictions, this kind of magic takes many different forms. The effect of the Magic depends heavily on excelia.

This is different from hieroglyphs, and different from any language of the races of people.

Nothing in common with itself, just a strange grouping of marks.

The passage...the sea of characters is pulling me in.

Next page.

Magic is interest. This is a vital factor for all acquired magic. What holds your interest—what do you accept, hate, want, grieve for, worship, swear to, long for? The trigger is already within you. Your Falna will carve your soul into a blazing sun.

A picture has appeared.

It's a head. It has eyes. It has a nose. It has a mouth. It has ears. It's a person's face.

A human face with closed eyes is drawn out in black. A picture made from the words of the passage.

Next page.

If you desire it, answer. If you desire it, break. If you desire it, focus! A terrible mirror of truth lies before you.

No. That's *my* face. My face, with nothing above the forehead.

No—it's a mask. It's another face of me. A me that I didn't know, another me.

Next page.

Now, let's begin.

The eyes open. It speaks with my voice.

The ruby-red letters that spell out the eyes shoot through me. Short passages that make up the small lips spin words.

Next page.

What is magic to me?

I don't know.

But it's something great and mysterious.

A finishing move to slay monsters. A mysterious power used by heroes to come back from near death.

Strong, fierce, merciless, overwhelming.

What I've always wanted to have, just once. What I've been yearning for.

Next page.

What is magic to me?

Power.

Great power.

A big weapon that will defeat my weak self.

A grand weapon that will inspire my weak self.

Not a noble shield to protect my allies, nor anything so elegant as a healing hand.

A heroic power to clear away the obstacles in my path.

Next page.

What kind of a thing is magic to me?

Thing?

What kind of thing?

Fire.

Magic has to be fire. It's the first thing I think of when I hear the word "magic."

Strong, ferocious, hot.

Burn the plains, scatter the ash, scorch the air, envelop everything in waves of flame and heat haze, crimson tongues of flame nothing like my normal weakness.

Hotter than anything else, never going out…immortal flame.

I want to become flame.

What do you seek in magic?

To become stronger, like her.

To become faster, like her.

Like light breaking through the clouds.

Like lightning racing across the sky.

More than anyone, more than anyone, more than anyone.

Faster than anyone.

Like her.

To be in her sight.

That's all?

If I can. If I can. If I can.

I want to become a hero.

I have always wanted to be a hero, and like a fool I've pursued that dream.

Just like the ones in the tales. A hero praised and loved by all.

No matter how pathetic a fantasy, how vain and indignant, how miserably unsuited I am for it.

I want to become enough of a hero for her to notice me.

You're such a child.

…Sorry.

But that's me, too.

The me inside the book smiles.

Then everything goes black.

"…ll…ell—"

I hear a voice.

My mind comes out of the darkness as a pretty voice echoes in my ears.

Light shines itchily into the darkness.

"Bell!"

The next moment, my eyes are open.

"Ah...G-Goddess?"

"Yes, Bell, it's me. What's wrong with you, falling asleep at the table? There are much better places to sleep."

I rub my eyes until the goddess's face comes into focus next to me. Raising my head, I take a look around.

I'm at home, in the hidden room under the old church. The time is...seven at night. It's already evening.

Even before I finish scanning the room, the goddess starts asking for details.

"Were you reading a book? Ah-hah! Maybe I just happened to walk in as your drowsiness finally got the best of you—not used to reading, eh?"

"Um...ah, yes......I think so?"

...I fell asleep?

The white book I borrowed from Syr is still wide open on the table. Apparently I was out cold and used it as a pillow.

I finished it...?

I hold down my temples. My head feels odd, like it's been spun in all directions.

There are some very strange memories in the back of my mind. They feel unreal, like daydreams.

Was I talking with someone? Did they ask me something? Or are all these memories just leftovers from a dream?

It's no use. I can't figure it out...

"Hee-hee, so cute. I'm usually really tired after work, but thanks to your playfulness, I feel like my usual self!"

"P-playfulness...?"

"Hee-hee! Now, let's eat some dinner."

With those words, my ears turn red and my head drops. But the goddess is smiling as she goes to her closet.

I step outside the front door for a moment, waiting until the goddess pokes her childish face out the door and says "All done!" before I join her in the kitchen. I feel bad that I was the first one home and haven't prepared anything at all. On the other hand, the goddess's cheeks are a rosy pink; she must be happy to be working next to me. That makes me smile, too.

"Bell, what were you doing with that thick book? You don't seem like the type of person who would buy something like that."

"Kind of sad that you put it like that…but yes. I borrowed it from a friend of mine."

"Ah, can I see it when you're done? I haven't seen many books that are that old. Got a bit of an itch to read it, you know."

"You really love books, don't you?"

After cleaning up after a modest dinner, we take turns in the shower before deciding to update my status. It's been growing faster these days.

The goddess must have finally gotten used to her job working for *Hephaistos Familia*; she has enough time and energy to do this now.

I take off my shirt and lay facedown on the bed while the goddess pricks her finger on a needle to draw out ikoru—the power in her blood.

"Huh…hmmm?…Tsk!"

"G-Goddess…Is my status still growing like before?"

"…Yep, no change at all. Full speed ahead, no other way to put it."

Her voice sounds a bit scary, so I have to muster up some courage to ask her. Sure enough, a very moody response came from behind my head.

She's still angry…No, she's angry *again*.

She seems to get angry every time she updates my status recently…

"Yes, that's right, you're a stubborn one. I know, I know, your feelings don't exactly change overnight."

I have no idea how to respond to those irritated whispers.

There's nothing I can do to clear the air but keep my mouth shut and hope the storm blows through on its own.

Suddenly, two sharp pinches drill into my back. It feels like I'm being pricked with a needle.

Hey, wait a second—it hurts!

"Goddess! That hurts! You're doing that on purpose?!"

"Hmmm?"

"What are you hmmm-ing for?!"

My pleas and tearful eyes don't have any effect on her. And as though she were saying "No backtalk," she sticks the needle into the back of my head. Direct hit.

Unable to fight back, I can only wipe my tears on the pillow, completely defenseless.

I'll make sure she doesn't sleep well tonight...

"...Well, with the exception of your Defense, all of your basic stats are almost an *S* rank, so of course your growth is slowing down a little bit."

"...Ah, I see."

"Still, this isn't normal..."

The maximum rank for all basic stats in a status is *S*. As each stat gets closer to the top, it takes more experience to improve. As a result, growth slows way down. I've heard in some cases, an adventurer could slay hundreds of monsters and not go up a single point.

Now in my case, the fact that my growth has slowed down might be due to this growth barrier, but the fact I'm still growing at all must mean that I'm still going strong.

But as the goddess said, there could be too much of a good thing.

"........."

"...Goddess?"

Seems strange that both her hands and her mouth aren't moving. Even after calling out to her, she just sits there silently until...

"......Magic."

"Eh?"

"Magic has appeared in your status."

That was the last thing I was expecting to hear.

"Whaaaaaa?!"

"Eeek!"

Astonishment wells up inside me.

I rear my back up like a startled horse.

As a result, the goddess, who was sitting on my lower back, flies off the bed and onto the floor—headfirst with a loud *thunk*, no less.

Wait, crap!!

"G-Goddess!! I'm so sorry! Are you hurt?"

"Didn't think you'd be getting revenge like that...You're something else, Bell."

She's at the foot of the bed, stuck halfway through a somersault cut tragically short. Her eyes are shiny with tears, her body shaking ever so slightly.

And...her boobs are hitting her chin...?! *No, focus, you idiot!*

I reach out to help her, doing my best to keep my eyes off her cleavage, my hands trembling with fear. Soon after that, the whole of *Hestia Familiar* is doing dogeza—the submissive pose on all fours with forehead on the ground, apologizing like mad.

It is quite some time before I see the details of my new status.

Bell Cranell

Level One

Strength: B-701 -> B-737   Defense: G-287 -> F-355

**   Utility: B-715 -> B-749   Agility: B-799 -> A-817   Magic: I-0**

Magic:

(Firebolt)

• **Swift-Strike Magic**

Skills:

( )

"...!!"

I really have to fight the urge to scream at the top of my lungs.

I hold the paper the goddess wrote my status on, my jaws clenched and my hands shaking.

My eyes sparkle with pure joy. Even though I can't see my mouth, I know I'm smiling from ear to ear.

"I can't believe Magic appeared...Could it be related to that Skill...? I can't tell."

The goddess mumbles something, her eyebrows down as she holds her chin like she's deep in thought. Completely different from my reaction.

She keeps looking at my back and then my face and back again, but I don't care.

"G-Goddess…Magic, I have Magic! I've become a magic user…!"

"Yes, I see that. Congratulations, Bell."

I'm happy, plain and simple.

Joy rushes through my body. I feel like I'm on fire.

At the same time, I can feel tears welling up in my eyes. This is a dream come true. My whole body is shaking in excitement.

I crumple up the paper in my hand and squat down to the floor. I get the feeling that the goddess is beside me, grimacing.

I'm happy—so, so happy! I can finally use magic!

Not just any magic, *that* Magic! The same one that the heroes used as a trump card in the tales of adventure, that one!

"I hate to throw water on your blaze of joy, but we need to talk about your Magic. There's something that's bugging me."

"Yes, Goddess!"

I stand back up and yell my response.

I really need to calm down. I tell myself that over and over as I take some deep breaths and try to make my tense body relax.

"Are you listening? This is just a summary, but Magic requires the user to speak an incantation for it to work. You already knew this much, right?"

I answer her question with a quick nod.

Every type of magic has many different attributes that can be manipulated by the user through a spell that is spoken aloud by the caster.

The incantation creates a launchpad for the magic so that when the spell is complete, it goes in the desired direction. Think of it this way: The longer the launchpad takes to create—the longer the incantation—the bigger and more powerful the magic will be.

On the other hand, the shorter the spell, the smaller the launchpad, therefore the weaker the magic will be. On the plus side, a shorter incantation can be said quickly. It's convenient because it can be conjured almost instantly.

"Then I'll get to my point. My friends have told me that when a person learns Magic, it shows up in their status. Said person learns their incantation by looking at their status. It's the trigger."

"Really? But there's no spell written on the status sheet you gave me..."

"Yes, that's right. Don't start thinking that I forgot to write it down, got that?"

"Firebolt" is written in my Magic slot, but there's nothing here that looks like an incantation. Without one, I won't be able to trigger my magic at all.

Just as my neck starts leaning to the side, the goddess tells me her theory.

"This is just my hunch, a complete guess. Judging by what was written in your status...your magic might not need an incantation to be triggered, Bell."

I freeze. Willing my body to move, I unfold the status sheet in my hand and take another look at it.

Sure enough, there is no incantation. The only description given is the words "Swift-Strike Magic."

...I think the goddess's hunch is spot-on. Heck, I can't think of anything else those words could mean.

"I don't know how powerful it will be, but it has zero conjuring time...'Swift-Strike Magic.' I don't think I'm wrong."

"So, then, this Fireb— Gholg!"

Both of the goddess's soft hands cover my mouth.

She's standing on her tiptoes, eyes locked on mine.

"I would advise not saying its name willy-nilly."

"Muhegeh?"

"I don't know what the trigger is, but it might conjure just by you saying 'Firebolt.'"

Ffffft. My face is turning blue. I still have no clue what this magic can do, but if I release it here by accident, I might blow our home to smithereens.

"Understand?" the goddess asks. I nod and she takes her hands down.

"The bottom line is that this is all a guess. We won't know for sure until you try it out...Use it in the Dungeon tomorrow. Then you will know for sure how your magic works."

"Eh? Tomorrow...?"

"Don't tell me you want to go now? You just took a shower, right? Your magic isn't about to disappear!"

"Ah, yes...you're right."

The goddess chuckles at me as I slowly nod in acceptance.

It's already late. The goddess is very tired from work, hiding a yawn with her hand and everything, so we decide to go straight to bed.

After brushing her teeth, the goddess jumps into bed before turning out the light.

I too feel a little sleepy and lay down on the sofa...

Sorry, Goddess.

...for a moment.

My eyes are wide open. Who could actually sleep at a time like this?

I jump up from the sofa. Listening to her breathing and being careful not to wake her, I grab my backpack, already prepped, and leave the room.

Throwing on my armor at all speed, I set my pack on the church stairwell before heading out.

I want to use it right now!

The moon and stars are shining brightly over Main Street. Light spilling out of shops' and bars' windows light up their patrons' faces. The drunken, noisy voices of demi-humans have a very nice rhythm; my feet tap right along with it as I pass by.

Orario still hasn't gone to sleep. And neither have I.

The white tower grows in front of me as I get closer. I lift the gear on the front gate with a grin on my face.

Once I'm into the first floor of Babel, I head straight down.

I reach the Dungeon entrance hole cover in the basement floor. Through the big hole I go, then down the spiral staircase as if I were on wheels. It's still not fast enough for me, so I put my hand on the railing halfway down and jump up and over the side into the middle of the hole.

I tear through the air and land with a solid *thud*. The impact feels so good it makes my eyes water, and my feet shake with excitement.

I'm now officially on level one of the Dungeon.

"......!!"

Crunch. I come to a halt.

It's a wide hallway. A short, fat green shadow has popped up in the middle of my line of sight.

A goblin.

This looks good...

The enemy's size, the distance between us—everything looks good.

I swallow all the spit in my mouth and wipe my sweaty palms on my inner shirt.

It sees me. Yelling at the top of its lungs, it slams its feet against the ground as it charges right at me.

I clench my right fist before thrusting my arm straight out and spread my fingers in front of the oncoming monster.

"......"

My heart pounds away in my ears.

I focus all of my built-up nerves, anxiety, and excitement into my right shoulder.

Short breath.

Raising my eyebrows as high as they would go, I release a roar of my own:

"FIREBOLT!!"

A scarlet light floods my vision a moment later.

"?!"

Scarlet lightning flashes through the hallway.

No, not quite. Electric flames.

The bolts carve sharp, random lines through the air before piercing the goblin.

That's all that I can see.

An explosive flash of light blinds me the instant the electric flame reaches the goblin's body.

An orange flower blooms.

"...ah."

The goblin stands there for a moment, covered in burns, its body smoking. Its eyes go white as it flops onto the floor. The last utterance of the monster echoes through the hallway.

"...No way."

It works. It really works.

My magic works.

I pull my arm down and take a long, hard look at the palm of my right hand in stunned silence. All those times I've tried that pose while working in the fields, and now it's here.

It's the hand I see every day. Nothing's changed.

But now it works.

Magic came from this hand.

"...H...haa-haa-haa!"

I know it works, but I'm not satisfied yet.

My entire body is sizzling. I close the open hand in front of my face into a tight fist.

Yes...!

Real results. Real progress.

This is something that I can see with my own eyes, not just my status on a sheet of paper. I'm finally getting closer to Miss Wallenstein—I can feel it!

Firebolt. Electric flame.

Conjured in an instant, it strikes at the speed of light with the power of fire.

Fire magic faster than anyone.

Magic just for me.

"_____!"

A new wave of joy envelops me.

I accidentally bite my lip while fist pumping over and over again. It hurts. I don't care.

I'm in the zone, my face flush with excitement.

My eyes haven't sparkled this much since the moment I registered for the Guild. Pure, naïve glimmering.

The emotion and excitement go straight to my head.

I sprint into the Dungeon, looking for my next target.

"FIREBOLT!"

"Gyuaaaaaaa!!!!"

I find a monster, then thrust out my arm.

"FIREBOLLLTTTT!!!"

"Ebbbsshhiiii!"

I feel like a small child, running around yelling as loud as he can.

"FFFIIIRRRREEEBBBOOOLLLTTT!!!!!!"

"BGYAAAAAAAAA!!!!!!!!!!!!!!!!!!!!!!!!!"

Explosion on sight.

"FIREBOLT!" "FIREBOLT!" "FIREBOLT!" "FIREBOLT!" "FIRE-BOLT!" "FIREBOLT!" "FIREBOLT!" "FIREBOLT!" "FIREBOLT!" "FIREBOLTTT!!!!"

"GYAAHH!!!"

"Whoops. I'm on the fifth level…"

I've gone too far in. I laugh to myself, looking around the room with a very satisfied smile.

The fact that the pale blue walls have turned light green is all the proof I need.

I was having too much fun, I reflect to myself as I make a quick U-turn.

'Bout time to go home, I say to myself, humming a tune when…

"—Whuh?"

Something feels…off.

Heartbeat in my ears, I can hear it.

"Uh……?"

It happens quickly.

I've never drunk alcohol before, but this must be what a drunk person feels like.

My legs are unsteady. I'm not even sure they're touching the ground.

My vision spins. I glimpse the rapidly approaching floor, and pass out right then and there.

"......?"

"What's wrong, Aiz?"

Two adventurers entered the fifth-level floor.

However, they didn't come from above. They arrived from below.

Standing firm without a scratch on them, Aiz and Reveria had spent three days climbing up from the Lower Fortress, level thirty-seven. Even though they'd been fighting off monsters for the past forty-six hours straight on their journey to the surface, neither of them looked all that tired.

Now their journey's end was right in front of them, but Aiz, who was walking a few paces in front of Reveria, stopped in her tracks.

The elf looked at Aiz's long blond hair as she asked what was wrong.

"A person is on the ground."

"Done in by a monster?"

Sure enough, alone in the middle of the room was the body of an adventurer.

He lay facedown on the dungeon floor, like he had tripped and not gotten back on his feet. The two girls approached him.

"No visible wounds, healing and detox appear to be unnecessary...Looks like a classic case of Mind Down."

Reveria continued her diagnosis in a matter-of-fact tone, saying that he'd probably used magic without thinking about the consequences.

Using magic was not free. It required energy. Magic uses mental energy, the opposite of physical strength, to activate. Of course, just as the body has its limit, the mind can only take so much.

Reveria was amazed that this boy had been able to keep using magic to the point of losing consciousness.

Meanwhile, Aiz crouched down over the adventurer with her hands on her knees, staring at his white hair.

"This boy…"

"What's that? Do you know him, Aiz?"

"Not really. We've never spoken directly…He's, um, the boy I told you about. The Minotaur…"

"…I see. He's the boy that idiot insulted."

She had heard many things about this boy, Bell, from Aiz. First, he was the coward who was chased around by the Minotaur. He'd also run out of a bar they'd been drinking at after he was slandered by Bete.

Even though Reveria had warned their party member and defended the boy, she hadn't realized that he had actually been there. She regretted not stopping the conversation sooner. She knew they had hurt him.

Even worse, Aiz had been dragged into the middle of that exchange.

"Reveria, I want to compensate this boy."

"…There are other ways of saying that."

Reveria let out a long sigh in response to Aiz's choice of words. Aiz looked up at her with pleading, sparkling eyes and blinked two, three times.

Realizing that Aiz didn't understand, Reveria gave up and decided not to say anything.

"Well, helping someone at a time like this is common courtesy…"

Aiz nodded twice, her clothing swishing with her head. Reveria leaned forward for a closer look at Bell.

Seeing that the boy showed no signs of waking up anytime soon, Reveria shifted her gaze onto Aiz.

"…Aiz, do for this boy exactly what I'm about to tell you. If you're going to compensate him, that should be enough."

"What?"

Reveria gave her a look to convey her real message.

"…Is it okay just to do that?"

"I'm not certain. But you will protect this spot. You don't have to do anything above and beyond that. Besides, any man would be happy because it's you."

"I don't…understand."

You don't have to understand, Reveria chuckled to herself.

The elf looked down at Aiz for a moment, like a mother watching her child grow up, before returning her expression to its usual refined, dignified state.

Her face back to normal, Reveria stood up.

"I'm returning to the surface. I'll just get in your way if I stay here. You two have to be alone to understand each other."

"Yes, thank you, Reveria."

The elf nodded with an affirmative "Ah" before leaving them behind.

She wasn't the least bit worried about monsters attacking them.

As far as guardians went, the boy had the best one on the planet to protect him.

A deep slumber envelops me.

A fragrance like a serene wind, warmed from the heat of the sun.

All the sensation my skin transmits is soft and pleasant.

I'm drowsy.

I'm so comfortable I don't want to move…

……?

Something is stroking my hair. Thin fingers run down my cheek.

So gentle, so reassuring.

My eyelids open slowly.

…*Mother?*

I call out to the person I've never met, don't even know her face.

The fuzzy outline filling my vision stops moving.

"Sorry. I'm not your mother…"

……*Huh?*

The person responds in a voice that goes right through me.

I blink to clear my clouded eyes.

As I do, the fuzzy shapes come into focus.

The first thing I can make out is shiny blond hair. Then a beautiful face.

Finally, golden eyes that match her hair.

"......"

"Are you awake...?"

My eyes are open. My head is awake.

But time isn't moving.

My mind still empty, I stare at the face looking down on me.

The back of my head is warm. Something soft is under it.

I think I know what's going on. My head is, probably, in her lap.

This person, Aiz Wallenstein, strokes my hair again.

She touches my eyelids, warm.

"......"

I clumsily raise my upper body.

I know it's a waste of warm comfort, but still I sit up.

She leaves my line of sight. In her place is a massacre of slain monsters and random bones. I pretend not to see anything and turn back to Miss Wallenstein. She's still there.

"...An illusion?"

"Not an illusion."

Miss Wallenstein's expression suddenly changes. The line of her eyebrows slants.

We exchange glances for an eternal moment.

Gold and ruby-red eyes. It looks like the silence is getting to her. My face is turning redder with each passing heartbeat. By the time Miss Wallenstein realizes it, my head is red enough that it might as well be an overripe apple sitting on my shoulders.

My eyes are out of focus, fluttering and quivering like lake-worms.

I scramble to my feet.

"GAAAAAAAH!!!"

I run away as fast as my legs can carry me.

"...Why do you always...run away?"

If someone had been there to hear her words, they would have heard a hint of loneliness in Aiz's voice.

WINE

DIVINE

Chapter 4

Suzuhito Yasuda

"Please have a look."

"All right."

An amulet was placed on the counter. The owner of the store, an old male gnome with a long white beard and a red hat, picked up the green jewel-encrusted necklace and made his way to the back room.

At the Gnome Trader, a very simply named antique shop, a small transaction was again taking place. A prum stood at the counter waiting for the owner to return, surrounded by a random assortment of odds and ends decorating the shop.

"All finished. Sorry to keep you waiting."

"What's the result?"

"Looks like it's got a full status boost…and resistance to poison attached to it. Very good, very good. So…how does forty-six thousand vals sound to you?"

The prum nodded with a very satisfied look. A deal had been struck.

"Is today's payment in cash?"

"No, the usual."

The two finished the transaction at a brisk pace.

A grandfather clock in the corner of the store ticked off the seconds.

The gnome slowly opened his mouth to speak. "It might not be this geezer's place to say this, but…"

Fiddling with the talisman in his hands, the owner gazed at his customer with a bit of concern in his eyes. The prum tilted his head.

"Wouldn't be a good idea to stick your neck into dangerous situations. Might already be too late, I know…"

"……"

"There's a rumor goin' 'round in some adventurer circles. Not too well known yet, but out there just the same. Talkin' 'bout a prum with sticky fingers pilfering their valuables. Sometimes even a whole party at once."

"…What are you trying to say?"

"No, no, my friend. I'm not suspecting you. The prum in question is a lady, and been stealing for a while by the sound of it. Suspecting a man like yourself would be barkin' up the wrong tree, I know. It's just..." said the gnome under his breath, his white beard twitching. "I've seen most of the valuables reported stolen with my own two eyes...yes? This geezer thinks you should keep an eye on your company and keep your nose down."

The owner's mood suddenly turned sour. The prum could see it in his eyes. In response, however, the male prum flashed an arrogant smile.

"Sounds like there's a bad prum out there. But then again, are the words of adventurers all that reliable? I mean, many of them do exactly the same kind of stealing and blackmail."

"That is...true..."

"If you ask me, they should all get off their high horses."

The prum continued with a nasty grin on his lips.

"It's harsh, but the fact is that it's their fault for being tricked."

"Hmm?" the owner replied angrily, but his voice was drowned out by the ticking wall clock.

"Hnngh...guhhh...?!"

"...Bell, what are you doing?"

I'm lying facedown on the sofa, holding a cushion against the back of my head with both hands. The goddess seems to think that me hiding my face with my butt in the air is funny, but I don't have any snappy comebacks in me at the moment.

I ran away from Miss Wallenstein.

I have absolutely no clue what chain of events led to it, but I know that all of it was real. I know that my head was in the lap of the girl of my dreams, and I know that I ran away from her at full speed like some crazy idiot.

Gaah...Someone, please kill me...

"Don't tell me, you wet the sofa?"

"No, Goddess, no..."

Normally I'd be all about getting back at her for saying that, but all that comes out is a pitiful voice.

After I ran away from Miss Wallenstein in an explosion of shame and confusion, I think I wandered around for a while, but I have no idea where I went. By the time I realized where I was, it was almost morning and I was staggering up to the front door at home and falling to my knees.

"I don't know the details, but you're a really sensitive boy…"

No, Goddess, not sensitive. I'm heartbroken…

I manage to peel my shaky body from the sofa, my ears still bright red. I even make it to the table for breakfast with the goddess.

I just want to stay in the room and wallow all day, but I know I can't. Just for today, I need to forget about Miss Wallenstein…Yeah, like hell I can do that.

Will the day come when I can thank her properly and express my gratitude?

"Oh, yes. Bell, show me the book you were reading yesterday. I've got nothing to do this morning."

"Ah, sure. Go ahead."

Her shift must start in the afternoon today. She's still working at the street stand in addition to her part-time job at *Hephaistos Familia*'s Babel Tower Branch Store…I wonder if she can physically keep this up.

I hold out the book, thick as an encyclopedia, that I borrowed from Syr, to the goddess.

"Hmm…the more I look at it, the book seems stranger and stranger…yes?"

She opens the cover and glances through the first few pages. Strangely, she stops moving.

But not completely. Her eyes start spinning. It's almost like someone had come to collect a debt she didn't know about and was looking at the paperwork.

Huh…? What's going on…?

"…Isn't this a grimoire?"

"G-grimoire?"

I repeat the word. I've never heard it before.

I don't have a good feeling about it, though. I break out in a cold sweat.

"So, um, what's that...?"

"To put it simply, it's a book that forces the reader to learn magic."

It feels like all the sweat glands in my body have opened at the same time.

"I don't think you know about Advanced Abilities, but they're special skills like Magic Control or Enigma. This book could only be made by someone who has mastered both."

—I know what you're talking about, Goddess.

Someone with two Advanced Abilities...In other words, a member of a *Familia* who has reached at least level three. An average smith could never make something like this. It would have to be someone much, much stronger.

It has to be the masterwork of someone on the level of a legendary individual known as "the Philosopher."

My body turns to stone, a broken smile on my lips.

"So this is how you learned magic...So Bell, just how exactly did this grimoire end up here in the first place?"

"I borrowed it from a friend...She said it was left behind by someone else..."

"......"

"What's it worth...?"

"At least as much as *Hephaistos Familia*'s highest-quality weapons, or possibly even more..."

Crack! My stone body breaks, right down the middle.

"By the way, it can only be used once. Once someone acquires magic from it, a grimoire becomes nothing more than trash. A big paperweight."

I'm dead.

Acquiring magic through external intervention was said to be miraculous, and I used a book containing precisely such a miracle. Not only that, I basically stole it, and now it's worthless. Millions of vals down the drain, and all because of me...

A heavy silence falls over our home.

I'm in despair. There is no way to undo what I've done.

The goddess stares at the floor, her face as emotionless as a mask. She suddenly turns to the table, grabs a chair, and walks over to me, her feet tapping lightly on the floor. She climbs up onto the seat, thumps both hands down onto my shoulders, and starts talking down to me from her high vantage point.

"Listen to me, Bell. You met the book's owner by accident. And you returned the book to him *before reading it*. So the book was never here. Even if there was a mistake, the grimoire had been used *before* you had it…That's how this happened."

"Goddess, that's wrong!"

Why is she trying to pull a fast one?!

"Bell, Gekai is not all sunshine and flowers; there are many dark, dark things. I've seen them with my own eyes. Being thrown out of home, being so poor that even buying potato puffs was impossible and starving, being forced to live under ruins…carrying an enormous debt. The world is full of injustices."

"Wasn't all of that your fault?!"

And what was that last thing you said there?!

What are you hiding, Goddess?!

"A-anyway, I'm going to go and explain everything to the person who lent me this book!"

"Bell, don't! You don't have to be that upstanding! This world is even more unpredictable than the gods themselves!"

"Please don't try to sound wise at a time like this! Even if we tried to hide it, the truth will come out! It's just a matter of time!"

The die has already been cast! Syr will ask me if I read the book, for sure. Even if I lied to her, everything would come out when the real owner came back for it! Done! Over! Out!

At this point, the only option is to explain everything and assume the *dogeza* position.

Grabbing the book and blowing past the goddess's attempts to stop me, I hold the book under my arm and kick the door open.

"Is Syr here?"

"Ohh, look who's here! Morning to ya, meow!"

One of the catgirl waitresses at The Benevolent Mistress responds to me while sweeping the street outside the bar.

If I remember right, her name is Chloe. She looks at me with a giddy smile, her tail swishing back and forth behind her.

"What's this, what's this? No morning greeting and calling on Syr at this early hour, meow? What are you planning to—"

"Please call Syr!"

"Wha—?! Okay, okay, meow!"

She finally understands my sharp words and jumps in surprise. Maybe she can tell I'm not my usual self. She runs into the building so fast she almost slips a few times. The bell on the front door rings as she flies inside.

A few moments later, Chloe sticks her face out from behind the front door and motions for me to come inside.

I step inside the café and bar; they're still getting ready for the day.

"Good morning, Bell. Is something the matter?"

"Syr!!"

Tap tap tap tap. I can hear her shoes on the floor as she comes running from the kitchen. She must have come in a hurry. She's still carrying a wooden tray in her arms.

Her blue-gray hair is tied back with a triangular bandanna. I start to tell her the gist of everything that had happened.

At first she wears a polite but confused smile, but her eyes grow larger and larger as I talk. The color of her face changes at some point…When I finish speaking, just like she had done at some point before, she breaks off eye contact.

"…Well, that's a very sticky situation you're in, Bell."

"Hold on there, Syr! How come you're acting like you're not involved?!"

I had to say something about her strange tone. What is she planning to use me as, some kind of sacrificial lamb?

She lifts the tray up to her mouth, hiding the lower half of her face. She looks at me with upturned eyes.

"So…I can't?"

"As cute as you look right now, no! Absolutely not!"

I strike down her request despite those imploring eyes, my own face a flaming cherry on my shoulders.

This woman really does seem like a witch!

"You're hittin' a nerve, boy! Burstin' into other people's shops this early in the mornin'."

The bar's owner, Mama Mia, must have heard our squabble and followed the noise all the way here. Despite being a dwarf, her frame is absolutely imposing. My body freezes as she walks up to me and plucks the book out of my unusually stiff hands, before glancing over the book herself.

"That's a grimoire, all right...But what's done is done. Boy, pay it no mind, ya hear?"

"Huh?? B-b-but..."

"The dimwit who left it here is at fault. Like saying, 'Here, please read this.' Boy, if ya hadn't read it, some other adventurer woulda said the grimoire was his and taken it anyway. That's just how it is."

She's rather persuasive. I close my still-open mouth as she lets out a long breath through her nose.

"He was prepared to lose it the moment he let it outta his sight. Think about it, boy: if ya lost a wallet full of cash, you'd come back to get it, wouldn't ya?"

"Well..."

"It's the same thing. Useless to worry about it, boy. Be happy ya got somethin' outta it and let it go."

Mia said her piece and leaves it at that.

I look back over to Syr. She has a small grimace on her face, tilting her head to the side.

This still leaves something to be desired, and I get a bad aftertaste from it. My face puckers up like I've drunk bitter medicine...

Mia glances at me through the side of one of her big eyes. "Real men don't brood over nothin'!" she says.

"Yes, ma'am!" Her voice is like a slap on the wrist. My whole body shoots to attention in response.

As I watch the dwarfess make heavy strides toward the back of the bar, I still can't help but wonder if it's really okay to just ignore what happened.

I rub the sides of my head, trying to untangle my thoughts.

"…Well, sorry to disturb you. I'll be going now."

I stand there in silence for a moment before turning on my heel. At the same time, a very sneaky Chloe brings a basket to Syr. She takes the basket and…nervously sticks it out in front of me.

"Would you be willing to take this again today?"

"…T-thanks."

I stutter as I take the basket from the outstretched hands of the shyly smiling Syr.

I always feel a little embarrassed when she gives me lunch, but Syr always looks very happy when I take it. Honestly, her smile looks more cheerful than usual…Not that it isn't always cheerful…I just can't put it into words.

My skin gets even redder as I express my gratitude one more time before finally making my exit from The Benevolent Mistress.

I set down the ex-grimoire when I get home and equip my armor to get ready for a day in the Dungeon.

I give the goddess a basic explanation of what happened at the bar before heading out. A very calm voice says, "Have a nice day" as I open the door to go outside.

Now that I think about it, didn't I use my last potion…?

I'm jogging down West Main when I suddenly remember my item situation. I used my last potion three days ago. The item holster on my left leg is completely empty.

They've helped me out before…Maybe I should swing by their shop first?

I decide to stop by a store I haven't been to in a while on my way to the Dungeon.

The shop is located off of West Main, but I have to go through a few backstreets to get there.

Basically, it's a house that was built in a dark, damp place. But there's a sign with the *Miach Familia*'s emblem, a completely healthy human body, above the front door.

"Ex-cuse me, good morn-ing…"

I open the wooden double doors a crack and peek inside. My eyes look up and down the rows of shelves, trying to find an animal-person girl in the dim shop. She hears my voice and turns her half-closed eyes my way.

"Morning, Bell. Long time, no see…"

With her slow voice and drowsy-looking eyes, you'd think she'd just woken up, but that's just how she is. The girl's taste in clothing is also a little strange. Her tail is sticking through her skirt, and her left sleeve comes down to her elbow, but her right sleeve goes to her wrist. She has a glove on her right hand only. She looks to be about the same age as Eina, maybe a little younger. She stops what she's doing and walks to the back of the shop and behind a counter.

"Sorry to come in this early. Are you busy?"

"No worries. No one will come in after you leave anyway, Bell… So, what're you going to buy today?"

She reaches under the counter and pulls up a closed case before setting it on the counter between us.

The wide case holds many tubes filled with various colorful liquids lined up in a row.

"By the way, is Lord Miach around? I would like to speak with him if it's all right."

"Lord Miach is on a personal errand and won't be back until tonight. I'm alone today…"

My eyes were scanning the tubes when I asked her, and that was her answer.

The shop is run by Miach and belongs to *Miach Familia*; it also doubles as the *Familia*'s home. The girl I'm talking to is Nahza, *Miach Familia*'s only member.

She pulls out a very expensive-looking potion from the case and holds it out to me.

"Say, Bell, what do you think? Isn't it about time to try a high potion…?"

"Uh, n-no, it's still too soon for me."

I dodge her proposal with a nervous smile. The high potion she's holding is worth tens of thousands of vals. This kind of conversation is almost a daily thing for us because we both belong to dirt-poor *Familias*. If there is a way to make or save a few vals, we'll find it.

That being said, I'm usually on the losing side when trying to barter with Nahza…

"Bell, you haven't paid us a visit in a long time…"

"…?!"

"Lord Miach was very lonely. His stomach was growling…'cause he was starving."

Ever since I hired Lilly, I haven't been to this shop. She'll prepare any item I ask for, so I haven't needed to go anywhere else to buy potions. Nahza's words stab at my conscience; I'm breaking out in a cold sweat.

This is bad! At this rate I'll end up buying something I don't need…

"Ah! I just remembered! Something strange happened to me in the Dungeon yesterday."

Desperate to change the topic, I bring up how I passed out in the Dungeon after using magic. Nahza listens to my story before letting out an affirmative "Ah!"

"That's Mind Down. It happens all the time to adventurers who've just learned magic but get carried away…"

"Mind Down…?"

"Magic requires mental energy to work. If you use too much, you go out like a light.

"So that's why…" Nahza continues as she rustles through a box under the counter, "…you need a mind-restoring potion to avoid that. This one was just brewed the other day…"

"Uh, but…that potion is really expensive…"

"No worries. I'll give you a discount, being a regular and all… Eight thousand and seven hundred vals."

I step back for a moment to think it over.

"All right…"

The dog ears on top of Nahza's head twitch happily when she hears my response, and she quickly bends over to pick up two more tubes.

"If you're willing to buy this for eighty-seven-hundred vals, I'll throw in these two potions for an even nine thousand…Sound good?"

Her suggestion makes my eyes go wide and my head spin. Is that really a good deal?

Miach Familia's cheapest potions are 500 vals apiece. Considering that, Nahza's offer is really good. But spending 9,000 vals in one go…that's almost painful. Then again, this item will let me use more magic, so it's very tempting.

The first rule of going on adventures is to prepare for anything and everything.

"No one knows what will happen in the Dungeon. It'd be a good idea to be thorough…"

With those words she's just sealed the deal.

I may be a bit of a coward, but if I have to choose between money and the safety of my party, I'll choose the latter.

"Okay. I'll accept your offer."

"Thanks, Bell. I love you…"

I feel a fire burning in my cheeks at her sudden words. Finishing the transaction, I take the items from the lazily smiling Nahza with her half-lidded eyes, and immediately feel the need to get the heck out of here.

Nahza waves good-bye as I make a break for the wooden doors and leave the shop.

"You're too easy, Bell…"

…I thought I heard something before the doors closed behind me, but no—it's just my imagination. My imagination, I tell you!

I leave the item shop and go down West Main—a street that I've traveled many times in the past few hours—toward the Dungeon.

A ton of fully equipped adventurers have already gathered in large, circular Central Park under a bright and clear blue sky.

Wonder if she's here yet…

I look around, hoping to find Lilly in the park. It's our meeting point, but I can't find a dog girl that looks like her.

Just as I was thinking this isn't like her, I happen to catch a glimpse of something strange on my way toward Babel Tower.

It's in a part of Central Park, under the shade of a tree with large leaves. Lilly is standing with three adventurers, sunlight dancing on their faces as the leaves sway in a soft breeze. It looks very comfortable.

However, the three large men are surrounding Lilly. They have their chests puffed out, looking down on her and saying something while Lilly frantically shakes her head from side to side. No one looks all that happy.

—Could they be members of *Soma Familia*?

As soon as the thought crosses my mind, I immediately go in their direction.

"…enough…hand…over!"

"Already…gone…Really…!!"

It sounds like they're having a heated argument.

I hide behind a tree in their blind spot and prepare to jump in at a moment's notice.

"Hey!"

"!"

But then, out of the blue—

Someone grabs my shoulder as if they're trying to get in my way. I spin out of it in a surprised reflex and turn to face the grabber.

It's a male adventurer. A human with black hair, excellent physique, and a longsword strapped to his back.

…*Wait a second, isn't he…?*

"Heh, yer that kid from before…Don't matter, got a question for ya: Ya working with that runt over there?"

That voice, that tone…No doubt about it. He's the man I met in the alleyway a while ago.

"Oi! Haven't got all day! Did ya hire that supporter or not?"

"…That girl is not the prum you were chasing in the alley that day."

I can tell he's pissed off just by looking at his eyes, but I still give him that answer. Part of it might just have been a reflex.

It's hard to tell because she's wearing an oversized robe and has a deep hood over her face, but Lilly isn't a prum. She's a Chienthrope, a dog person.

I just want to say, "Don't get the wrong idea…" The man curves his lips into a sneer.

"Moron…is what I wanna call ya, but what ya think is yer own business. Ya wanna play the fool, be my guest."

Sounds like he's giving me an angry lecture, but there's something in the tone of his voice that bothers me.

It's like he's saying I'm being tricked.

But I'm not just going to take him at his word…

I squint my eyes in suspicion, and the man makes a jeering smile back at me.

"But that don't matter; yer gonna help me…We're gonna snatch her."

"Wha…"

"Not askin' ya to do it for free. I'll pay ya a bit up front and a share of what we get out of the runt."

This guy sounds serious. I'm so shocked by his sudden proposal that words leave me.

"All ya have to do is go into the Dungeon like usual. After that, find an excuse to leave her alone and I'll do the rest. Piece of cake, ain't it?"

The man's mouth opens wide as he laughs with all his might.

I don't like that laugh at all. It reeks of a malice I've never heard before.

Even as a chill of nervousness sweeps through my body, I clench my fist.

"Why are you saying things like that…?"

"Huh? What's with the backtalk, kid? This is where ya nod 'yes' like a good boy. Think of all the money yer gonna get from this. Hell of a sweet deal.

"Ha-ha!" The man lets out another round of ridiculing laughter. "Use yer brain, boy! That's just a supporter—the runt carries the bags! Yer no worse off if that useless piece of trash were gone, now are ya? Wring her dry while ya can and ditch the rest."

I'm way past my boiling point.

This is different from the back alley. I don't have room to be scared—a fierce rage is taking control of my body.

"Not a chance in hell…!"

"Friggin' brat…!"

The man's face contorts into a gruesome visage. My forehead tightens as power flows into all of my muscles.

A fierce energy surrounds us. The leaves on the branch above us shake, almost as if in fear of what's going on below.

We stare each other down for a minute or two until he turns on his heal with a loud "Tsk" and walks away.

I watch him go, the mask of fury still on my face.

"…Mr. Bell?"

"!"

A voice from behind me.

I turn around, almost as if drawn in by it, to find a dumbfounded Lilly standing there, looking up at me.

The flames of rage that had been burning inside me cool. I return to my normal self.

"L-Lilly? How long have you been there?"

"Lilly just got here…What were you talking about with that honorable adventurer?"

"Ahem…Nothing much, he was just trying to pick a fight…"

I manage to come up with something. I can't exactly tell the person in front of me that he was trying to set up a trap for her.

Lilly can tell I'm not calm. She stares at me with her mouth closed. Her expression seems a little dark.

"Oh! You seemed to be tangled up in something a minute ago. Is everything okay, Lilly?"

"So you saw that…Please don't worry. As you can see, Lilly is fine."

She holds out her arms and does a small twirl before looking up at me with a big smile.

No bruises or tears on her robe. It looks like nothing happened. That's a relief.

"Lilly, who were those—"

"Just like what happened to Mr. Bell, they were picking a fight with Lilly. Maybe Mr. Bell and Lilly look weak?"

She jumped in before I could finish.

Smiling her usual bright smile and telling more jokes, she didn't let me get another word in. I don't think she wants to talk about what really happened.

"All right, let's go, Mr. Bell! Since Lilly hasn't worked in two days, Lilly's counting on your efforts today, Mr. Bell!"

She passes right by my side, heading toward Babel Tower. Her bangs sticking out of her hood shake as she turns back around for a second. I catch a glimpse of her chestnut-colored eyes—they're perfectly normal. It's like nothing happened at all.

I decide to let it go and not say anything else. I close my mouth and follow her.

I can't tell what her face looks like now because she's in front of me. But I think about it as we weave through the crowded and noisy street on our way to the Dungeon.

"…Looks like the time is right."

"What's this? You're already finishing up, Eina?"

"Yes. About to."

Eina nodded at her coworker.

They were in the lobby of Guild Headquarters. The floors and walls of the first floor were constructed from white marble, giving the space a somber feel. Evening sunlight shining in through the windows lit up the lobby like the neighboring houses.

Eina looked around the Guild lobby as she cleaned off her desk and stood up.

"Wow! Right at closing time?! The Eina I know never leaves right away…Could it be…surely not…a date?!"

"Why is that the only…"

Eina waved off the idea, politely refuting the idea, and forced a smile before taking her leave.

Saying a quick good-bye to her other coworkers, she left the building through the employee exit.

"Well, then…"

Tat, tat, tat. The funny excuse for shoes the Guild provided her echoed off the stone street as Eina set off in the opposite direction from her home.

This area of West Main was completely devoid of street vendors and stalls. The evening sun bathed long rows of large stores on both sides of the street in red light. Being very close to the Guild, almost all of the stores targeted adventurers as their main customers.

People who lived and worked in this neighborhood referred to this Main Street as "Adventurers Way" for that reason.

The street was wide enough that adventurers wearing heavy armor could easily pass by one another without incident.

After all that searching through the Guild's resources, I couldn't find anything other than the usual information on Soma Familia...

Eina had been trying to find information about the inner workings of *Soma Familia* for the past few days.

If she was asked why, she simply answered, "There's something I need to know." If said person asked for more details, Eina would add that she was concerned about the possibility of Bell being caught up in a difficult situation.

Even talking to people in charge of Soma Familia's *adventurers, they all say the same things...Let's see what I can find out myself.*

Despite going through all of the Guild's records and talking to as many people as she could, the results were less than promising.

She'd gotten as far as understanding, superficially, that all of the members of that *Familia* were obsessed with money, and it seemed as though there was something forcing them into a frenzy. Eina did her best to focus on the important points as she organized her thoughts.

A god uses their Familia *to further their own ends...No, nothing makes sense.*

Where there was smoke, there was fire. The "smoke" seemed to be coming from two places: the members' unending desire for money and the sheer number of members in that group.

Soma didn't have the type of reputation that could bring in the large numbers of members and followers that belonged to *Soma Familia*.

What if the god Soma isn't the cause? What if there is something else...something making the members of Soma Familia *act like that?*

Eina stopped walking for a moment as she reached that point in her train of thought.

A large bar was in front on her.

"Hmmm…It might be useful to go in here, but…"

It had always been true that a bar was the best place to gather information.

However, it was the one place that Eina preferred to avoid.

For her—no, for all elves—bars where large numbers of adventurers gathered were usually unlucky places.

Basically, men of all races swarmed to her like bees to a flower.

"Ah-ha-ha…No, don't think so."

Thinking about what might be waiting for her beyond those doors, Eina laughed quietly to herself before walking past the bar entirely. Her pace quickened when the wild voices of the adventurers inside echoed through the entrance.

Not trying to flatter myself…

Eina was always very conscious of her appearance.

Despite being half human, the blood of elves—considered to have the most beautiful men and women among all the races—also ran through her veins. She had to accept the fact that, to a degree, men of other races would be attracted to her.

It's not that I'm not open to the idea of dating…

The surprised look on her coworker's face after she asked about a man or a date just before leaving work jumped into Eina's mind.

Eina wasn't trying to come across as some innocent virgin. She was already nineteen; it was perfectly acceptable for someone that age to have a partner. She did feel a bit empty from time to time.

That void was normally filled by work, however.

But then again, I've never really felt like "That one!" about anybody…

Most of the men who had approached Eina in the past were robust, capable adventurer types.

All of them were dependable men who could sweep her off her feet as well as protect and support her.

But because they were like that, there was one thing about them that made her a little nervous:

Maybe it would be better if they weren't so reliable...

She was a workaholic, so perhaps someone who was a little more unpredictable would be a better fit...Never before had she been so honest with herself.

She'd be struggling with problems alone, trying to overcome them by herself, but then in the end someone would just come into her life. She wanted that kind of person. She laughed to herself as she envisioned getting a little too involved with him, working together to make something great, a hold-and-be-held relationship. Someone who would depend on her and let her feel like a protector would be just right for Eina.

Ahhh, I wonder if there's a man like Bell anywhere—

Yes, that was it.

The answer was clear. It was hard to miss, putting it into words.

*So a man like Bell would be perfect—ahhh...*Eina had found the most satisfying answer.

...Wait.

Hey, hey! Her hand flew into the open air beside her.

A man like Bell...Well, then—that was it, wasn't it?

"Hee-hee-hee..." No one was there to see Eina's ears turn pink or to hear her giggling.

"Ah! There it is, there it is!"

She was alone but still said her thoughts out loud and much louder than necessary.

Her face still flush with heat, she entered a two-story item shop made from stone. The billboard above the entrance to the shop read RETAIL.

The reason she wanted to come here was to investigate *Soma Familia's* wine.

Part of it was that she had exhausted most of her options, but the fact that they sold so little wine didn't seem right to her. While she didn't think she'd crack the case with this, Eina thought there was some value in looking into it.

I haven't been here in ages. I wonder if they have a larger selection.

Transparent cases that were many times stronger than glass lined the inside of the shop like army camps. Eina craned her neck to look at the highest shelves.

Many products were stored on each shelf. Round-bottomed flasks filled with blue liquid were potions. Green fluids in cylindrical tubes were antidotes, and elixir was sold in fancy bottles with intricate designs. All of them were made by *Familias* that specialized in sales.

Many item shops sold items produced by only one *Familia*. This particular shop had secured a spot on Adventurers Way by having a good reputation and carrying many different types of items.

Eina walked right past the adventurer items and over to a corner of the store marked GROCERY.

Yes! Here it is!

Eina happily clapped her hands together when she spotted *Soma Familia's* label on a shelf lined with wine.

The container on the shelf wasn't very appealing, being nothing more than a typical glass bottle. The liquid inside was clear. For something so highly sought after, it didn't look very good at all.

However, out of all the varieties of alcohol on the shelf, there was only one of *Soma Familia's* wines left. Its popularity must be the real deal.

"...Soma"?

Eina blinked her emerald eyes a few times as she looked at the most boring and thoughtless label in the shop.

Same name as its creator...Had the god Soma named it after himself?

Eina tilted her neck as she thought about it. She was thinking about calling over a sales clerk to open the closed case for her when her eyes saw the price tag.

Sixty thousand vals.

Thunk! Eina's forehead hit the shelf.

Wha...huh—? This is just wine?!

Unbelievable! It cost more than all of Bell's equipment combined!

Eina rubbed the red spot on her head and looked at the bottle one more time.

The price was equal to or above the value of specialized weapons and armor for ádventurers. While it wasn't impossible for an average person to purchase a bottle of this wine, at that price it was highly unlikely.

The value of the contents and the shoddiness of the bottle didn't match in the slightest.

How much money do I have on me? No way I brought enough...

The average pay of a Guild employee was more than what a run-of-the-mill adventurer made but nowhere near enough to justify walking around with 60,000 vals in their pockets. Buying even one bottle would put immense strain on Eina's living expenses. Not to mention the fact that she'd bought a piece of armor as a present for Bell just a few days earlier.

Eina stood in front of the wine shelf, a fierce debate raging in her mind.

"...Aren't you Eina Tulle?"

"Huh?"

A clear voice caressed her eardrums. Eina turned around to find the person who said her name.

Behind her stood a stunningly beautiful and surprisingly tall female elf.

Her glimmering jade-colored hair was tied into a single ponytail that hung halfway down her back. Her ears stuck up like leaves on a tree, guiding her gorgeous long hair backward. Even among the beautiful and refined elves, the woman looked on par with royalty. Her looks could even be described as otherworldly.

Fitting right in with her elegance, the woman's emerald eyes were the same emerald green color as Eina's, if not a little deeper shade.

Eina's body snapped to attention.

"Lady Reveria?!"

"So it is you...It's been a long time. You have become very beautiful in my absence. I almost didn't recognize you."

While it wasn't quite a smile, the lips of Reveria Riyos Ahrve softened and curved upward. Eina was very quick to show respect.

"I am honored, my lady. To receive such high praise, I will hold your words dear..."

"Stop talking like that. This isn't the elven homeland. You were not born in the homeland in the first place. You have no reason to hold me in such high regard."

"Even so, I mustn't forget to be humble and show the utmost respect to royalty such as yourself. Mother always told me—"

"So even that Aina would force this upon her daughter...It is regrettable. She escaped the homeland alongside me, to end up like this."

Eina looked on as Reveria let out a wistful sigh before fixing her piercing gaze on her.

"It is prudent to carry the smallest amount of respect, but any more than that is needless. I find it tiresome to be placed in that particular cage. If you say that you want to respect and honor me, then you must comprehend what my heart desires."

"M-my lady…"

Reveria's overpowering words left Eina speechless.

The fact remained that Eina was born in a free city with its doors wide open to any and all races. Her knowledge of elves in the homeland was very limited but…she knew that the elf in front of her was royalty, a high elf.

The elven half of her blood was forcing her to bow her head.

"I'm not asking you to break the system. Only don't go overboard."

"U-understood."

"Good."

Reveria gave a satisfied nod, but Eina wasn't sure how to feel. Even her eyebrows weren't on straight.

Eina felt like she had lost an argument and tried her best to keep that feeling hidden. So rather than dwell on it, she decided to be happy about their reunion.

When they were both young, Eina had met Reveria many times at her childhood home. However, they hadn't seen each other even once since then.

Eina knew about Reveria's activities as soon as she entered the Guild. Due to their schedules and job responsibilities, there hadn't been a good opportunity to meet again.

Not that there wasn't the possibility, but neither of them had made an effort.

"I'm glad to see that you are well. To think you would work for the Guild, of all places…"

"Please forgive me, I meant to contact you…"

"Pay it no mind. I've spent my days in the Dungeon ever since arriving in this city. There has been no time for much else. Our meeting would have been delayed over and over, no doubt."

All of Reveria's movements, even her short head bow, were extremely polished and refined. Eina had grown up watching her mother carry herself with dignity and grace, but the high elves were on another level entirely. The two girls came from completely different walks of life.

"Why are you here today, Lady Reveria?"

"What? I used up the last of my items the other day in the Dungeon. Simple as that."

"Would it be silly to think...that Lady Reveria can't use healing magic?"

"Why, yes. However, magic is not perfect. If an item is on hand, nothing is better. What about you, Eina?"

"Oh..."

Reveria's question reminded Eina of her mission. Her knees wobbled for a moment before she decided to answer as best she could without bringing up her investigation of *Soma Familia*.

This was to avoid the possibility of rumors going around that someone working for the Guild was investigating a specific group.

"Ahh, this wine. There are many in my *Familia* who adore it."

"Um...can I ask you a question, Lady Reveria? Do any of them show signs of dependence or act strangely?"

"Everyone who drinks alcohol looks strange to my eyes...but no one has done anything I would consider out of the ordinary. Why do you ask?"

"Well...a friend of mine recommended it to me. But from the things I've heard about *Soma Familia*..."

There was some truth in Eina's words. Even though she didn't feel right, purposely misleading Reveria with her answer, the chance of getting valuable information from her was too good to pass up.

"I see. I too have heard a few things about members of that *Familia* being odd, almost cold."

"Lady Reveria, do you know anything about them?"

She got her hopes up, and her voice cracked with excitement.

Her cover was blown.

Reveria closed one eye and stared at the excited Eina for a moment.
*Oh no…*Eina froze. She realized her mistake a moment too late.

Reveria was very sharp. She could sense the emotions of whomever she was talking with and figure out their true intentions. Reveria was the only person Eina couldn't keep a secret from when they were children.

Reveria had more than likely figured out that Eina was investigating *Soma Familia*.

A wave of cold sweat passed over her body as Eina waited for the high elf's response.

"…Whatever. I'm sorry to say that I don't have any information concerning that *Familia*. No more than you know, probably less."

"Oh, is that so?"

Reveria had seen right through her, but Eina was relieved that the high elf hadn't asked for a reason why.

She gazed at Eina for a few moments before opening her mouth to speak.

"While I don't know about them…I do know someone who knows something concerning that group."

"…Yes?"

"Would you accompany me to my *Familia*'s home?"

The head residence.

That was this building put into words.

I never heard anything about them…but this is just how the home of a prominent dungeon-prowling Familia *should be…*

The building was located on the northern edge of Orario. It stood on the side of a backstreet, one block away from North Main.

Long and thin, it was as if the builders had to squeeze it onto the spot. Several pointed towers protruded from the roof like a line of spears standing on end, supplementing one another.

Of course these bronze towers were nothing compared to Babel but were still tall enough to make someone crane their neck to look up at them. The very tips of the towers were dyed black by the evening light.

It was a dwelling carved from flames.

"Lady Reveria, welcome back."

"Excuse me, this person with you...is she with the Guild?"

"She is the daughter of a friend. I request that you overlook her position."

After being questioned by male and female guards at the doorway, Reveria and Eina walked into the building.

The two of them looked as though they could be sisters, walking side by side. In reality, Reveria was many times older than Eina.

Elves live the longest of all the races of demi-humans.

"I suppose it's a little late for this, but...but are you sure this is all right?"

"What is?"

"Inviting me, a member of the Guild, into a home like this...If private information about *Loki Familia* became public because of me..."

"Do not speak of impossibilities, Eina. If I felt you had the potential for something like that, I would not have brought you here. Or perhaps you are trying to insult me?"

"N-no, not at all..."

More and more childhood memories came flooding back into her head as Eina followed Reveria through the main hall and into a reception room.

The room itself was completely open to the hallway and decorated in a calming, light orange color scheme. There were many expensive-looking sofas and round tables draped in cloth. While every furnishing there was of the highest quality, it seemed less a reception room than a space for repose and conversation.

Eina got a good feel for the overall atmosphere and mood of *Loki Familia* just by looking around this room.

Hey, not bad. I wouldn't mind living here myself— Hmm?

She noticed something as her gaze reached the far corner of the room.

It was in an armchair facing away from her. There seemed to be a big fluff of golden string attached to the side of it.

No, not string—blond hair. It was the back of someone's head, their hair flowing down the side of the chair and sticking out.

The person sitting there slowly turned her thin neck to face the elves.

Eina suddenly swallowed a lump of air.

"Welcome home, Reveria."

"Yes, Aiz. I have returned."

The speaker was a beautiful girl, even younger than Eina.

What stood out more than her soft, delicate features was her refined solemnity. Still, her eyes glimmered like pools of gold on her face. The word "innocent" seemed to fit her very well.

A noble beauty and a childlike purity seemed to coexist within her.

As Eina had said once before, just seeing the girl's beauty made her heart skip a beat.

Aiz Wallenstein.

The blond-haired, golden-eyed adventurer whom Bell couldn't get out of his mind.

"Who is…that person?" Aiz asked.

"I…um, I'm…" Eina stuttered.

"She is like a member of my family. You two, introduce yourselves."

They followed suit and exchanged greetings. Aiz didn't break eye contact with Eina as she spoke, her words clear and concise.

Without any armor on, Aiz looked like a very sheltered girl. She was very feminine, with her slender body wrapped in a pure white one-piece dress. It accentuated her generous bosom, as well.

Aiz's bare feet were pearl-white, like alabaster, smooth and vibrant.

…Breathtaking.

Eina didn't feel right, looking at Aiz this way. Even though he wasn't here, it felt like she was wedging herself between Bell and Aiz.

Moving slowly and carefully, Eina walked around the armchair and took a seat on the sofa facing her. Reveria joined them, with a table situated between the three girls.

"Aiz, have you purchased replacements for the items used during the last trip? We set out again in ten days."

"Yes…I'll go tomorrow."

Aiz's voice was muffled by her knees; she was holding them to her chest while sitting in the chair. Her words sounded dull, like a bell fallen on its side.

Eina could tell something wasn't right. She glanced over at Reveria, only to see a look on her face that the high elf often gave Eina years ago—a warm, motherly expression. Eina finally worked up the courage to say what was on her mind.

"Um, Lady Reveria?"

"What is it?"

"Don't you think that Aiz looks…a little upset?"

Eina couldn't feel any energy coming from the girl, her face half hidden behind knees covered in white cloth. Even Aiz's hair seemed to be missing its usual luster. It hung limp over her shoulders.

Eina hadn't known the girl for long, but she could tell Aiz was very sad.

Reveria laughed quietly at Eina's question, letting a rare smile onto her lips.

"Oh, a boy she's been interested in for a while now apparently ran away from her."

Reveria's shoulders shook as she laughed again, teasing Aiz about the situation. Eina, on the other hand, didn't feel like this was a laughing matter. "That's terrible…" she said, her hand on her forehead.

It looked as though the chances of her cute little subordinate getting a girlfriend were rather low.

Eina decided to hide this information from Bell and seal it within her memory.

"…Lady Reveria. About the reason I came here today…"

"Oh yes, my apologies. Let's call her here."

A still-smiling Reveria reached into the bag she had brought back with her.

She pulled the bottle of Soma out of it.

"Um…Lady Reveria? Weren't you going to summon someone for me…?"

"It would be a waste to go looking for her. She has always been very elusive; I don't know how much time finding her would require. It would be more effective for her to come to us."

Before Eina could ask another question, Reveria removed the lid of the wine she'd purchased herself, though the fact that she'd put all of her purchases on *Loki Familia*'s tab seemed somehow more striking.

Soon, the surprisingly sweet smell of the wine filled the reception room.

"Wow…a frosty smell."

"I may be quite accustomed to it, but this smell still has that effect."

Eina enjoyed the aroma for a moment before realizing that Reveria was holding out a glass in front of her and took it out of reflex. Before she knew it, a high elf was pouring her a drink. Eina was on the verge of passing out from shame and embarrassment.

Feeling bad that Reveria had gone through the trouble, she cautiously raised the glass to her lips.

Oh my…!

Her eyes shot open the moment the glass touched her lips.

It was heavenly. Too heavenly.

It was so sweet that her tongue almost went numb. But somehow it had a smooth, almost melting texture.

Its sweet bouquet instantly filled her nose. The aftertaste was so invigorating that her very consciousness seemed to be tossed around inside her head until the very last drop. That feeling made its way into her body, right down to the tips of her toes.

*No wonder so many people like this wine…*In just one gulp, Eina learned firsthand where the wine's reputation came from.

"I know that smell…"

It was only a heartbeat after Eina put Soma to her lips.

Thump, thump, thump, thump. The sound of excited footsteps drew ever closer, as if being pulled in by the smell of the alcohol.

"Hey, you—is that Soma?!"

With that, the vermillion-haired goddess of this *Familia*, Loki, appeared from around the corner a second later.

"She has arrived."

"So that's what you meant by her coming here…"

"I knew it! I knew it! That's Soma, all right! Did ya get me a present, Reveria? You devoted child, you!"

Eina took a look at the glass in her hand, the source of the mellow smell around her. Next she looked at Loki, in awe of how well Reveria's plan to summon her had worked.

Even in the dimly lit reception room, Eina could clearly see Loki's vermillion hair and eyes.

"While it was I who purchased the wine, the idea was not mine."

"Well then, musta been Aiz! And here ya were actin' all sad since you came back from the Dungeon! It was ta keep this a surprise! Geee! Aizuuu, yer soo cute!"

"Not me."

Loki was ready to jump onto Aiz and give her a big hug, but an intimidating glare from the depressed girl stopped her in her tracks. Aiz's eyes were saying "Touch me and I'll slice you."

"Huh...?" Loki was confused as she took a few steps backward, sweating.

"A-Aizuu...Isn't that a little too prickly, even fer you? What ya think?"

"If you want my permission, use words I can understand. More importantly, the person who brought the wine is standing right there."

Ah, so that's how this is going to work.

Eina realized this was part of Reveria's plan as well.

The person who had information about the inner workings of *Soma Familia* was in fact the goddess of her own *Familia*, Loki. By appeasing her with a gift, Loki might be willing to answer a few questions.

Directly asking a god for their opinion made Eina rather uncomfortable, but she forced herself to relax.

"Huh? Who's this girl here?"

"This is our first meeting, Lady Loki. It is my pleasure to make your acquaintance. My name is Eina Tulle. I know that my being here is very unexpected..."

"No need ta be so formal. Yer makin' my neck itchy. Talk normal, got it?"

Loki waved off Eina's formality like it was too much trouble to bother with as she turned to face her. Loki stiffened when she noticed Eina's uniform and planted her gaze firmly on the half-elf.

Her thread of a right eye opened; a catlike smile popped up on her lips.

"What's this here, a Guild member payin' my *Familia* a house call?......Old man Uranus, claimin' neutrality and all that, yet havin' a dagger armed and ready. That how this is?"

"N-no, it's not! I...I..."

"This girl is my guest. I won't allow such slander."

"Ah, ehh. So yer Reveria's guest, my mistake, then. Sorry 'bout that, Einy. Beg yer pardon?"

"I-I'm fine. Please pay it no mind..."

Feeling Reveria's quiet gaze, Loki tried to pass the moment by shrugging and laughing it off.

She then plunked herself down on the sofa.

"That's enough with keepin' up appearances, let's get ta it. Ya brought me one of my all-time faves, which means ya wanna ask me somethin'. Am I right?"

"...Well then, I'll get right to the point. If you know any details about what goes on behind the scenes at *Soma Familia*, would you be willing to tell me?"

"Bringin' Soma fer that? Ha-ha. I see how it is."

Holding the bottle in one hand, Loki rudely grabbed a glass from the table and poured her own drink. One big gulp and a long, satisfied sigh later, Loki turned her reddening face in Eina's direction.

"It's not like I got a good connection with that idiot Soma. Don't know if I have the info ya want, Eina......But what the heck, I'll spill the beans on anythin' ya want. So, what'll it be?"

"...Do you know the reason behind the strange tendencies of the members of *Soma Familia*?"

"Hmm, right ta the good stuff, eh?...But how to explain it."

Loki swirled the wine around in her hand a few times, watching the waves wrap around the inside of the glass.

After a few moments, Loki downed the remainder of the wine in one loud swig.

"Got it! I'll tell ya a story 'bout me and Soma. Ah, just bein' clear, the wine Soma. Not that idiot god, just t'be clear."

"Ah, um, okay?"

"Well then…Ya know me, I love me some wine. Goin' ta different shops, tryin' and comparin' all brands every day. Gettin' drunk off my ass, pukin', passin' out…Livin' the dream in a loop until one day…I ran into this li'l beauty, Soma."

Reveria was staring at Loki with her eyes half closed, with no notion where the goddess was going with this. Loki, however, didn't care, and continued her story.

"One of those fated meetings, I guess you could call it? It was love at first taste! Some *Familia* made it, but I didn't care. Went 'round Orario, buyin' Soma left 'n' right…But while I was doin' that, I heard somethin' very interestin'."

"Something interesting…?"

"Can ya wrap yer head 'round this, Eina? This wine is defective, a failure."

Wha…Eina remembered Bell saying he heard that from Lilly.

Loki's smile grew deeper.

"Makes ya wonder, don't it? A failure that's this good? What about the successes, huh? I had ta know. Found my way to *Soma Familia*'s home base by myself."

Eina was shocked and Reveria looked down on Loki with disgust. While the two gods weren't exactly enemies, a god going directly into another's territory was almost an open invitation for an attack.

Even the gods had manners. While part of this was to protect personal information, there was no reason for a member of one *Familia* to go waltzing into another's home.

"Went up ta the porch, yellin' 'SOMA! Marry me! I'm beggin' ya!' But I was ignored, ta the point of gettin' lonely…I was gettin' ticked off, so I went inside without askin'."

Eina rubbed her fingers up and down her temple as though she had a bad headache.

However, *Soma Familia*'s lack of resistance to an intruder added to her curiosity about the members themselves.

"Place was totally silent. Not a single child anywhere. This is their home, y'know? Why'd everyone be out at the same time? I could tell somethin' wasn't right, and it gave me the chills…But I ignored it and perked up a bit. Went snoopin' 'round the whole place."

"……"

"I implore you, Loki. Do not reveal any more embarrassing information."

"Ge-hee-hee, you're no fun, Reveria. Anyway, couldn't find the real Soma anywhere. Finally got to the point o' gettin' fed up with it, turn ta go home…and there he was, that idiot himself."

Loki lowered her head as if remembering every detail of that meeting. Her smile vanished.

"I let out a big friendly 'Hey, there!' and that idiot responded with only 'Welcome.' Nothin' else. It was our first time meetin', y'know? Hardly ever looked at me, either, just stood there with a hoe in his hand. Was tendin' ta his garden. Only heard 'bout this later, but he grows all the ingredients fer his wine. Ah, nothin' too alarmin' goes in, though."

Loki continued to refill and drink the wine even while telling her story. Her bright pink cheeks were getting redder by the minute.

The tone of her voice went up.

"This Soma god…really pissed me off."

"Huh?"

"Tried talkin' 'bout everythin', but all he did was answer 'yeah' or 'hmm' and kept on hoein'…He was implyin' that his shit-filled fertilizer was above me."

Just talking about this memory made Loki's gaze grow more and more serious.

Eina was damp with sweat.

"That god was nothin' more than an indecisive, pitiful coward. But he acted like I was some dumb scarecrow and ignored me… Makin' me sick just thinkin' 'bout it!"

"……"

"On top o' that, Einy, on top o' that!"

"E-Einy…?"

"Overlookin' all of that, all of his rudeness and whatnot, I still asked ta taste the real 'Soma,' bein' real polite and everythin'! Even bowed ta him! Me! What ya think that idiot's answer was?"

Since Loki hadn't sensed any kind of hard feelings from Soma, she thought there was a chance she could try the good stuff—if not a full bottle, then at least a cup or two. However, Soma finally stopped working and turned to Loki for the first time and said:

"I refuse."

Apparently that was the first time he had shown any kind of emotion.

"Geeyahh! He's supposed ta be on my side, but that kinda tone pissed me off more than ever!"

"Loki, get a hold of yourself. Stop going off on tangents and get to the point."

"Hee-hee-hee." Loki took a few quick, deep breaths to calm down before her face relaxed. She sank back into the sofa.

"Sorry, sorry. Beat 'round the bush a bit, but I asked that idiot about his *Familia*. When I asked, what he said made me sick, that idiot. He's got absolutely no clue how to run a *Familia*, no sense at all. Like his heart wasn't in it from the start."

Eina's thin eyebrows flicked up.

His heart wasn't in it from the start…?

Well then, what was his goal? Eina had a new train of thought take off in her mind.

"Eina, don't be thinkin' too hard on it, y'know? The god known as Soma has only one thing in his skull: his hobby. Plenty o' those types, right? Their head's so far in the clouds, they can't see nothin' else. That idiot is case number one, the ultimate example. Not barbaric or evil, just purely livin' fer his craft. A god o' pure amusement. Guess you could say he's the wise ol' hermit of the gods—ha-ha!" joked Loki.

There were many strange and usual personalities among the gods, but Soma was weird even among them.

At least that was the impression Eina was picking up from Loki.

"Now, the problem is that wine, Soma. That idiot made his *Familia* for one reason only: his hobby. But they weren't bringin' in enough money. Not enough ta support his pastime, anyway—makin' wine's expensive, yeah? Couldn't keep it goin'. What little brain he had told him to give them a 'prize.' Somethin' really special—a trigger ta get them ta work harder."

"Don't tell me…"

"Yep, that Soma. The good stuff, yeah?"

A drop of wine from her last swig started to roll down Loki's lip. She licked it up a second later.

"Eina, ya drank the failure, so ya probably know, but the real stuff isn't playin' 'round. It *takes* ya. Not talkin' 'bout getting hammered outta yer mind, now. The deepest part of yer soul, the spirit, gets taken. Like it takes hold of the mind and body, like they're not yer own."

Whoosh. A sudden chill ran through Eina.

She thought back to the warm, elated feeling she got from drinking the failure before.

Her senses had been swept away by the wine, in a good way. Her spirits had been lifted.

Something even more euphoric than that?

Goose bumps quietly erupted on her skin beneath her suit.

Loki then said, "Maybe if I put it like this, you'll get it easier," as a way of leading into her next sentence.

"The children who follow him aren't there fer the idiot, but the Soma itself."

Members of that group weren't worshipping a god, but divine wine.

That meant that the reason *Soma Familia* had more members than the god Soma's reputation would allow was because their spirits were taken by the wine he gave them.

His followers had fallen in love with wine that could give them more happiness than anything else with as little as one sip.

"That idiot is a real monster. He's not gettin' help from members with Enigma, he's just growin' ingredients, mixin' 'em, and brewin' them himself. That idiot has driven his hobby ta utter perfection."

It suddenly came to Eina.

Part of the reason Loki referred to Soma as "that idiot" was out of fear and awe.

"He ain't usin' 'our' power, either. He's usin' the same abilities as his children, maybe even less, ta make somethin' like that. Can ya believe that? In other words, human hands can make the wine o' the gods. It's, like, what the hell'd he do up in Tenkai, right?"

"Hmm, I think I see the gist of your story. The god Soma uses his wine as bait to lure in members…"

"Yep, that's right. Once the members knew the flavor of Soma, they did anything they could ta get money. While I did call it a 'prize,' not everyone in the *Familia* gets an equal share. On top o' issuin' a quota, the idiot only gives the highest earners the good stuff. That *Familia* is at war with itself. Ah, yeah, those who fill the quota get a sip, most likely."

Loki racked her brain, trying to remember. However, Eina had a realization.

This was why the *Soma Familia* members she sometimes saw at the Guild were obsessed with money.

They were thirsty for Soma.

"The more I hear about this, the more it sounds like a dangerous drug. Is it acceptable to let this continue?"

"Might just be my bad choice of words. The spirit 'gets stolen,' but yer brain doesn't go up in smoke like that other stuff. Ya don't go mad, just feel *really* good. Makes yer whole body tremble. Makes ya want ta take another sip, no matter what. But, just like with normal alcohol, that feeling will go away."

Loki explained the difference between Soma and drugs like this:

There was no withdrawal with Soma. Its addictive qualities were not particularly strong.

Since Soma's followers' condition was only temporary, everyone would return to normal in time.

However, in the case of *Soma Familia*, members were given their next drink before the effects of the first dose had worn off. They were stuck in a hellish cycle.

"Can you explain what you meant by the addictive period being short?"

"Well then, there are loads o' children who have tasted Soma but got cut off and managed ta recover, right?"

To add to that, it appeared that even Soma drinkers became tolerant of it over time. The strongest members of *Soma Familia* were almost always at the top, and therefore received the wine all the time. However, somehow they could drink it without their spirits being stolen, and stay normal.

Come to think of it, thought Eina, *of all the members of* Soma Familia *who demand money at the Exchange, the ones who have reached Level Two are always much calmer and more collected.*

"To sum it all up fer ya, the leadership of a careless idiot obsessed with his hobby, the allure of Soma, and the members cravin' fer it all mix together ta make the craziness that infects *Soma Familia*."

Normally, if the god at the top of a *Familia* had real interest in it, things wouldn't turn out this way.

This was because if the one who empowered everyone raised their voice, the *Familia* would fall silent. If they didn't, they would be stripped of their Falna.

All this information seemed to indicate that, although he was not at fault for the current conditions, Soma himself was responsible for setting them in motion and not putting them to an end.

"That's all there is ta it, Eina. Anythin' else ya wanna ask?"

"No, that's all. Thank you very much for your time."

Eina understood what was happening at *Soma Familia*.

While their craving for that special wine was a bit scary on its own, this was a case of her being too focused on appearances.

Eina came to this conclusion because their yearning for alcohol and large amounts of money were not much different from other adventurers trying to strike it rich quick in the Dungeon. The only scary part of it was how they chose to reach their goal.

However, according to Loki's explanation, this was only a risk for part of the *Familia*, not every member. The supporter whom Bell had hired sounded as though she was perfectly normal, by the way he described her last time they talked.

A feeling of relief flowed through her as Eina deduced that it was highly unlikely that Bell would be thrust into a life-threatening scenario.

Loki watched her carefully and, upon seeing the look of relief on her face, opened her eyes a little wider.

"Eina."

"Yes?"

"Do ya know what happens ta donkeys that have a carrot hung in front of 'em but can never reach it?"

Eina was dazed by this sudden, strange question.

Loki stuck out all of the fingers on both hands one by one and continued without waiting for Eina's answer.

"The weaker ones get run over as the stronger ones go fer the others' carrots, kickin' and thrashin' their competition outta the way."

At first, Eina was confused. The answer dawned on her a moment later.

"That's what's happenin' at that *Familia*. All the idiot does is hang carrots. Nothin' can stop them now."

Then Loki folded all of her fingers together, expect for the pinkie on her right hand.

"There might be a donkey that doesn't care how many times it gets kicked down by its 'allies.' One who can't do nothin' alone…but in exchange skillfully spurs sympathy and pity from a different 'master.' A smart, uncompromisin' donkey."

The face reflected in Loki's vermillion eyes suddenly tensed. Eina's face.

"The new master might realize his carrots are gone, yeah?"

Loki sat up to peer into Eina's eyes, sliding all the way into the sofa.

Pouring what little was left of the wine into Eina's glass, Loki continued:

"Just thinkin'. If ya got a friend connected with one of 'em, ya might wanna let 'im know, just in case? Don't think it'll be serious, but there might be some problems. Gotta take care o' adventurers at the Guild, yeah?" said Loki, crossing her legs and grinning.

She had seen through Eina. Loki was truly worthy of the title of goddess.

Eina took a slow breath and nodded with a very concerned look on her face.

"Sayin' it outta kindness might not be my place, though."

"…No. I'm taking your advice to heart."

She was a good goddess.

Loki was much more compassionate than her reputation indicated. Either that or Eina was getting special treatment because of her relationship to Reveria.

Feeling Eina's gaze on her, Loki flashed another grin.

"All right, the wine's gone. Shall we go our separate ways?"

"I apologize for taking this much of your time."

"Don't worry 'bout it. Glad I got ta chat with the cute little beauty Eina."

"A-ha-ha-ha…"

Loki stood up from the sofa and stretched out as high as she could before going over to the one person who was silent this whole time: Aiz.

"Hey, Aiz. How long ya gonna beat yerself up?"

"……"

" 'Kay, then, how 'bout updatin' yer status? Haven't done it since ya been back, yeah?"

"…Okay."

"Fu-hee-hee, been a long time since I got my hands on Aiz's soft skin…!"

"Do anything else and I'll slice you."

"Huh?! Ya serious?"

Aiz's harsh tone made Loki crouch down slightly as the two of them left the reception room. Just before turning the corner, Loki looked back at the elves, winked, and gave a quick wave.

"She's…an interesting goddess."

"I am inclined to agree that she is interesting, but she's much more. We have a lot of faith in her."

"You too, Lady Reveria?"

"Yes, me included."

Eina giggled to herself, looking at Reveria's closed-eyed half smile. Eina picked up her glass from the table and drank what was left.

Tomorrow, I wonder if I'll have a chance to talk with Bell.

Loki's warning was still fresh in her mind. The Soma tasted a little bitter on Eina's tongue.

"AIZUU'S A LEVEL SIIIIIIIIIX!!" Loki suddenly yelled.

"PFFFTT—"

"…Eina."

"Aaaaaagh! I'm so sorry!"

Chapter 5 RESET

The sun set, the moon came out, and then the sky brightened as the sun rose once again, heralding a new day.

I'm usually still at home at this hour, but today I've come to Babel Tower.

While Lilly and I were in the Dungeon yesterday, I couldn't get the words of the man who'd tried to capture Lilly out of my head. I'd been on edge, and I could tell it was making Lilly uneasy.

I didn't want to worry her, so I didn't tell her the details, but I could still tell she was worried—she'd kept stealing glances at me with a nervous, desolate expression as I looked out for anything unusual.

"……"

I invited her out here so early to try and protect her from this mess. So here I am, just staring at the blue sky. I have nothing to do until Lilly arrives, so my mind wanders off into a conversation I had with the goddess last night.

Once I got home from the Dungeon, I told her everything I knew about Lilly and her situation.

My plan was to have her live with us under the church until I was sure the danger had passed—once I had explained everything to the goddess, anyway.

"Bell, is this supporter worthy of your trust?"

"Huh?"

She listened quietly to every word, and then she slowly asked that question.

At first, I didn't realize what she was saying. Then it hit me and I stood up, leaning over the table to say something in Lilly's defense. But when I opened my mouth to speak, the tranquil look in the goddess's eyes sent me for a loop and I fell silent.

"Just from what you have told me, something about this girl smells fishy. Like the day you lost my knife...Oh, I'm not accusing her of anything, so don't give me that look...I just can't help but think she was somehow involved because the two of you worked together that day."

A very sudden meeting, separated from her own *Familia* for mysterious reasons, targeted by adventurers...The goddess repeated my main points back to me, cutting out all the unnecessary filler.

There was nothing I could say in response. I pitifully sank my shoulders.

"Sorry to put it all like that. But I've never met this girl, so I only have what you tell me to go on. You have interacted with her, so your decision might be the best. I won't be very pleased with it, though."

She continued by saying she was more worried about me. Then her aura changed, and she acted rather high and mighty as she quietly asked more questions about Lilly.

"Do you think this girl is hiding something from you? Something that adventurer suspects—no, *knows* she's guilty of?"

She said that I should know this, too. Her words shot through my heart like arrows.

I might have been trying to avoid thinking about that possibility.

Lilly had done many things for me as a supporter, including saving my life from a monster. Was that making me turn a blind eye?

I just kind of sat there for a while, looking at the goddess as I went through my memories of Lilly. Everything. I was trying to find the moments when Lilly had shown me a piece of her true feelings.

"Goddess, I..."

"Mr. Bell?"

"!"

My thoughts cut off.

The voice calling my name makes me focus and return to the present.

"Ah!...L-Lilly, morning."

My response is a little slow, and I lightly shake my head to get the final remnants of last night out of my mind.

Seeing that, Lilly's face shifts to a smile, her eyes hidden behind her bangs as usual.

"Good morning, Mr. Bell. Lilly didn't think that you would arrive so soon—Lilly couldn't believe her eyes."

"Ah-ha-ha, you're right. You're always here before me no matter the time, Lilly."

At least it looks like nothing has happened to her. That's a relief.

Just as I thought, that adventurer wouldn't dare put a finger on Lilly aboveground.

Adventurers who cause problems get put on the Guild's blacklist. Life in Orario is extremely difficult for them. For starters, if they have their registration revoked, the Exchange will no longer pay them for magic stones and drop items, instead unceremoniously taking them away. Not long after that, they'd be kicked out of their *Familia*—which was tantamount to being abandoned by their god.

They could even be punished and put in jail if their violation was severe enough.

These laws would make the blacklisted adventurers a kind of outlaw, but the Guild has no choice but to take a firm stance against them. You could say that they are keeping criminal activities under control.

So, that's why if anyone is going to cause a problem, they'll do it in the Dungeon. With no witnesses, the attacker could say that they were defending themselves or they thought the victim was a monster and attacked by accident. Their escape routes are limitless.

"Mr. Bell."

"Ah, sorry. What is it?"

"Shall we go to the tenth level today?"

"Um…"

I look down at Lilly, her smiling face hidden under hair and hood, almost in shock.

"It's very sudden, don't you think…?"

"Mr. Bell, did you really think that Lilly wouldn't notice? Mr. Bell has more than enough power to do well on the tenth level, right?"

"……"

The "power" she is talking about must be my status.

It's true that many of my basic stats, especially my Agility, were already in the *A* and *B* ranges. The Guild has declared that the lowest level that Level One adventurers are allowed to enter is the twelfth level.

The reason that I don't go down there now is the fact that I'm solo. Plus, the layout and difficulty of the Dungeon get especially hostile below level ten.

You could say the Dungeon starts baring its fangs. In any case, having an average status grade of *G* on the seventh level and an average grade of *A* on the twelfth couldn't be more different.

Actually, I've already entered and returned safely from the ninth-level floor. At this rate, I should be able to go into the eleventh level, even solo. Lilly must have decided it was a good time for me to try the tenth.

Honestly, I feel like I can do it. I might be a little overconfident in my abilities, but I can see myself thriving there.

Even still, there is another more depressing reason that I don't want to set foot on that floor.

They come out on the tenth level.

Large-category monsters. There are none of them down to level nine.

……Just like that Minotaur.

"…But I almost died on the seventh level the other day. Are you sure someone like that is ready for the tenth level…?"

"That's true, but because Mr. Bell has that experience of failure due to overconfidence, the Mr. Bell of today won't have that problem, right? Lilly believes Mr. Bell has more credentials of being an adventurer now because of it."

"……"

"Don't forget that Mr. Bell now has magic. That magic is strong. The new Mr. Bell has no weaknesses."

I showed her the Firebolt magic yesterday.

It wasn't much of a presentation— I wanted to see how much my Magic had improved from getting my status updated the night before. That, and I wanted to get used to using the magic, so it was good timing. Lilly had been very impressed.

Since I'm solo, being able to use Swift-Strike Magic is very valuable to me.

"Lilly has been as far down as the eleventh level with other adventurers, so you can take Lilly's word. Mr. Bell will have an easy time on level ten. Lilly's guarantee."

Even before I had magic, Eina gave me permission to enter the lower tenth (as well as a stern warning). So when I think about it like that, just as Lilly said, now that I have magic, the tenth level shouldn't be a problem.

To advance or to stay put.

"...The truth is, Lilly has to gather a large amount of money in the next few days."

"Wait a minute, is that...!"

"Lilly can't say the details, but it involves Lilly's *Familia*..."

As if she were guiding my thoughts, she hits me with her real motivation.

I can't help but remember her being surrounded by those three adventurers.

My mind goes off on its own, and my neck starts to twitch.

"Can you blame Lilly for being selfish, Mr. Bell?"

Lilly bows down in front of me, looking up at my face.

If this is really about her contract with her *Familia*, then my interference—basically shouldering the load to help her gather the "large amount of money"—would work against her. It would depend on who was there at the time, but if it were discovered that someone from another *Familia* helped her gather the money, they would have some hard feelings toward said *Familia*. It might be humiliating.

I don't have any way of knowing if Lilly's claims are true. I doubt she'd tell me honestly if I asked her.

I know I wouldn't if I were in her position.

I make up my mind and clench my right fist.

"All right. Let's go to the tenth level."

A large smile blooms on Lilly face when I say that. She bows over and over again, saying, "Thank you, thank you, thank you!!" I scrunch my eyebrows down and force a smile.

"Should we leave right away? Or should we buy some more items inside Babel, just in case?"

"Lilly bought extra items yesterday. Lilly has a suggestion, though: why don't you try this?"

"This is…"

Lilly set her backpack down on the pavement as she spoke. She pulls out the ink-black sheath of a short sword.

The Divine Knife is about twenty celch long, so I would guess this weapon is about fifty, just by looking at it.

A shortsword—no, a baselard?

The simple round sheath is flush against the blade's hilt, perfectly hiding the blade within. It's a very simple design for a sword.

"So, why?"

"Don't feel bad, Mr. Bell, but this was part of the preparation. Mr. Bell's current weapons don't have enough reach to fight against larger monsters. Also, Lilly has been thinking for a while that Mr. Bell needs more range."

"So you're…giving it to me? I don't feel right, not paying you for it…"

"Mr. Bell has accepted Lilly's selfishness; this is a thank-you gift. Please accept it."

"…Well, if you're going to put it like that…"

I draw the blade of the baselard she's given me.

The silver blade is thin on both sides. It's very light, and not that much bigger than my dagger, so for someone like me who has never used a sword, it might be pretty useful…

"I wonder if it suits me. I've never used something like this before…"

"How about testing it on the way to the tenth level? The monsters down to the seventh level would be perfect for practice. If Lilly's eyes aren't playing tricks on her, Mr. Bell would do very well using a shortsword."

Lilly's been with many parties and seen many fighting styles; I can trust her on this. She's been with me a while now; she knows what she's talking about.

There is no reason to doubt her; I'll take her word for it.

"Ah…I don't have a belt for a sword…"

All I can do is hang it from my waist. I was a little slow to realize that the sheath would get in my way.

"Mr. Bell, Mr. Bell."

"?"

"If Lilly remembers correctly, Mr. Bell's protector can hold weapons about that size, right?"

Ah, forgot about that. I even told her that myself.

I take the Divine Knife out of the protector for a moment to see if the baselard will fit inside. Yep, no problem.

"You have an amazing memory, Lilly. I completely forgot."

"Hee-hee, Lilly only just remembered now, too."

Lilly puts her hands behind her head and shyly turns away for a moment.

I can't help but laugh as I watch her, but soon I realize I have another problem: Where do I put the Divine Knife?

"......"

Suddenly, I hear the goddess's words from last night in my head:

—*Is this supporter worthy of your trust?*

It's almost like the Divine Knife in my hand speaks to me, as the goddess's voice asks me the same question for a third time.

"..."

I quietly close my eyes, asking for forgiveness.

When I open them up again, I slip the knife into my leg holster.

It has slots big enough for potion tubes; the knife and its sheath fit securely.

"..."

Lilly watches me silently, giving a light nod.

"Well then, shall we go?"

Lilly raises her head at my invitation. Bobbing her head slightly, she smiles and says, "Yes."

"I'm counting on you, Tulle. It may be an inspection, but don't go overboard."

"Yes, sir."

Eina's supervisor at the Guild saw her out the door as she stepped onto West Main.

She was assigned to go to Babel to inspect the shops renting space from the Guild. This was just a routine job—entering the shops themselves and making sure that none of the *Familias* were doing anything shady.

Slipping an official armband up her sleeve and wrapping a scarf around her neck, she set off into the early morning streets of Orario. This set identified her as an inspector from the Guild. There were other Guild employees assigned to Babel Tower, but Eina was a few minutes behind them.

I didn't get a chance to talk with Bell after all...

The information she collected at *Loki Familia* yesterday had been churning in her head all night.

Loki's warning was still fresh in her mind, and she was itching to tell Bell just how much danger he was in right now.

She regretted not trying to do more yesterday evening to see him; she should have stopped at nothing to tell him.

I'm overstepping my bounds...But since I'll be there anyway, I should inform Goddess Hestia.

Eina was going to inspect *Hephaistos Familia* today. The face of the goddess who recently started working there in her mind, she decided talking to her was the best course of action. The serious, law-abiding Eina realized that doing this would be an abuse of power as well as mix her personal and professional lives. However, she kicked those thoughts out of her head with a "Think I don't know that?!" and continued on her way.

"Ah."

".......?"

It was when Eina had just entered Central Park from West Main that Aiz Wallenstein came into Central Park from North Main and walked toward her.

"...G-good morning, Miss Wallenstein."

".......Good morning."

Aiz gave a small head nod, greeting the stuttering Eina. Her long blond hair, sparkling as if it were filled with golden dust, shook lightly as her head dipped.

While Eina didn't know how to proceed, she would feel guilty not saying more than "good morning" to someone she had formally met yesterday. So she said the first thing that came to mind:

"Miss Wallenstein, what are you doing today?"

"I was thinking about buying some items."

"Umm…at Babel?"

Aiz nodded again as their conversation continued. It sounded as though she was planning to go into the Dungeon today as well.

Eina thought it was a little strange that Reveria used a different item shop, but looking at the fully equipped and battle-ready Aiz, she nodded to herself.

While it might be difficult to imagine just by looking at her, this beautiful girl was known by two other names. Her first nickname was "kenki": sword princess, or lady of the sword. However, she wanted to be known as "senki"—lady of combat, or lady of the battlefield—by other adventurers.

…*She still looks depressed.*

Eina had seen Aiz's condition the previous night at *Loki Familia*. She did her best to engage Aiz in conversation, despite the blond girl's spiritless voice and constant downtrodden eyes.

It must have really been a shock to her, having a boy she liked run away.

Even as she wanted to see the guy who would run away from a girl as breathtaking as Aiz, Eina decided to do some meddling on the behalf of her favorite younger-brother figure.

"Miss Wallenstein, please allow me to express my gratitude for saving one of my adventurers."

"……?"

"Don't tell me you have forgotten? A short time ago, you slew a rampaging minotaur on the fifth level just in time to save him."

"………A minotaur."

"Yes. The adventurer's name is Bell Cranell. He's extremely grateful to you…"

The instant Aiz heard Bell's name, her neck twisted to an almost shocking degree. Eina was trying to let her know how Bell felt about her, but took a step back in stunned silence.

They stood there quietly beneath Babel Tower for a few moments. Aiz then looked at Eina with a hint of sadness in her eyes and nervously opened her mouth to speak.

"…He's not afraid of me?"

"Wha…Huh?"

Eina was so confused, only a few sounds escaped her mouth in response.

"—?"

Just then, Eina happened to catch a glimpse of something.

Four adventurers had gathered under a tree with wide leaves just inside her line of sight.

Three of them had an emblem with a crescent moon over a glass of wine on their armor…*Soma Familia*'s symbol.

Almost out of reflex, Eina did what she could to lip-read their conversation from afar.

"—just as planned—make a mistake—"

"—know that—Erde needs to—"

There was quite a distance between them, but Eina's emerald eyes were able to pick up those words from their conversation.

While they didn't mention Bell's name directly, they said the name of his supporter.

The group then broke up, but all of them made their way toward Babel. Eina was almost certain they were heading for the Dungeon.

"…Is something wrong?"

Aiz must have sensed something wrong with Eina. She raised her head as she spoke.

Eina's expression was much more intense than usual, her eyes shaking. Eina stood silently for a few heartbeats before lowering her head in a crisp bow and releasing all of her anxiety at once.

"I know this is incredibly rude of me, but I have to ask. Please, help my subordinate. Save Bell Cranell."

"……"

"I might just be overthinking it, but I have reason to believe he is in a very dangerous situation. I realize I'm asking a lot from you, but I beg you, come to his aid."

"Is that yesterday's...?"

Aiz had heard the conversation in *Loki Familia*'s reception room the night before and instantly connected the dots. The still-bowing Eina nodded and proceeded to tell Aiz everything in detail, from the beginning up to the party of *Soma Familia* adventurers that was now headed for the Dungeon.

Aiz listened quietly to every word. She nodded back and, when Eina finished, said, "I understand."

"Are you sure this is okay?"

"Yes...I haven't gotten a chance to apologize to him properly yet."

While Eina was a little confused about the meaning of Aiz's words, she stepped aside to let the girl pass.

Eina was just going to see her off, but watching her golden blond hair go into the distance, she had an urge to yell out one more thing.

"Um, Miss Wallenstein!"

"......?"

"Bell is...Bell Cranell really is extremely grateful to you for saving his life!"

Eina's words brought a new level of focus and clarity to Aiz's face—as well as a bit of softness around her eyes and the very slightest of smiles to her lips.

The layout and interior of the Dungeon change dramatically on levels eight and nine.

First of all, the number of rooms increases and they become much wider. The corridors connecting the rooms are all very short. Next, the ceiling that had been three or four meters above my head before is now about ten meters high.

The walls in these levels are yellow and covered in moss. Since the floor is covered with short grass, these levels look like a vast prairie. The light above is concentrated into one spot, like the sun over a massive plain. It feels like I've stepped into the countryside.

The monsters that show up here are like a review of previous floors—rather than new ones roaming the floors, stronger versions of goblins and kobolds show up. As long as adventurers don't underestimate their strength, all of the techniques they've learned fighting these monsters on the upper levels will work here, too. Conquering levels eight and nine should be relatively easy.

As proof of that, Lilly and I have come down here many times in the past few days.

Now, our main destination: the tenth level.

This floor is…

"Fog…"

It's not that bad, but there's a cloud of mist hovering in this floor that's thick enough to make it hard to see the other end of the room.

The look and pattern of the tenth level is more or less the same as eight and nine. However, the bright "sun" shining down from above is gone. Instead, it looks like a morning fog just before sunrise in here.

This is the first time that visibility has been an issue in the Dungeon.

"Lilly, stick close to me."

"…Yes."

I don't know how many times I've said that to her, but I say it one more.

Of course I'm worried about getting separated and losing her in the mist, but I'm also keeping a sharp eye out for that male adventurer. Who knows when he'll strike. I've been on the verge of pestering Lilly to stay by my side long before we got down to the tenth level, so it wouldn't surprise me if she's sick of it by now.

In any case…this thing isn't half bad.

Keeping Lilly in my line of sight, I take a look at the baselard in my right hand.

It's been very useful. I've never used a blade longer than my dagger, so it felt a bit awkward in my hand at first. But I think I'll be giving it my seal of approval. It turns killer ants into mincemeat.

The baselard's longer reach is like a breath of fresh air. I never knew how it felt to launch strike after strike from a safe distance.

It doesn't have the cutting power that the Divine Knife has, but I can't complain.

"......!"

A room opens up in front of us as we exit the corridor.

It's another room of open savanna. The fog is still hanging in the air, but I can make out the dimensions of the room.

There are leafless, limbless dead trees scattered all around.

"......"

They stand eerily still within the haze. I frown as we set foot inside. For now, the best plan is to get away from the wall before a monster is born.

We approach a small group of the dead trees. Each stands somewhere between one and two meters tall. Abnormally thick bark covers a wide base, but the trunk becomes thinner and thinner the taller the tree grows. Very strange indeed...

—Ah, this must be them.

After giving the dead trees a once-over, I turn to talk to Lilly.

"What do you think? Should we cut these down?"

"No, we don't have time for that."

Lilly's voice jumps in surprise as she stares past me.

I feel a wave of dread run down my back as I turn around to see what startled her.

A large silhouette is moving through the fog. Not only can I hear its gigantic feet hit the floor as it walks, I feel the vibrations of the impacts through my boots. My whole body is shaking.

I put up my arms defensively, with my face cramping up as I clench my jaw, hard.

"Ughaaaaaaa......"

The orc—a monster solidly in the Large category—appears through the fog with a low growl.

It has brown skin and a boar's head. With old hide wrapped around its waist, it looks like it's wearing some kind of beat-up old skirt. I think it's about three meters tall—just a bit taller than the Minotaur.

However, compared to the thickly muscled Minotaur, the orc is round—squat and hugely fat.

"Well, they really are large..."

"You mustn't run away, Mr. Bell!"

Lilly always says that escape never leads to the way forward. I swallow and nod.

She's right. If I can't slay this orc, then I'll never be able to take down other large-category monsters later on…like the Minotaur.

I can't let it scare me just because it towers over me.

I take a deep breath and make up my mind.

"Gahhh, ungahhh…!!"

The orc catches Lilly and me in its beady yellow eyes.

Locking onto its prey, the orc quickens its pace and the floor shakes even more. It makes its way through the group of dead trees, holding out its arm.

Grabbing onto one of the trees with its meaty hand, the orc pulls it out of the floor.

What was once just natural scenery inside the Dungeon has become a crude club in the monster's hands.

A landform—the Dungeon's own armory.

Yet another one of the Dungeon's troublesome characteristics.

The living Dungeon itself provides natural weapons to the monsters that roam around inside it.

Landforms first appear on level ten and give the monsters here that much more power.

The Dungeon's support has given one or two extra stones to monsters that could be taken down if unarmed.

"Lousy timing…"

Landforms can be destroyed, but since they are part of the living Dungeon, they grow back after a certain amount of time. It's the same as the monsters themselves. However, I've heard that these dead trees grow back almost instantly.

Normally, adventurers would cut down the landforms before monsters arrived to prevent them from being used as weapons. The timing here couldn't have been worse.

Now I have to confront a fully armed orc with almost no room to spare.

"……"

The orc's heavy breathing is getting closer.

Its eyes are sparkling, like it could jump at me any second.

This will be my first battle with a large-category monster. I couldn't be tenser.

My chest feels like it's going to explode. Trying to get a handle on my beating heart, I take a deep breath and relax my shoulders.

That's when the orc roars with all its might.

"GUOOOUUUHHHHHHHHHHH!!"

The starting bell. It's time for battle.

Hearing the signal, I charge.

I can't take a hit!

The difference in size is just too great. There's no way I can block an attack.

If I'm hit, I'll go flying. The protector on my arm isn't going to stop anything.

On the other hand, if I'm on the attack…

First target: the lower body. Especially the feet planted firmly on the ground.

Just because it's big doesn't mean it's invincible. Sure, I've been scared of its size from the start, but just like all big monsters, it has weaknesses.

When the enemy is big, it can't hit a smaller, nimble target very well.

This is particularly true for the slow and sluggish orc. Its body is so heavy that it loses its balance very easily.

One hit.

Just one hit.

If I can avoid the first hit, it'll be wide open to a counterattack.

The orc is getting closer, charging right for me!

"UGHOOOOOOOOOOO!"

The orc builds up a head of steam, raising its club as it comes barreling forward.

The dead tree's roots are round, making it look like a big hammer or club. The orc swings it around over its head, lining me up for its first strike.

Over its head…That means—!

"!"

I shoot forward with no hesitation.

It's much easier to dodge an overhead arcing strike than a sideways sweep. If I can just figure out where the weapon will land, I can get out of the way. Once the club hits the ground, I don't have to worry about a follow-up attack.

And the orc can't defend itself until it raises the club again, so that's my chance.

I'll hit with everything I've got!

"GHOUUUU!"

"Gotcha!"

"—Gwouhhh?"

I handily dodge the falling club.

I use that momentum to get close to the orc's right side and thrust the baselard into the beast just below its ribs.

The orc lets out a piercing scream as greenish liquid squirts out of its wound.

The grass below is stained a slightly thicker green.

"Ha!"

I quickly decide to follow up my stab attack with the original plan, and attack the legs.

I spin around, getting the blade as low as possible before bringing it up and into the monster's thick right leg.

I grasp the shortsword in both hands as it skims the top of the grass before the blade makes contact just below the orc's knee.

"—??!!"

A deafening roar hits my ears like a wall.

The baselard hits bone and comes to a stop. I can feel both the bone itself and the monster's weight bearing down on it; the blade won't go any farther.

But I grit my teeth.

I use all of my strength to lift the orc up, forcing the baselard's cutting edge forward.

"TAKE THIS!!"

Its leg comes clean off.

The baselard shoots out of the back of the monster's shin. Its lower leg no longer attached, the orc falls to the ground.

The room shakes with the beast's scream of pain. The orc is in serious agony, but I can't stop now.

Thok, thok. I dash up onto the orc's back and run to the back of its head. Holding my shortsword upside down, I take aim and thrust the baselard into its skull.

"GIH, GOUghhh…"

"Mr. Bell!! Another one!"

"!"

The orc beneath me violently shakes before expiring. I look up from its corpse to see, just as Lilly said, one more orc charging at us from the way we came in. It must have heard the sounds of battle and become enraged because even as it plows through the fog, it's ignoring the landforms entirely.

I jump down from the lifeless orc and stick my right arm out, straight forward.

I won't miss.

I lock my eyes onto its massive frame and pull the magic trigger all at once.

"FIREBOLT!!"

"BAGOUUGHHHH?!"

A bolt of flame sears the air as it hits the newcomer square in the chest.

It lets out a scream and loses a step, but that's all.

The orc's ragged chest is burned to a crisp, but it's not about to fall, either.

It looks like my magic isn't strong enough to slay an orc in one blow right now. Not surprising—I just learned it the other day. Fire-bolt's power is still low.

However…

"—FIREBOLT!!!"

Round 2.

Another Swift-Strike spell hits the orc in quick succession.

I wasn't really aiming for it, but the magic hits the orc in almost the same spot, and the explosion knocks it back. The blast catches its chin, and the orc looks up at the ceiling as it wavers on its feet, stumbling away from me…and stops.

"......"

The orc silently turns to ash.

The two direct blasts of Firebolt opened a hole in the orc's chest. The magic stone inside must have gone up in flames and disappeared.

I watch the monster dissolve from between the fingers of my outstretched hand. Only when the last of it disappears do I slow my breathing and lower my arm.

I won...

It worked.

The sword, my fighting style, my magic—everything worked.

They worked on a monster much larger than me, on a large monster not unlike the Minotaur.

As my heart finally slows down, a new flame swells within me.

It's the feeling of accomplishment. Maybe the feeling of progress.

I'm enjoying every second of the feeling of triumph that's bubbling up inside me, making my lips quiver in joy.

"Lilly! I did...it..."

I turn around to find her, a look of pure happiness on my face. But all that's there to greet me is white fog.

The partner who's traveled with me up until today has disappeared.

My euphoria is gone.

"Lilly?!"

My voice is just a pitch shy of a scream as it leaves my throat.

My head spins as if I had been slapped in the face. But no matter what direction I look, I can't see hide nor hair of Lilly, just the fog.

I fear the worst at first, but I take a deep breath to calm down, then take off running.

If that male adventurer is responsible for Lilly's disappearance, she would have fought back somehow, yelled out at least. A monster seems a lot more likely.

I make for the corner of the room where the fog is thickest.

"...?"

Weaving my way through the dead trees, a horrible smell hits my nose like a ton of bricks.

I bury my nose in my sleeve and look around for the source. It doesn't take long.

There is a hunk of bloody, raw meat at the base of one of the trees.

"Isn't that…a monster lure…?"

I kneel down next to the oily mass of processed flesh to get a closer look.

No doubt about it. These things are sold in item shops. Adventurers like me can use these trap items to draw monsters to them and increase their haul of magic stones and dropped items without leaving their usual route in the Dungeon…

But why is there one here…?

"—"

The sound of heavy footsteps reaches my ears. Orcs.

As in not a lone orc. The impacts of many sets of feet are coming all at once; it sounds like the world's worst drum line.

And then I notice something else. There are masses of glistening, slimy meat scattered all over the place.

I stand there, stunned. The footsteps are close enough that I can get some idea how many orcs there are. Air leaves my lungs.

…*Oh shit*…

—Four.

I curse to myself in a numb silence as their shadows appear in the fog, all walking in a line, side by side.

Taking down even one of these took everything I had. Four at once is impossible. I don't stand a chance. I'd be surrounded and sent into the afterlife in seconds. And then there's their size. If they used any of the natural weapons around here, there'd be no escaping their wide range.

I have to get out of here, now.

There's no way I can get out of this alive.

But what about Lilly?

What if she's lying injured in this room or can't escape for some reason?

Do I leave her behind? Do I leave Lilly to die?

The orcs lured here by the smell of the bloody meat notice me, and they're less than pleased. The dark green veins in their thick, muscular arms slowly pulse as they glare at me.

It's to the point now that I won't be able to get away without drawing my sword, but I still can't move an inch.

Suddenly, something flies at me from out of sight, whistling as it cuts through the air.

"Huh?!"

Clang! The thing strikes my left leg holster, sending a piece of it flying. The piece containing the Divine Knife. *That* piece.

I see a small golden arrow sticking out of the holster as it flew up and away.

The orcs see my wide eyes following the holster, figure that's their chance, and all come at me at once.

"OOUUUUUGGGGHHHHHH!!"

"!?!!"

Two of the orcs grab landform weapons and take a big swing in my direction.

I make one of the most ungraceful dives ever but manage to get out of the way.

I don't have time to catch my breath. As big and clumsy as they are, the remaining two orcs cover the distance between us in no time flat.

"E-gaaa!!!"

I scream out as massive arms come at my head from all directions.

This is serious! What the hell am I gonna do now?!

I've never felt this vulnerable as a solo adventurer before. I don't even have time to breathe as I dodge the storm of fists and strikes raining down from the orcs around me.

When I dodge an overhead strike and happen to glance past the monsters, that's when I see her.

She's a safe distance away from the orcs, walking as if she were in Central Park.

"Lilly?! Eh-dahhh!!!"

The next attack comes down the moment I yell for her. I can't lose my focus, even for a moment.

While I'm dodging for my life, Lilly picks up the piece of my leg holster and takes out the Divine Knife.

She then looks it over carefully before tucking it into her shirt and looking in my direction with her usual smile.

"Sorry, Mr. Bell. This is where it ends."

"Lilly, what the hell are you saying?!"

"Lilly thinks that Mr. Bell shouldn't be so trusting of others."

I catch another glimpse of her between orc limbs: she's tilting her head to the side like a cute little girl, even though I'm screaming at her.

Her eyes aren't covered by her hood or her bangs, and as always, her cute little smile.

But she looks somehow…lonely.

"I hope you find an opening and escape."

Lilly speaks from the other side of the orcs, like she's leaving her last bit of advice.

Then she adjusts her bulging backpack before turning her back to me.

"Good-bye, Mr. Bell. We won't be seeing each other again."

She takes one last look over her shoulder before running off into the fog.

"Lilly! *Lilly!*—Dahhh! Enough already!"

"BUGOuuhhh?!"

"You're too nice, Mr. Bell."

Lilly ran through the halls of the Dungeon, carrying bags that no normal person could hope to lift.

Grasping the straps of her backpack, she kept on going forward with no hesitation in her steps.

Lilly had told Bell a total of two lies.

The first was that she was a dirt-poor supporter.

Lilly was a thief. Or "con artist" might be a better way to put it.

She targeted adventurers with high income and class, especially ones who had valuable weapons and armor.

For example, she'd worked with Bell up until this point because he'd been her target. Or rather, to be more precise, the *Hephaistos Familia* knife he carried had been her target.

The story about being poor was nothing more than a way to approach him.

And the second lie…

"Hmm."

A breeze blowing against her as she ran pushed her hood down. Her fluffy, furlike hair and dog ears were exposed.

Lilly reached up to lightly pet her ears as her lips recited an incantation:

"*Stroke of midnight's bell.*"

As if she had been dosed in ash, a gray dust covered her head.

A light flashed without sound, and the ears on her head were gone when it cleared.

That wasn't all. The bangs that covered her eyes and the furry tail behind her had disappeared as well.

"Looks like a full transformation isn't necessary. Changing out a few parts is just as effective."

If Bell had been here to see this, he would surely have been shocked.

Her big chestnut eyes looked cheerful, her face that of a cute girl. The dog-girl child was gone.

There was no doubt now—Lilly was the prum girl who had run into Bell that day in the back alley.

Lilly's second lie: Who she really was.

She had been running away from that male adventurer and used her "Cinder Ella" magic to change her appearance from a very suspicious prum girl to someone else entirely.

Lilly had used this special magic to fool many, many adventurers.

Her victims would charge after her in a rage, but she would change her appearance and make them think she was someone else. They had made a mistake; they couldn't do anything to her. The rumors going around among adventurers about a "group of thieving prums" was a testament to the power of her magic.

Sometimes she became a supporter. Other times she was an innocent civilian.

Lilly had used this magic not only to change her appearance but also to change her race, and she had committed hundreds of crimes up to this point.

Looks like being careless enough to let that adventurer see me transform was a big mistake...

The man who had pursued her the other day was a victim of one of Lilly's schemes, and he happened to see her reverse the effects of Cinder Ella. He saw her true face. That was the full story behind the incident in the alleyway.

She'd made a clean getaway, but now it seemed like that adventurer had told Bell some things he didn't need to know.

Ever since she'd spotted them having a secret meeting that day in Central Park, the boy started acting much different toward her. He was always looking at her, and he hid information from her anytime she tried to ask why. It was almost as though he was suspicious of her, or he knew that she could change her appearance and was on the lookout for it.

It looked as though deciding that this was her last chance and making her move was correct...

...This really is it...

What a waste, she thought to herself as she remembered all the money she made while working with Bell.

It was over—the good mood and security he'd provided were gone. A part of her felt the loss.

This was a strange feeling for a thief such as herself. She didn't understand.

But there was something that she did understand: No matter how much she thought about this odd feeling, it was nothing more than a useless emotion.

There was no way to continue any connection with the boy.

She couldn't ignore the risks of continuing the contract after what that man had told him.

Now that Bell knew everything, there was no way he would forgive her.

"......"

Lilly's face became downtrodden. But she took a deep breath and shook her head from side to side.

Who cares? she thought to herself as she dismissed any feelings of guilt. For someone like her to be moved by the kindness of an adventurer—what a joke.

Because all adventurers were the same.

Adventurers...adventurers...!!!   •

Lilly had been born into *Soma Familia*. Her parents were members, which meant that from birth, Lilly had no choice but to join *Soma Familia* herself.

Just by being who she was, the gears of fate might well have been snarled from the beginning.

The world had not been kind to Lilly.

Both of her prum parents said over and over how they wanted to save money to support Lilly when she was just an infant. However, they never did anything that could be considered parental, and before she knew it they were dead. Their desire for money—for Soma—drove them to prowl dungeon levels that were way out of their league. Apparently they were killed by a monster before they even realized what had hit them.

This left Lilly on her own in *Soma Familia* to fend for herself, in a group that was always stealing Soma from one another. She was alone. No one in the *Familia* looked after her. Those were very painful days.

Since the moment she drank Soma when being officially inducted into the *Familia*, she too had fallen under its spell.

There was no one she could depend on. So she decided to go it alone and make money by herself. But it was futile. She didn't have what it took to become an adventurer and was forced to work as a supporter.

Then she was exploited.

Whenever she worked with a party, they would always say: "You stole some magic stones for yourself, didn't you?" "You swiped some cash, didn't you?" "You should be punished." "You're not getting any of our shares."

She frantically tried to tell them there was a mistake, that she was innocent. But all they did was turn their backs on her, smirking.

When she was in the clutches of a monster, inches from death, they didn't help her. They even refused to heal her afterward. She was kicked around all the time. They threatened to do all sorts of things to her if she lost the bags.

She'd never fit in with *Soma Familia*. After returning from the Dungeon, a fierce argument and fight over the money earned were always waiting for her.

Lilly hates adventurers...Lilly loathes them...!

After the effects of Soma wore off, she ran away from the *Familia*, a waterfall of tears in her wake.

She threw away the title of being a member of *Soma Familia* and tried to live a normal life in the city. Once she had acquired a sense of stability and happiness, it was taken from her. Members of *Soma Familia* destroyed her new life.

How they found her, she didn't know. But they came, their eyes driven mad with greed, and stole everything from her. Not only that, they ransacked where she was living.

The nice elderly couple who had let her stay at their flower shop kicked her out after that. Lilly could still remember how they looked at her, like a soiled, rotten piece of garbage.

Even here, *Soma Familia* tormented her.

Lilly held a grudge against the god at the top, Soma. She wondered why he had created such a *Familia*.

She bore no ill will or malice toward him. Soma wasn't interested in them, anyway. There was no connection of any kind.

Soma never did anything for them. He wouldn't. She didn't even think he knew what was going on in his own *Familia*.

Perhaps, from his point of view, it was pointless to take pity on any of his "children" despite being their "father," their god. But Lilly's grudge against him never went away.

In the end, Lilly's only option was to return to *Soma Familia* and work as a supporter to survive. If she made a bad choice—if she failed to play her part as the faithful little supporter—all it did was invite more hurt. Even if she was on good terms with a few members of the *Familia*. Even if she worked for free.

Yes, all adventurers were exactly the same.

All of them did horrible things to Lilly, just because she was weak.

Even that boy, surely…surely…

Even Bell…Even Bell—!

No matter how nice he was, he would have eventually raised his hand to her. There was no doubt.

What was so wrong with betraying someone before they betrayed you?

The elderly couple had treated her like their own granddaughter. Just thinking about them made Lilly remember their eyes. Yes, no matter what she did, she would always be thrown away at some point. She would always be abandoned.

Her thoughts did nothing to ease the ache in her heart. She picked up her pace, trying to drown out the pain.

"A Guild inspector will come today. Even if you make a mistake, don't do anything stupid, newbie."

"Yes, sir!"

Hestia returned to her post after the half-dwarf store manager finished his lecture.

Hestia had learned much about how to work with store employees who didn't treat her as the goddess she was. Her twin black ponytails swished lightly from side to side as she set to work.

Her main job was to interact with customers, so she was the one to greet the Guild inspector. When the inspector arrived, she looked like a half-elf Hestia had seen somewhere before.

"Ah, aren't you…"

"I have come here on behalf of the Guild. My name is Eina Tulle. I am here to conduct an inspection, as scheduled."

Eina greeted her very professionally. Hestia thought about it for a moment but dismissed it as common sense and led her into the shop.

Keeping her visit completely by the book, after introducing herself to the store manager, Eina pulled out a piece of parchment and a pen before walking around the shop.

"Goddess Hestia."

"Eh?"

"I would like to speak with you. Do you have a moment?"

While looking over weapon racks and the magic-stone air-conditioning, Eina made her way to Hestia's side. She spoke in a low voice and never made eye contact. Hestia was a bit surprised at first, but then took a quick look around before casually filling her role as guide and leading Eina into a corner.

"I'm surprised you'd approach me like that. You plan for everything, don't you, Ms. Adviser."

"Sorry to trouble you."

The two of them continued their conversation while pretending to work, never looking at each other.

In response to Eina's "Do you have a moment," Hestia shook a weapons rack to cover her as she nodded yes.

"I have information concerning the supporter employed by Mr. Bell Cranell."

Hestia's hands stopped as a shiver ran up her spine, making her shoulders twitch. She turned to face Eina.

"I'm going to tell you about the *Familia* she belongs to, so please listen well."

The more Eina told her about what she'd learned last night at *Loki Familia*, the tenser Hestia's expression became.

Even though the possibility of her being under the influence of Soma was rather low, the supporter working with Bell might have had another motive—like depriving him of all his possessions—when she'd approached him.

Eina said that she would encourage Bell to break off all interaction with said supporter before something serious happened.

"Goddess Hestia, can I ask you to convince him for me?"

Eina looked down at the goddess with her emerald-green eyes.

Hestia looked back at her, speechless.

Since leaving Bell behind, Lilly had stayed on one clear path straight to the upper levels. She cleared the tenth level and ninth level with no trouble at all before arriving on the eighth-level floor.

Lilly knew every twist and turn of the Dungeon down to the eleventh level like the back of her hand.

Her method for relieving adventurers of their valuables was, like she had just done to Bell, to create a diversion and make her move during the ensuing commotion before making her escape—before the mark even noticed she was gone.

However, if they caught up to her, it was all for naught. The only way she had to avoid this was to memorize the dungeon maps sold at the Guild.

Even if she encountered monsters, she had become an expert at leading said monsters to other adventurers and letting them take care of it. In fact, that was about all she did.

Once she got to the surface, all she had to do was return to her normal self and sell off the goods. There was no way any of her victims could catch up at that point.

Alone, she could do nothing. But with a bit of planning and a vicious mind-set, Lilly had tricked many adventurers.

Her reason for stealing from adventurers? To put it simply, revenge.

She decided that she'd take back what was once hers from the people who had tormented her all of her life. She had repeatedly bared her fangs at members of *Soma Familia*.

She felt no remorse for her actions; it was her right as the victim.

All adventurers were *adventurers*. That had always been her reasoning, and that was never going to change.

…Everything so far had been the same, until she felt cruel looking away from one boy's face.

Now that it's mine, Lilly almost has enough money…

She had no interest in Soma. Actually, quite the opposite—she hated it. A piece of her had a grudge against it as well.

Even just the smell of it might make her fall under its spell again, make her go crazy like an animal.

Therefore, this money was going toward her salvation.

Someday, she was going to trade a large sum of money for her release from *Soma Familia*.

The point was, Lilly was a possession of the god Soma. She tried to get the Guild involved, but they didn't have the resources to help her and did nothing. The only thing she could do was convince Soma to let her go by offering an extraordinarily large amount of money in exchange for her freedom.

She made up her mind; she would get her freedom with her own two hands.

"Hmmm!"

Lilly came to a halt as she stepped into some tall grass.

An eighth-level goblin was walking around in front of the only exit from this room, directly in front of her.

There were no signs of other adventurers. The goblin blocked her path. Even if she tried to sneak around it, she couldn't go forward.

Doubling back and taking another route would take far too long.

While Bell surely had his hands full with the onslaught of monsters heading his direction and wouldn't be able to pursue her at top speed, there were other dangers in the Dungeon. Time was of the essence, so Lilly decided to break through.

"Lilly's not built for this kind of roughhousing, yeah?" said Lilly under her breath as she rolled up the right sleeve of her cream-colored robe.

She pulled out a small handheld bow gun.

The magic sword would be wasted on a goblin!

Stepping forward with her right leg, she leveled the bow gun at the monster.

Prums in general were known for having amazing eyesight. Lilly's round chestnut eyes zeroed in on the goblin, lining it up dead center. The monster finally noticed her as well.

"Bah—ffftt!"

A golden arrow shot out of the bow gun with frightening speed.

The arrow carved through the air and bore straight into the goblin's right eye.

"GiGYAAAAAAA!!!!!!"

"Excuse me!"

The goblin screamed out in pain, clutching its eye as Lilly used the opportunity to scurry by the monster and to the exit.

Lilly could fight, too, as long as she had a strategy. However, she had to rely completely on weapons and items. Slaying a single monster did not justify the amount of money required to take it down, not by a long shot.

Lilly only fought against monsters in self-defense.

"Lilly's jealous of Mr. Bell. He could do everything by himself!"

Starting with her magic, Cinder Ella, Lilly's strengths were not suited for combat. Lilly was very weak physically.

She gained her magic shortly after swearing revenge against adventurers, and hoped that it would transform her into something stronger than her weak self. She was extremely depressed when she learned the truth about it.

However, she soon learned how to use it in a different way to exact revenge. She pushed her magic to its limits and figured out what it could really do.

As proof of its power, her magic allowed her to consistently steal many items, using the same strategy on many adventurers.

Lilly had become powerful enough to laugh at the weakling she once was.

And...seventh level!

She made her way up the staircase jutting out of the wall, to the next floor up.

Lilly kept her speed up as she raced past the light green dungeon walls.

After this floor, the rest is a piece of cake.

In terms of the monsters, the seventh level was the last mountain she needed to climb. It was too early to lose focus.

After this floor, she could handle everything on her own. Her lips started to curve into a smile as she bolted into the next room.

"Ain't this a surprise. I've hit the jackpot."

"Eh?"

It happened when she came out of a small corridor and into a room.

A leg appeared from the side and caught Lilly's short body just under her knee.

Her balance gone, Lilly fell face-first onto the dungeon floor.

Wha...what was that...?

Dazed and confused, she put her hand into the dirt to push herself up. That's when a long shadow fell over her.

She was yanked up before she could turn around; half a second later a boot was slammed into her nose.

"Gyhaaa?!"

"I'd better be gettin' an apology, ya piece-of-shit prum!"

A powerful fist nailed her left cheek. A river of blood flowed from her nose.

Just as her eyes were beginning to focus, she took another kick to the chest. Her oversized backpack dislodged from her shoulders, rolling backward like a snowball.

The next hit wasn't far behind—the heel of a boot bore into the small of her back.

"—hhhh?!"

Her body bounced off the floor like a ball, bouncing once, twice.

Lilly was swept up in a whirlpool of pain as her body finally came to a halt.

"Ah...! Gahaahaa...!!"

"Ha! Ha-ha-ha-ha-ha-ha!! That's a good look for ya! Plastered in blood and dirt!"

With the world spinning around her, Lilly finally caught a glimpse of the voice's owner.

It was a human adventurer. The same one who'd been talking to Bell yesterday. Her former employer.

The man's jaw was pointing at the ceiling as he looked down on her with a sneer.

"Thought it was about time for ya to throw away that kid. I wet up a net for ya. Been dyin' to say hello!"

"A…net?"

"The Dungeon is huge. Waitin' for ya by myself woulda been as borin' as lookin' for a needle in a haystack. Got myself some part- ners, increased my chances."

The Dungeon itself was extremely large; the floors below level five were wider than Central Park. Despite its size, there were only three or four ways to get this far down.

The man had stationed his partners at each of the pathways and waited for her arrival.

Of the four, Lilly had chosen the route that the man was watching.

"Couldn't believe my eyes when I saw that white-haired kid run- ning around with a runt…Don't tell me, the kid had something that made yer eyes go all a-twitter? Are ya dense?"

"…!"

"But I don't care 'bout that. Before I tear you limb from limb as a thank-you for stealing my sword, think I'll make you play along…!"

He declared with a sadistic twinge in his eyes that he would take everything from her.

Lilly did her best to cup her still-bleeding nose as the man ripped off her robe, causing everything inside to fall to the ground. She was now wearing only her underclothes, unable to do anything to resist him.

"Magic stones, a gold watch…Hey, hey! You had a magic sword?! Haaa-ha-ha-ha-ha! So ya stole this, too, eh?"

The man was overjoyed by his discovery.

His mood improved greater still when he saw a knife with a glossy shine.

Spinning the crimson knife in one hand, a dark smile grew on his lips.

"Hee-hee-hee-hee…All right, I'll let you off the hook, ya piece- of-shit prum. After gettin' a present like this from ya, I'll show ya a bit of mercy. Nice guy, ain't I?…Hyaa!"

"Ahgg…!"

Two swift kicks to the stomach and Lilly was reeling in pain.

This is bad, this is bad, this is bad. Lilly's heart raced inside her small chest, her brain in all-out panic mode.

She knew at that moment that if she didn't get away now, she would meet a miserable fate at the hands of this man's brutality.

Just as she took in a deep breath, another man's voice came from somewhere distant.

"You certainly went all out, Master Gedo."

A new person was coming toward them.

"…?!"

Looking in the direction of the new voice, Lilly saw someone she recognized.

He was one of the adventurers who'd tried to get money out of her the other day. Just one of the many members of *Soma Familia* who had tried to do the same thing many times before.

Then it came to her. The man's partners were members of *Soma Familia*. Most likely, after talking with Bell, he had seen them arguing with her and decided to ask them for assistance.

"Get this, Kanu. The runt had a magic sword! Just as ya thought, looks like she's been stealin' all over the place. Ha-ha-ha-ha!"

"…Is that so?"

An adult male animal person, the one called Kanu, narrowed his cloudy, dark eyes at the happy man, the adventurer called Gedo. But Gedo was in such a good mood that he didn't notice.

"Master Gedo, I have a suggestion…"

"What's that? Hand it over? Hey, now, I caught the prum, I should have first dibs on—"

"That's not quite it. Not just the magic sword, but everything you took from her. I suggest you leave it all on the ground."

"Huh?" Gedo looked at his partner with a confused smile. Before he could ask any questions, however, Kanu pulled something out from behind him and threw it. It landed just in front of Lilly.

"KEEEEI!!!!!!!!!!!!!!!!!!!!!!!" Lilly screamed. "K-killer ant…?!"

It was only the top half, making it easier to carry. The bloody mess was still oozing purple liquid from many gashes all over its body; it had likely been slain only a few minutes ago. No, not slain. Its mouth was still moving; an arm twitched in agony.

"You might have thought at first that all of us were hunting together. There's a chance that Master Gedo, who has conquered many floors, is stronger than we are. So the three of us put our heads together and came up with this plan here."

Plop, plop. Two more barely alive killer-ant bodies landed close to them.

Two more adventurers had arrived in the room from separate entrances, both of them working with Kanu. The three masses of dying ant let out cries that united to create eerie echoes throughout the room, like a curse from another world.

Both Gedo's and Lilly's faces turned pale.

Killer ants released a special pheromone when they were close to death. It was a call for help, and other killer ants would answer.

The three balls of still-breathing ant flesh had been releasing the pheromone for some time. The room had become a ticking time bomb.

"Are you serious?!!" Gedo said.

There were three ants in that state calling for help. Just how many of their friends would answer?

The expressions on Kanu's and his allies' faces were surprisingly calm and unchanging, even during Gedo's screaming.

Only Lilly correctly understood the adventurer's irrational obsession with money, having been under the influence of Soma herself.

"You don't want to become their prey while you're fighting with us, now do you, Master?"

"Hyee?!"

Five killer ants poked their heads into the room entrance behind Gedo.

This room had four entrances. Kanu and his cronies were standing in front of three of them; the last one now had killer ants in the way. Gedo gritted his teeth, shaking in a mixture of fear and anger. His pale face hardened as he threw everything he'd taken from Lilly to the ground.

"Damn! Damn you all!!!"

Kanu grinned as he stepped aside to allow the man to pass. Gedo took one last look around the room before running past him.

Not a moment later, a barbaric roar erupted from the corridor, followed by the sound of a sword clang. After that, silence.

A shell-shocked Lilly had no way to see what happened; there was a wall of giant ants between her and the exit.

"Gii…!!"

"?!"

A killer ant stepped in front of Lilly as the room was flooded with the monsters.

Her injured body wouldn't move like she wanted it to, and she couldn't get out of the way of the monster's incoming claws.

Blood suddenly sprayed into the air.

The injured killer ant fell to the floor.

"Are you okay, Erde?"

"Mister…Kanu…"

Kanu looked down on the girl, his mouth nothing more than an upward rip in his face and a purple blood–splattered sword resting on his shoulder.

"I came for you, to save you. We are in the same *Familia*, after all."

Lilly bit her lip and clenched her fists as the man in front of her spoke like some kind of hero.

His partners were holding the killer ants back, for now.

"That's right, we all came for you, Erde. In this desperate situation, we didn't abandon you, see?"

"…Yes."

"…You know what I'm saying, yeah?"

He wrapped his arm behind Lilly's shoulder as he spoke. His tone sounded as though he were acting in a play rather than facing death.

His eyes might have been looking at Lilly's quivering body, but in reality he didn't see her.

All he could see was money—to be more specific, the Soma that the money would get him.

Kanu's expression was calm and collected, but on the inside he was overwhelmed with anxiety.

"Hey, speed it up! We can't hold them!" said one crony.

"I know!" Kanu looked to Lilly. "You, yesterday you said you had no money. Drop the act. If you try to pull something like that again…"

"Okay! Okay-okay-okay…!"

Seeing the direness of her situation, Lilly nodded with a defeated look on her face.

She had no time to be angry, so Lilly grabbed a small key that was hidden as part of a necklace and held it out to him.

"The hell is this?"

"A key to a gnome rental storage unit in Orario's eastern ward…"

"Talking about a safepoint? To think you kept large amounts of vals in a box that small…"

"Gnome jewels are in there…"

"Ah…now I gotcha…"

The jewels and minerals that gnomes collected were highly valuable. Their worth rarely changed so there was always a buyer. Lilly had exchanged most of her ill-gotten gains from coins into gnome jewels at the Gnome Trader because carrying large amounts of money would look suspicious if she were caught.

Another dark grin graced Kanu's lips as he nodded and grabbed the collar of Lilly's shirt. With a big wad of fabric in his hand, he pulled Lilly to her feet and then up off the floor, placing her level with his eyes.

"Mr. Kanu…what are you…?"

"We're in quite the pinch, you know. Look around. We're being surrounded."

At least twenty killer ants had made an almost complete ring around them. There was only one exit that was still open for escape.

Lilly futilely kicked her legs as she hung in the animal man's grasp, but it was like trying to swim in the air.

Kanu, five o'clock shadow and all, made one last big smile.

"Buy us some time."

"?!"

"We'll make our escape while you draw them away, Erde. That exit over there isn't blocked yet, so we can take a few of them while you act as a decoy."

Terror filled Lilly's eyes as she looked back at him.

Chancing a look to the side, she saw Kanu's partners had the same savage smile on their faces.

"Without money, you're useless. At least do your job to help us one last time, *supporter.*"

Lilly was thrown.

Making a tall arc in the air, she cleared the ring of killer ants.

The monsters quickly locked onto her airborne body and followed her.

For Lilly, time stood still. She watched the adventurers make a break for the exit, smiling their evil smiles, before finally hitting the dungeon floor.

The impact knocked the wind out of her, but nothing else.

"...haa-haaa..."

She lay on her back, staring at the ceiling and laughing awkwardly, broken. The killer ants were all coming in her direction.

So this is how it ends, she thought to herself. There was no reason to laugh, but she couldn't help it.

Adventurers truly were not worthy of trust.

If this is some kind of punishment for everything up till now, it's far too cruel, her train of thought continued.

...But wait.

If this is punishment for what Lilly did to Mr. Bell, maybe it's okay.

Despite being an adventurer, he didn't act like any adventurer Lilly knew. If this was her reward, then strangely she felt as though it was her duty to be punished.

"Giyaa......!"

More killer ants than she could count were making noises and advancing on her in a wave of pincers and claws.

There was no way for her to escape. She had landed against a wall.

The monsters had surrounded her. They approached in an ever-closing arc around Lilly as she lay helpless on her back.

"...Lilly's...sad."

Her words were drowned out by the continuous pounding of hundreds of killer-ant feet on the floor.

A professional supporter. Always treated like something else.

Adventurers never felt remorse for the luggage carrier, even if the supporter fell. They were useless.

Right where Lilly, who could do nothing by herself, belonged. That was, in fact, who she was.

Her pathetic self.

Lilly hated the person she was most of all.

"Gods…why…?"

No one ever called out to her. No one ever depended on her.

She was always used, never needed.

She hated how weak she was. She hated the fact that her life was always directed by someone else's hand.

Lilly wanted to become someone else, anyone else but Lilly.

Even the magic she learned showed that she didn't want to be herself.

"Why…why did you make Lilly, Lilly…?"

She didn't know how many times she had thought about dying.

She had wished that she could go to the gods and ask for a reset more times than she could remember.

She wanted to become a different Lilly—any Lilly was better than this one.

In the end, Lilly was too weak to go through with it.

But somewhere in her heart, Lilly always wanted a reset.

"Gisyaaa…!"

"……That's right. It doesn't matter anymore."

The half ring of monsters around her was getting closer and closer.

Flop. Her cheek hit the floor as she turned her head to the side with a small, accepting smile on her face.

One killer ant was so close it looked gigantic from her new line of sight. Its leg stopped right in front of her face.

"…So lonely."

Lilly was surprised by the words that rolled off her tongue.

It was how she really felt. Only at the end did she realize it.

Oh…Lilly was lonely.

She was used to not being needed.

Used to it, but the loneliness never went away.

Alone.

Not having anyone to rely on or depend on her made her lonely.

She got used to being alone but never got used to being lonely.

"So that was it, Lilly…"

She wanted to be with someone.

She lamented the fact that only now did she see the truth.

"SyyyAAAAAAAAAAAAAA!!!!!!!!!!!!!!!!!!!!!!!"

The closest killer ant raised its claws. They glinted in the light shining down from the ceiling above.

Good-bye.

She could finally die. It was finally over. She could go to the gods.

The tiny girl whom no one would save, the girl who was worth nothing, the lonely girl…

She could reset at last.

Finally, Lilly can…

…And Lilly was so close to finding someone, too…

Is Lilly…finally going to die?

She lightly smiled, a tear rolling down her cheek.

And then…

"FIREBOOOOOOLT!!!"

An explosion of flames.

"…Huh?"

A scarlet inferno engulfed the room.

"It's not possible."

Hestia looked up at Eina and answered with a long sigh.

"What do you mean…?"

"That's not going to happen. Bell has already decided not to cut ties with that supporter."

Eina stood completely still, not expecting that response. Hestia let out another sigh.

Hestia gently closed her eyes and remembered what had transpired last night.

"Goddess, I...Even so, if she is in trouble, I want to help."

Hestia had mentioned that the supporter, the girl, shouldn't be trusted. That was Bell's response.

Maybe Hestia hadn't heard him the first time, but Bell quickly put those words together as the goddess tried to sway him. However, Bell wouldn't—no, *couldn't*—listen to her and change his mind.

"That girl, she seemed lonely. I don't think she knows it, though. It's like she's numb, just smiling a cute smile...She thinks she's fine on her own."

Bell kept on talking about Lilly and the things he had seen. Hestia had never seen this girl, but she kept listening.

On top of that, Bell added his own memory to the conversation.

"Wasn't it you, Goddess, who helped me when I was lonely?"

He saw a bit of himself in Lilly.

Before meeting Hestia, Bell wandered around Orario by himself, on the verge of being crushed by anxiety and loneliness. Lilly had the same look in her eyes as he did then.

"If I'm wrong, then that's fine. But if I'm right...This time, I want to be the one to help."

Bell said that he wanted to become someone like the goddess who saved him, to be like Hestia. He left it at that.

"That boy...Bell. He's the type of person who can pass on the kindness he receives to anyone. He recognizes pain that he has felt in others..."

Hestia had kept her eyes on the shelves in front of them while speaking. She once again looked up at Eina.

"He's really stubborn when he makes up his mind. No one can reason with him now."

Eina looked as though she had been thrown for a loop. Hestia's shoulders dropped as she looked at the troubled expression on the half-elf's face. Eina's lips quivered as if she wanted to say something.

"Not convinced?"

"No, no…That does sound like something Bell would say. But what's he basing it on……?"

Hestia crossed her arm and let out a small "hmm" as she looked at the unease written all over Eina's face.

Hestia puffed out her cheeks as she chose her words; it felt strange even to say them out loud.

"About that. Bell has an extraordinary ability to read people. He's as good as we, the gods, are. Probably."

"LILLYYYYYYYYYYYYYYYYYYYYYYYYYYYYYYYY!!!!!!!!!!!!!!!!!!!"

A voice calling out to her cut through the swarm of monsters.

Echoes of explosion after explosion of fire filled the room. The startled killer ants all tried to turn and face this sudden attack from behind but ran into one another as they moved.

Flashes of fire reflected off Lilly's eyes as they came closer, carving a path through the massive ants. The moment Lilly clearly saw lightning flames…The wall of monsters collapsed and a white-haired boy jumped through.

"OUT OF MY WAYYYY!!!"

"GIGAA?!"

The boy, Bell, dove toward Lilly, wielding both his dagger and the shortsword as he tore through the mass of killer ants.

The killer ant standing over the girl froze for a moment before its head was separated from its body in a flash.

"Lilly! You're okay, yes?! Do you know who I am?"

At first, Lilly didn't recognize the boy embracing her.

His ruby-red eyes were shaking as he held her. The fingers around her shoulder were clamped down so tight that it hurt.

Bell quickly took out a potion and raised it to her lips.

Lilly's blank eyes looked as if she already had one foot in the grave. But her mouth opened just enough to allow the blue liquid to roll down her throat.

Koff! Koff! A moment later, a cute little cough escaped her lungs.

"...Mr. Bell?"

"Yes, it's me! You're okay, right?"

Bell's voice cracked as he spoke, tears gushing from his eyes—like Lilly's were, a moment ago—and a smile on his face.

Heat filled Lilly's body, which had been cold until now, as she was pulled into a strong and somewhat painful hug.

Seeing that Lilly was all right, Bell immediately looked up from her.

The sharp claws of the surviving monsters were closing in.

Lilly's hand moved on its own underneath her shirt, where she had hidden a jet-black knife up until now. She pulled it up and held it out to Bell.

Bell grinned from ear to ear as he took the Hestia Knife from her.

"Wait for a minute, just like usual."

Saying those words, Bell stood up.

Angry, clicking sounds reverberated around the room. Many spots on the floor were burning from Bell's magic, smoke rising into the air.

There was no greater feeling of isolation that this.

No less than thirty monsters had Bell and Lilly surrounded. Even more were coming from the exits, born from the walls.

All of them looked as though they could charge at any second. And yet, Bell wasn't afraid.

The Bell of a few days ago would have faltered in the face of this many enemies for sure. Even now, Bell could never contend with this many monsters at once.

However, now Bell had magic.

"Here I come...!"

He withdrew a vial filled with yellowish liquid from his leg holster.

Bell now knew about the limits of the Mind Down and had purchased this 8,700-val trump card to be ready to face death.

"Magic Potion." Medicine that healed the mind.

Popping the cap off the vial with his thumb, Bell downed it all in one gulp.

"...—RIGHT!!!!"

"Hh!!"

Another one of the ants stepped forward, and Bell raised his right arm. "FIREBOLT—!!!!"

The killer ant was blasted backward the moment electric flames erupted from Bell's palm.

That was the signal. All the ants charged at once. Bell started yelling over and over at the oncoming onslaught.

Rapid-fire explosions of flame and electricity blanketed them all.

Every time Bell shouted, a new jet of electrical inferno shot forward, illuminating the room.

Every time his scarlet lightning was released, at least one killer ant was rent asunder. Some of his lucky shots slew two of the beasts at once.

The army of killer ants took Bell's assault head-on, giving no ground.

Magic was turning the tide of battle against overwhelming numbers.

"HAAAAAAAAAAAAAAAA!!!"

Bell reached for his weapons once a good portion of the killer ants had fallen.

Gripping the Hestia Knife in one hand and his dagger in the other, he charged headlong into the mass of wounded killer ants.

Lilly watched on in silence as flashes of purple light were followed by a severed head or torso flying into the air.

"......"

She sat quietly in stunned silence, watching the scene unfold before her eyes.

Whenever she caught a glimpse of his white hair, another killer ant was sliced down in a surge of purple liquid.

He was fast, sharp, and strong.

Before she knew it, Bell was the only one standing. There had been so many killer ants just a few minutes ago; now they were all motionless on the dungeon floor.

Bell returned both blades to their sheaths with a look of relief on his face. He took one last look around the room before returning to Lilly's side.

"How...did you get here?" she asked.

"Well, orcs kept coming in after you left, but I think another adventurer came, probably. I couldn't see clearly because of the fog, but all the monsters between the exit and me suddenly weren't there anymore..."

That was how Bell had managed to do the impossible and cover that much ground to come straight here.

Bell forced a smile, scratching the back of his head as though what he did was no big deal. However, something inside Lilly snapped when she saw that.

"...Why?"

"Eh? Did you say something, Lilly?"

"Why did you do it?"

The floodgates were open; Lilly's mouth started moving on its own.

There was something else she should be saying right now, but other words were spilling out.

"Why did you save Lilly? Why didn't you just abandon Lilly?"

"...What?"

"There's no way you couldn't have realized by now Lilly was fooling you! Does Mr. Bell think Lilly wanted to surprise him by taking that knife, or something stupid like that?!"

The confused look on Bell's face only served to make Lilly's voice even more heated.

Lilly's sudden rage burned through the last wall of self-restraint.

"What are you, Mr. Bell? An idiot? A buffoon?! An airheaded moron beyond all hope of recovery?!"

"Moron......?! Wait, Lilly, calm down...?!"

"Impossible!! Mr. Bell doesn't notice anything?! Lilly took money for herself at the Exchange! Mr. Bell's and Lilly's shares should have been fifty-fifty, but it was closer to forty-sixty! There were times Lilly got greedy and made it thirty-seventy! Lilly charged you more than double the price of items when Lilly prepared them! Twelve of them! Lilly doesn't know how many times Lilly was shocked by your lack of knowledge about items, or how careless you are with equipment!!"

Bell's mouth twitched as all this information suddenly came to light.

Lilly would not stop. A little voice in the back of her head was frantically saying "Stop!" but it was no use. She kept on confessing to everything.

"Do you understand now?! Lilly is a bad, bad person! A thief! Lilly's a piece-of-shit prum who lied to you over and over! Lilly's not worthy to be your supporter!"

"U-um…"

"Even still…even still, Mr. Bell saved Lilly?!"

"Y-yes."

"WHY?!"

Lilly was gasping for breath as she looked at Bell.

She had no clue what she was hoping to hear.

But her heart was beating a mile a minute, faster than it should be even now.

A little frightened by Lilly's barrage, Bell opened his mouth to speak almost as a reflex and said these words:

"B-because you're a girl."

—HUH?? Lilly's entire body felt like it was on fire.

Her fists clenched; her shoulders rose to her ears in anger.

Her emotions were boiling over, and she had no idea why.

She couldn't understand this explosion of discontent.

"ID-IOT!! Mr. Bell is an IDIOT!!! Saying something like that again, it's the same as before?! Would Mr. Bell save ANY woman just because?! Lilly can't believe this!! You're horrible!! Playboy!! Pervert!! Enemy of all women!!!!"

For some reason, tears leaked out of Lilly's eyes during her rant.

She was in no position to be saying any of it, but she unloaded all of her discontent on the boy standing in front of her.

Discontent? About what?

He saved her; just what did she have to be discontented about?

What was this flame in her chest—no, her whole body—trying to say?

She didn't have any idea.

Bell withstood the latest tirade, Lilly once again panting for breath.

Relaxing his shoulders and smiling, Bell leaned forward and placed his hand gently on the cheek of the dog-earless Lilly.

"Well then, because you're Lilly."

"—"

Chestnut eyes went as wide as they could go.
"I saved you because you're you, Lilly. I didn't want you to disappear."
"Fuu, ehh......!"
"There's nothing else to it. Why would I need a better reason to save Lilly?"
Her tear ducts gave out.
A waterfall of tears gushed from her eyes, flowing down her face in all directions.
Lilly couldn't hold back any longer and cried out.
"*Hic*...waaaaaah!"
"Lilly, if you're in trouble, come talk to me. I'm an idiot, so I won't know unless you tell me."
"*Hic*...! Waaahhh..."
"I'll help you, you can count on it."
Lilly dove into his chest and hung on tight.
His metallic armor got in the way, but she didn't care. She embraced him with all her might, her hands around his back.
She could feel the palms of Bell's warm hands gently stroking her head and back over and over again.
She knew. She noticed.
Bell had thought of her when he rushed to this room.
His light clothes were trashed, torn to shreds.
The pale skin showing through the holes was covered in cuts and bruises.
Lilly knew that he had taken on hordes of monsters to come to her side.
She wanted to call out to him, to say something to acknowledge what Bell had done.
Lilly wanted him to accept the one thing she hated most: Lilly.

"Sorry...so, so sorry...!"

"...It's okay."

The sound of Lilly's cries echoed far and wide.

The scene of a giant ant massacre filled one corner of the Dungeon. Slowly but surely, their magic stones broken one by one, the slain killer ants turned to ash amid smoke rising from still-burning embers strewn about the room.

The ashes slowly fell off the crying girl's face, along with her tears.

The human kept the small prum girl in a tight embrace, the same calm smile on his face.

The sky was clear.

Just like on the day that someone called out to him, not a cloud in the sky.

Bell walked toward Babel Tower, his white hair bathed in sunlight.

Two days had passed since then.

He hadn't seen any trace of Lilly since they broke up.

The room she had used up to that point had been completely cleared out; she'd left no messages.

There was no point going to *Soma Familia* for help. Lilly had disappeared altogether.

He felt worried and anxious.

He didn't know how many times he had considered searching the city.

But at the same time, Bell had a feeling.

A feeling that he would see her again soon.

It really was just a thought, but he kept to his usual routine.

So he could be found easily.

"!"

Bell stopped. And then started right back up again.

He caught a glimpse of something at Babel's west gate: a small figure standing still, wearing a cream robe.

The figure's hands were clasped around straps of a backpack while she looked at the ground.

The figure's round, cute eyes were clearly visible between bangs in the sunlight.

Bell set out toward the figure at a brisk walk. He didn't want to scare her or make her jump.

The prum girl noticed him in no time.

Her shoulders dropped to an almost pitiful level. She stood still as she watched him approach.

"......"

"......"

They were close enough to shake hands—if only one of them would reach out.

Lilly looked up and opened her mouth to speak over and over again, but each time she couldn't get any words out.

She couldn't start a conversation; it was very unlike her.

Bell waited patiently for Lilly to speak, but seeing her struggling with it, he flashed a quick smile before starting the conversation himself.

"Miss Supporter! Miss Supporter! Are you looking for an adventurer?"

"Huh?"

Lilly looked up again.

Bell's big grin reflected off Lilly's round, chestnut-colored eyes.

"Are you confused? This is a pretty simple situation, you know. An adventurer in need of a supporter has come to you, asking to buy your services."

Lilly realized what was going on.

Her eyes filled with tears of joy. Her cheeks turned a warm shade of pink.

Bell shyly held out his right hand, as though he were embarrassed.

"I was wondering if you'd be willing to prowl the Dungeon with me."

Today was a fresh start.

Bell and Lilly really joined forces—their own two-person party.

Their relationship had been reset.

A new beginning.

"—Yes! Please take Lilly with you!"

With a smile as big as a sunflower, Lilly took Bell's outstretched hand in her own.

Epilogue BACKSTAGE

"He's gone…" Aiz quietly said to herself.

She was on the tenth-level floor. She stood alone in the fog, surrounded by the corpses of all the monsters she had slain.

She had seen the boy through the fog not too long ago, but the moment he cleared the next set of oncoming monsters, he'd left the room as if he were shot out of a cannon.

At Eina's request, she had collected information from other adventurers about the whereabouts of a white-haired boy, and she finally managed to track him down…only to have him run away from her once again. Her shoulders drooped.

But…

Aiz thought vaguely to herself that maybe he was used to his power.

While she couldn't be sure because of the fog, she felt as though he was fighting with impatience, full of desperation. And when she cut an opening for him, he shot off like a madman driven by thoughts of something that wasn't her.

Aiz got the impression that the boy had a reason to rush, but she didn't know why.

What should I do now…?

She had accepted Eina's request to confirm the boy's safety. She should go after him.

However, going after him now would be another wild-goose chase. She was considering her options when suddenly…

Something glinted through the fog.

"…What's…"

She bent down to pick up the source of the light from the grass. It was an emerald-colored vambrace.

The vambrace, the exact color of Reveria's and Eina's eyes, was somewhat the worse for wear. It looked as though it had taken a bad hit or three before falling off, and the surface was covered in nicks, scratches, and cuts.

But why here? she wondered to herself before it came to her. "Ah!"

An important thought occurred to her.

"Could this be…?"

—Behind her, a lost needle rabbit hopped around the prairie field on the tenth-level floor of the Dungeon.

【LILLILUKA◆ERDE】

BELONGS TO: SOMA FAMILIA
RACE: PRUM
JOB: SUPPORTER
DUNGEON RANGE: ELEVENTH LEVEL
WEAPONS: SHORT KNIFE, BOW GUN
CURRENT WORTH: 300 VALS

《SUPPORTER GLOVES》

- SUPPORTER GEAR DESIGNED TO ASSIST IN
  DISPOSAL OF MONSTER BODIES. DISPOSABLE.
- PROTECTS THE HANDS FROM POWERFUL ACIDS.
  PROTECTS AGAINST OTHER ABNORMALITIES AS WELL.
- THEY COME IN A VARIETY OF COLORS. LILLY PREFERS BROWN.

STATUS

Lv. **1**

STRENGTH: I 42   **DEFENSE:** I 42   **UTILITY:** H 143
AGILITY: -285   **MAGIC:** F 317

《MAGIC》

【 **CINDER ELLA** 】

- SHAPE-SHIFTING MAGIC
- TARGET WILL TAKE THE ENVISIONED SHAPE AT THE TIME OF THE SPELL.
- MAGIC WILL FAIL WITHOUT A CLEAR IMAGE.
- IMITATION IS RECOMMENDED.
- TRIGGER SPELL: "YOUR SCARS ARE MINE. MY SCARS ARE MINE."
- RELEASE SPELL: "STROKE OF MIDNIGHT'S BELL."

《SKILL》

【 **ALTER ASSIST** 】

- ACTIVATES AUTOMATICALLY WHEN WEIGHT CARRIED EXCEEDS A CERTAIN LEVEL.
- AMOUNT OF ASSISTANCE IS PROPORTIONAL TO WEIGHT CARRIED.

《LITTLE ✦ BARISTA》

- MADE BY *GOIBNIU FAMILIA*. DESIGNED FOR SHORTER RACES LIKE PRUMS.
- HAS POWER BEYOND ITS SIZE. THE AMMO IS LIGHT, WITH LITTLE TO NO RECOIL. HOWEVER, RANGE IS LIMITED.
- DIFFERENT ARROWS CAN PROVIDE MORE POWER AND RANGE. SOLD SEPARATELY.

Afterword

This is the second book in the series. Thank you for picking it up. This is Fujino Ohmori.

While this story has a fantasy world–type feel, I was very conscious of building the story like a video game. My greatest challenge was figuring out how to incorporate an experience-point system, the most basic role-playing game element, into the story in a way that readers could accept without any misunderstandings. I spent many long hours trying to solve this problem.

This book casts the spotlight on baggage-carrying "supporters," a job that came to mind while working on the first problem.

Since there are no "magic pockets" that adventurers can put as much as they want into, how are they going to take all their loot out of the Dungeon? Could they fight at full strength while lugging around large bags? If not, then who would carry the load? This is how the "supporter" role came to be.

As you have read, being a supporter is not a glamorous job by any means. Their position is so low that they have to be content to sip muddy water. It's not surprising that the heroine of this story, and others like her, wasn't satisfied and went astray. Yes, for sure.

However, not just in terms of this story, but I think life itself is easier when someone is there to help shoulder the load. It's only when we have people there to help us that we can face new challenges.

I don't want to be thought of as someone who got too caught up in the moment and forgot to express gratitude to those who helped me along the way. Writing this book reminded me of that fact.

So I would like to take this opportunity to do just that.

First, to my editor who supported me again and again. To Mr. Suzuhito Yasuda, who overcame a very difficult schedule to provide amazing artwork. And to everyone who put their heart and soul into making this book a reality, thank you from the bottom of my heart.

Thanks to overwhelming support from readers, a third book is now in the works. I'm working as hard as I can to get it on the shelves as soon as possible. Thank you all for your continued support.

That's all for now.

Fujino Ohmori